Kentucky
State Facts

Nickname: Bluegrass State

Date Entered Union: June 1, 1792
(the 15th state)

Motto: United we stand, divided we fall

Famous Kentucky Men: Muhammed Ali, *boxer*
Jefferson Davis, *former president of the Confederacy*
Casey Jones, *locomotive engineer*
Abraham Lincoln, *former U.S. president*
Hunter S. Thompson, *writer*

Flower: Goldenrod

State Name's Origin: Based on the Native American word *ken-tah-ten*, meaning "land of tomorrow"

Fun Fact: The Kentucky Derby is the oldest continuously held horse race in the country. It is held at Churchill Downs in Louisville on the first Saturday in May.

Dear Diary,

I met the weirdest guy today. A real stuffed shirt named Stuart Greyson. Here this guy is at one of the most exciting events of the year, the Kentucky Derby, and he's making a to-do list. Can you believe?

He definitely needs to let his hair down...not that his hair is long enough to let down, mind you. He wears it cut real short, but, boy, oh, boy, it's just long enough for a woman to knot her fingers in and hold on.

I have his suit jacket. Promised him I'd take it to the cleaners. Not that I consider myself totally responsible for the stain, mind you. What was I supposed to do? Wipe my hands, then hug him? No way! Not when I'd just bet the long shot and won *big money!*

Got to go, Diary. I've got a farm to save, and that's going to take all of my energy...though I might save a little for Mr. Stuart Greyson. Somebody has to show that man how to have a good time.

Alyssa

American
HEROES
AGAINST ALL ODDS

PEGGY MORELAND
Run for the Roses

Published by Silhouette Books
America's Publisher of Contemporary Romance

For all the color and laughter she adds to my life,
this is dedicated to my sister Debbie,
who planted the seed for this story
when she bet the long shot and won.

And to Hubba,
a dog blessed with more personality than most humans
and the only canine I've ever known who owned a tux.

SILHOUETTE BOOKS
300 East 42nd St.,
New York, N. Y. 10017

ISBN 0-373-82215-4

RUN FOR THE ROSES

Copyright © 1990 by Peggy Bozeman Morse

This edition published by arrangement with Harlequin Books S.A.

® and TM are trademarks of Harlequin Books S.A., used under license. Trademarks indicated with ® are registered in the United States Patent and Trademark Office, the Canadian Trade Marks Office and in other countries.

Visit Silhouette at www.eHarlequin.com

Printed in U.S.A.

About the Author

Peggy Moreland published her first romance with Silhouette in 1989. She's a natural storyteller with a sense of humor that will tickle your fancy, and Peggy's goal is to write a story that readers will remember long after the last page is turned. Winner of the 1992 National Readers' Choice Award and a 1994 RITA Award finalist, Peggy frequently appears on bestseller lists around the country. A native Texan, she and her family live in Round Rock, Texas.

Books by Peggy Moreland

Silhouette Desire

A Little Bit Country #515
Run for the Roses #598
Miss Prim #682
The Rescuer #765
Seven Year Itch #837
The Baby Doctor #867
Miss Lizzy's Legacy #921
A Willful Marriage #1024
Marry Me, Cowboy #1084
A Little Texas Two-Step #1090
Lone Star Kind of Man #1096
†*The Rancher's Spittin' Image* #1156
†*The Restless Virgin* #1163
†*A Sparkle in the Cowboy's Eyes* #1168
†*That McCloud Woman* #1227
‡*Billionaire Bridegroom* #1244
†*Hard Lovin' Man* #1270
•*Ride a Wild Heart* #1306
•*In Name Only* #1313

Silhouette Special Edition

Rugrats and Rawhide #1084

*Trouble in Texas
†Texas Brides
‡Texas Cattleman's Club
•Texas Grooms

Dear Reader,

Thoroughbred horses. Steeplechases. Bluegrass. Mint juleps. The Kentucky Derby. These and more are what I think of when I think of Kentucky and the years that I lived in Louisville. Though Texas is my home, Kentucky will always hold a special place in my heart, as will the many memories I gathered while living there.

One of my fondest memories—and one sure to produce a chuckle when I reflect on it—is my first visit to the Kentucky Derby. I invited my grandmother and my younger sister to come to Kentucky and attend the Derby with me. My sister arrived with a purse stuffed full of money—mostly one-dollar bills given to her by friends for whom she was supposed to place bets. By the time the Run for the Roses rolled around, she was weary of standing at the window, placing bets for other people, and panicked when the warning sounded that the race was about to begin. Frantic because she hadn't yet placed her own bet, she threw eighteen one-dollar bills down and pulled a horse's name out of thin air. The horse was Gato del Sol, a field horse. The chances of a field horse winning the Kentucky Derby were slim, but that didn't dampen my sister's spirit. She stubbornly cheered Galo del Sol all the way around the track...and right across the finish line.

The opening scene in *Run for the Roses* was inspired by that memorable event. I hope that you enjoy reading Alyssa McCord and Stuart Greyson's story, and how Alyssa, like my sister Debbie, went to the Derby, bet the farm on a field horse...and came out a winner.

Happy reading!

Peggy Moreland

Please address questions and book requests to:
Silhouette Reader Service
U.S.: 3010 Walden Ave., P.O. Box 1325, Buffalo, NY 14269
Canadian: P.O. Box 609, Fort Erie, Ont. L2A 5X3

One

It was there. Money. Excitement. The thrill of victory. She could smell it, almost taste it in the breeze that warmed her uplifted face. It surrounded her, absorbed her and filled her with an expectancy she could barely contain.

This was her last chance, a last-ditch effort to save all that she had grown to love. That fact alone drew her anticipation to fever pitch. *I'm going to do it, Granddaddy,* she silently vowed to the stretch of blue sky above. *I don't know if you'd approve of my methods, but I'm going to try.*

"And they're off!" At the sound of the announcer's voice, Al McCord snapped her gaze from the billowy clouds drifting above Churchill Downs and centered it on the eleven powerful Thoroughbreds already racing down the backstretch. The announcer's voice rose above the noise of the race fans, calling the horses' positions on the track.

Al ignored him. The only horse she cared about was the sleek black colt wearing the number three blazoned across his flank. Her fingers tightened on the racing program as the horses streaked down the backstretch.

"On the inside, it's Mariah in the lead, Wild Card second at the rail. Moving up fast on the outside is My Boy. Bygone trails by a length."

"Come on, Foolish Pride. Come on, baby," Al urged as she rose to her feet. From behind her she heard a low growl of frustration. She ignored it as well as the man who had made the impatient sound. If the guy resented her standing...well, that was just too bad! She'd come to the Kentucky Derby to see the race, and if that meant standing, so be it.

Besides, she reasoned further, *she* hadn't complained when he'd leaned across her to conduct a minimum of two business conferences with men who had passed by on their way to the betting windows. The man was way too uptight. Anyone who would jot down a "To Do" list in the back of his appointment book and ignore her attempts at conversation while waiting for the races to start had to be.

If he didn't know how to relax and have a good time, it certainly wasn't her concern. She had enough problems to deal with. Serious problems, she reflected as she narrowed her eyes on the pack of horses making the final turn on the track.

One hundred dollars rode on this race. Another nine hundred warmed her purse, one hundred for each of the day's remaining races with an additional hundred to be wagered on the Run for the Roses itself. To say she had bet the farm wouldn't be exaggerating much.

"Mariah continues to lead by two lengths with Sugar Baby taking second. As they round the second pole, Thunderous Applause slips up the middle to fourth while Bygone drops to fifth. On the outside now it's Foolish Pride, moving up fast."

The horses streaked by in a blur of red, black, green, blue, and gold silks while the floor beneath Al's feet reverberated with the thunder of their hooves. As the horses raced toward the finish, Al held her breath, not daring to hope, but hoping nonetheless.

Stuart Greyson bit back a frustrated oath as he strained to see around the woman standing beside him. Why people insisted on standing for the race was beyond him. If everyone would simply remain in his or *her* seat, he thought angrily as he glared at the woman's back, it wouldn't be necessary for anyone to stand for a better view of the track.

He rolled his knee inward to avoid the woman as she leaned in his direction. Race crowds amazed him. The people always leaned as if they themselves were perched on top of the horses' backs, jockeying for position on the fast track. And *this* particular person seemed intent on driving him crazy. Chattering and flapping about like some kind of magpie.

"At the finish line, it's Foolish Pride first by a

nose, Thunderous Applause second, and Wild Card third.''

The woman leaped into the air, waving her arms above her head and totally obliterating Stuart's view of the finish line. She was still screaming and jumping around like a cheerleader when the stragglers crossed the finish.

Last to pass by was Mariah, the horse Stuart's money had been riding on. He glanced at the woman dancing in the aisle beside him and stifled a low growl. For God's sake, it was only a race! She was acting as if she'd just won a million-dollar lottery.

This thought had no sooner formed than the woman flopped down in the seat beside him, fanning her flushed face with her program and sending her too-long bangs flying. ''Can you believe it?'' she gasped to Stuart. ''I won! I really won!''

He pulled his elbow from the chair rest and away from the pressure of her arm. ''Good for you,'' he mumbled irritably.

Without warning, her arm shot out, nearly dislocating his shoulder. A slender index finger wavered just beneath his nose, pointing toward the tote board where the payoffs were displayed. ''Look! Foolish Pride pays $8.40. That means I win—what?'' she demanded as she whirled to face him. ''How much do I win?''

He frowned, then turned his attention to his program. ''Depends on how much you bet.''

''A hundred dollars. I bet a hundred dollars.''

''Then you win four hundred and twenty.''

She fell back against the seat, clutching her racing

program to her breasts, her eyes wide in awe. "Four hundred and twenty," she whispered, then repeated, "Four hundred and twenty," as if she couldn't quite believe her luck.

Luck was what it was, too. Stuart knew that for a fact. Mariah should have won the race. The statistics were there in his hands as proof. The jockey's record, the horse's past racing history. Hell, Mariah had been the favorite. Foolish Pride shouldn't even have placed, let alone won.

"Who did you bet on?"

Groaning inwardly at the woman's persistent chatter, Stuart mumbled, "Mariah."

She patted his arm consolingly. "That's too bad. Better luck next time. Which horse are you betting on in the second race?"

He glanced up to find her peering over his arm at the notepad on his lap. Flipping it closed, he said somewhat coolly, "I'm not sure." He lifted a shoulder as a barrier between them and turned his gaze on the infield in the distance where a record-breaking crowd milled around, looking for all the world like ants swarming on an anthill.

Undaunted by his inattentiveness, she glanced at her own racing program. "Me, neither." She pulled a pencil from behind her ear and dragged the eraser down the narrow page, murmuring aloud the horses' names listed for the second race. "Oh, look," she said in amusement. "Risky Venture. Isn't that cute? I think I'll bet on him."

"'Him's' a her."

She cocked her head, the furrow of her brow just visible beneath her mass of bangs. "What?"

Already sorry he had responded to her remark, he mumbled, "Risky Venture is a filly."

One bare shoulder rose and fell in a careless shrug. "Oh, well, then I'll bet on *her*." A smile played at the corner of her mouth as she circled the horse's name on her program, then broadened as she glanced up at Stuart's frowning face.

The smile was wasted on Stuart. He was immune to feminine charm. He stood and eased past her. "Excuse me, please."

She raised her gaze to meet his towering glare. "Where are you going?"

"Not that it's any business of yours," he replied tersely, "but to the men's room if you must know."

She grabbed for her purse. "Would you mind getting me a mint julep on your way back? I feel the need to celebrate." She dug for her wallet amongst the clutter filling the oversize purse. "I never can find anything in here."

His frown deepened. Now the woman was going to turn him into her personal gofer. "Forget it. I'll buy." He brushed past her and was immediately swallowed by the crowd of people working their way up the aisles to the betting windows beyond.

He hadn't really felt the call of nature but had been desperate to get away from the talkative woman. She seemed bent on driving him crazy with her incessant gabbing. He stepped into one of the lines at the betting windows and waited impatiently for his turn to place his wager for the second race. He'd made his choices for each race prior to arriving at the track. The fact was he'd made them at his breakfast table while he'd studied the racing forms he'd picked up at the corner grocery.

When his turn came, he tossed a crisp fifty-dollar bill on the counter and placed a bet on number six, Comanche Pride. The harried woman behind the window typed his wager into the computer and shoved a ticket at him. He started to step away then turned back and pulled a twenty from his leather wallet. "And twenty on Risky Venture."

After accepting the second stub, he slipped both tickets into the inside pocket of his linen jacket and frowned. Now why did I do that? he wondered as he made his way to the portable bar. Always a careful man even at the track, the impulsive action surprised him.

It's only twenty dollars, he reminded himself as he ordered two mint juleps. He could well afford to lose that much...and more. After paying for the drinks, he wove his way back through the crowd and to his seat. "Here's your drink," he said and held out a glass for the woman to take.

She accepted the souvenir glass topped with a sprig of mint and turned her knees so that he could pass. "Thanks."

She held out three dollars, but Stuart waved it away. "My treat."

She grinned. "Well, then, thanks again. By the way—" she shifted the glass to her left hand and extended her right "—I'm Al McCord."

He took the offered hand and frowned when his

palm met the cool condensation the glass had left there. "Al?" he echoed.

She laughed. "Short for Alyssa. My dad wanted a son. And yours?"

Now why in the world would the woman want to know whether my father had wanted a son or a daughter? Hoping to silence her questions, he replied dryly, "I don't think he cared one way or the other."

At his unexpected answer, she laughed again. "No, I meant your name. What's your name?"

"Oh." Momentarily flustered, he pulled a handkerchief from his pocket and wiped the dampness from his hand before replying, "Stuart Greyson."

"Stuart?" The last time Al had heard that name had been in a European history class when she'd studied England's royal lines. She wrinkled her nose at him. "Kind of stuffy, don't you think?" She eyed the charcoal linen jacket covering his broad shoulders then dropped her gaze to the precise crease in slacks a shade darker than the jacket. Visions of monarchs and kings dressed in the staid fashions of court leaped to mind.

Pursing her lips to hide her amusement, she raised her gaze to meet dark eyes narrowed at her in a disapproving frown. "No?" she asked innocently enough. "Well, I guess it does suit you." She lifted her glass in a toast. "Here's to you, Stuart Greyson. May we both leave the track a little wealthier than when we arrived."

He watched the glass touch her lips and her eyes close as the cool, bourbon-laced drink hit her tongue. The thickest eyelashes he'd ever seen swept down to touch a high slash of cheekbones the afternoon sun had painted a rosier hue. A pink-tipped tongue snaked out and made a slow, sensuous journey around her lips. As much as he wanted to, he found he couldn't take his eyes off her.

"Ahh. Nothing like a mint julep, don't you agree?" She balanced the glass on the chair arm between them as she shifted to retrieve her program. The glass slipped, and the syrupy liquid sloshed over the side, splashing onto Stuart's linen-covered thigh, making him jump.

"Oops. Sorry." She yanked the handkerchief from his hand and mopped at the stain. "No harm done. It'll dry." She stuffed the handkerchief into his jacket pocket, gave it a satisfied pat, then settled back in her chair and took a sip of her drink.

Dipping his head, Stuart frowned at the wad of stained silk. The woman was a disaster looking for a place to happen.

"Are you from Louisville?" she asked as if nothing out of the ordinary had happened.

"Yes." He removed the handkerchief and refolded it properly before tucking it back in place.

Al noted the movement and mentally confirmed that the man's name did in fact suit him. A stuffed shirt if ever there was one. "Me, too. At least now I am. I'm originally from Dallas, but I've been living here for the past ten years. This is my first Derby though. How about you?"

"I come every year."

"Really? You must know the right people. Tickets are hard to come by."

"Yes, well..."

She laughed gaily. "But then I'm sure you *would* know the right people, wouldn't you, Stuart?" Not waiting for an answer, she chatted on. "A friend of mine at the gallery where I work got my ticket for me. She knows somebody who knows somebody who—well, you get the picture. Anyway, here I am!"

The bugler sounded the traditional call to post, obviously startling Al. "Oh, gracious! I haven't placed my bet." She gathered her mammoth purse and slung it over her shoulder, unknowingly knocking Stuart on the jaw. Apparently oblivious to his discomfort, she turned to ask, "Do you want me to place your bet for you?"

"No," he replied dryly as he rubbed a hand across his throbbing jaw. "I placed mine while I was out getting *your* drink."

"Oh, well. I'll be back in a minute."

What she offered in conversation, Stuart accepted as a warning. Sighing deeply, he slumped down in his seat. A minute was all she had promised, and he intended to enjoy every second. With her scatterbrained ways, the dizzy woman would probably get lost. That wishful thought drew a hopeful smile. He glanced at his watch, noted the earliness of the day and frowned again. With jabber jaws in the seat next to his, it looked as if it was going to be one hell of a long afternoon.

Her minute turned into ten. Stuart knew because he counted every one, relishing each for the welcome silence it offered. Unfortunately, she took her seat just as the announcer pronounced the horses in their starting positions.

Seconds later the horses broke from the gate, and Al lurched to her feet again. Stuart dropped his chin onto his palm in frustration. He hadn't missed a Derby in over ten years and not once in those ten years had he been subjected to a seat partner the likes of this—this *Al* person.

The skirt of her sundress grazed his thigh, followed quickly by heart-shaped hips which swayed dangerously close to his face. Bold bands of varying shades of blue blocked his view of the track. One of the shades matched the blue of her eyes. Stuart shook his head and sat up straighter in his chair, uncomfortable with the knowledge that he'd noticed the woman's eye color, much less the shape of her rear.

Suddenly she whirled and leaned down, bracing an arm on either side of him, her face bare inches from his. An exuberant smile stretched her lips to their limits. "I won!" she screamed in his face, then whirled back around, waving her arms above her head. "Way to go, Risky Venture! Way to go, baby!"

Stuart had no way of knowing how his own horse had placed. With Al blocking his view of the track, he'd missed the finish. He couldn't even hear the announcer's voice because his ears still rang from Al's piercing scream. The fact that he, too, had twenty dollars riding on Risky Venture didn't mollify him. He'd reached the limit of his patience. He caught Al's arm at the elbow and pulled her none too gently into her chair.

She seemed unaware of his action. Her gaze remained glued on the tote board where the payoffs were being listed. "Risky Venture pays sixteen eighty. I bet a hundred dollars so that means I won—" She grabbed for her purse and started digging. "Now where is that pencil?"

"Behind your ear." Stuart slumped farther down in his chair. "You win eight hundred and forty dollars."

She cocked her head toward him, her surprised expression asking, "How did you do that?"

He shrugged. "Come often enough and you learn the payoffs by heart."

"Wow! You must have a computer for a brain." She dropped her purse and pulled the pencil from behind her ear. "Four hundred and twenty on the first race, plus eight hundred and forty on the second." She scribbled the numbers on the back of her program. "Twelve hundred and sixty dollars. Can you believe it?" she demanded of Stuart. "I just turned two hundred dollars into twelve hundred and sixty!"

"I think the horses deserve a little of the credit," he muttered dryly.

"I'll have to remember to send a thank-you note or better yet, a bucket of oats. Oh, look!" Al said, gesturing to a man passing by. On his head the man wore a hat shaped in the form of Churchill Downs's famous twin spires.

Unimpressed, Stuart looked away. "He's here every year."

"Really? I just love hats. Don't you? There was a lady standing behind me at the betting windows and she had on the most darling hat. It was straw with dried flowers circling the crown and about a hundred different colored ribbons cascading down the back.'' A wistful sigh escaped her lips. ''I'd kill to have one like it.''

''No need to kill,'' he said sarcastically. ''You made enough on the first two races to buy a different hat for every day of the year.''

''No, siree.'' She shook her head for emphasis. ''I'm not spending this money on anything as frivolous as hats. This money is going to keep the buzzards away.''

Buzzards? Stuart pressed his lips together in a firm line, determined not to respond to the curious statement.

For the next three races, he ignored Al. It didn't keep her from chattering away at his side, but it pleased him to know he hadn't been suckered into answering any more of her endless questions. Although he did succeed in ignoring her, he found he couldn't ignore her method of betting—if there was a method to her madness.

She chose one horse because it looked friskier than the others when they had paraded in front of the stands. Another for its name. On the sixth race she'd changed her mind at the last minute and bet on a different horse altogether because the horse she had originally chosen was wearing blinders. Her reasoning had been that the horse couldn't see his competition, therefore wouldn't put forth his best effort.

But the most illogical choice of all was in the last race; she'd chosen the horse because the jockey had a cute rear end. The hell of it was, the woman kept winning—even the horse ridden by the jockey with the cute rear end had crossed the finish line first.

Her illogical, unearned success was doing nothing to improve Stuart's black mood. The only money he'd won so far had been on Risky Venture, his impulsive, last-minute wager placed solely on Al's recommendation. Just to prove he didn't agree with her logic, he purposely avoided betting on any horse she favored.

"Hold this please."

Before he could decline, Al plopped her program and pencil into his hands and then proceeded to empty the contents of her purse onto her lap. Wallet, lipstick, hairbrush, key ring, screwdriver—*screwdriver!*—package of chewing gum, a toothbrush, toothpaste and a wad of tissues landed on her lap.

Disgusted by the sight of such disorganized clutter, he looked away. His gaze settled on the program she had shoved into his hands and to the numbers scribbled on the back. His eyes widened. The woman had tallied almost six thousand dollars in winnings during the day. He thought of the measly one hundred and sixty-eight dollars he'd won and turned to frown at her.

Just as he turned, she took a bite of a roast beef sandwich which dripped mustard down her chin. Judging by the sandwich's mashed state, he assumed it must have been pulled from the bottom of her purse.

She glanced over at him and offered the other half. "Hungry?" she asked.

He eyed the drippy mess and tried not to curl his

nose. "No, thank you." He turned his attention back to the program and flipped it open to the eighth race, the famous Run for the Roses.

Al leaned over, reading over his arm. "Have you decided who to bet on yet?"

Avoiding the sandwich—which dripped dangerously close to his sleeve—he pulled his arm closer to his chest. "No."

"I have."

One dark brow arched up, appraisingly. "Oh? And what did you base your decision on this time? The color of the jockey's silks?"

Al laughed good naturedly at his sarcasm. "No. This one is special." She switched the sandwich to her left hand and licked the index finger of her right before pointing at the program. A slim almond shaped nail rested on number 12-F.

"A field horse?" At her nod, Stuart tossed back his head and laughed.

The rich sound of his laughter drew a smile from Al. She hadn't known the man had it in him. She'd seen nothing but a perpetual frown all day. "And what's so funny about that?" she asked.

"In the entire Derby history—over one hundred and fifteen races—only one field horse has ever won the Run for the Roses." His shoulders shook as he continued to laugh.

She settled back in her seat and took another bite of her sandwich. After she'd swallowed, she replied, "This one will."

Still smiling, Stuart hooked an arm over the back

of the seat and twisted around to better see her. "And what makes you so certain?"

She decided she liked him better when he smiled. His eyes lit up, and he didn't appear nearly as stuffy as when he frowned. "The horse's name is Ripcord. My dad's nickname was Cord."

Stuart waited. When she didn't offer anything else, he said, "Is that it? Just because your dad's nickname was Cord you're willing to bet on the horse?"

Her chin lifted defensively. "That's enough of a reason for me."

He pulled his arm down, shaking his head in disbelief. He gestured at the tote board. "Look at the odds. Ripcord is listed at 20-1. Surely that should tell you something."

She smiled smugly. "Yes, as a matter of fact, it does. It tells me I'm going to win *big*."

Voices, harmonizing the song "My Old Kentucky Home," filtered through the public address system. Al swallowed back the lump that quickly rose in her throat. The song always had that effect on her. It brought forth memories of Clairemore Farms and the sense of home it had provided her throughout the years. No matter what sacrifices she had to personally make, she knew she would gladly make them if it meant she could hold on to the farm.

When the song ended, the bugler blew the call to the posts, and the horses stepped onto the track, led by their outriders. While the horses made the post parade, Al sprinted to the betting windows and placed her wager. Stuart followed at a slower pace. Al placed her money on Ripcord, Stuart on Knight Rider.

When they returned to their seats, the horses were loping toward the far end of the track and the starting gate for the mile-and-a-quarter race.

Stuart folded his arms across his chest, his eyes narrowed on the track. "It's not too late, you know. You could always take some of your prior winnings and put money on a horse with better odds."

His attitude was condescending and too darn cocksure for Al's liking. She batted her eyelashes prettily and replied in a voice dripping with enough Southern charm it would have made her mother proud, "Why thank you for the advice, Mr. Greyson, but I'm pleased with my bet as placed." She picked up the other half of her sandwich and took a bite. In an attempt to control her growing anger at the stuffed shirt sitting beside her, she chewed slowly, counting to thirty before allowing herself to swallow.

"They're off!"

At the sound of the announcer's voice, Al rocketed to her feet. With the sandwich clutched in one hand, and the program in the other, she searched the field until she found the saddlecloth bearing the number 12-F. Ripcord was running third from the last in a field of thirteen horses.

A sliver of doubt worked its way into her confidence. Instead of the two hundred dollars she had planned to bet, she had been challenged by Stuart's skepticism to raise her bet to five hundred. It wasn't the first time in her life she had acted without thought to the consequences. She just hoped her impulsive action paid off...and big. So far, she'd won enough to pay the five thousand dollar payment on the farm's

mortgage. But she needed more: a stake for the future.
The continuation of Clairmore Farms lay in the success or failure of this race. "You can do it, Ripcord,"
she whispered under her breath. "You can do it,
boy."

"At the first pole, it's Dover first, Johnny's Boy
second, Windsong third. Coming up the middle is
Knight Rider."

Without thinking, Stuart rose to his feet, his hands
clenched into fists at his sides, his gaze riveted on the
chestnut squeezing his way through the pack of muscled Thoroughbreds. More than his money rode on
this race. His pride rode on the horse's back, as well.
And damn it, this time logic would win out.

Al's sandwich slipped from her fingers and plopped
against Stuart's Italian leather shoes. He ignored it.

"Dover continues to lead. Passing Johnny's Boy is
Windsong now in second. Knight Rider moves to the
outside. On the second pole it's Dover first, Windsong
still holding on to second, and Knight Rider running
third on the outside. Coming up fast on the rail is
Ripcord in fifth."

Al grabbed Stuart's arm as the horses thundered
past. He felt her nails dig into his sleeve, but he never
moved his gaze from the track. Every muscle in his
body was tensed, pulsing energy toward Knight
Rider.

"On the homestretch it's Knight Rider in the lead,
Dover second and Ripcord third. Ripcord moves to
second and is running nose to nose with Knight
Rider."

The pressure was too much. Al buried her face

against Stuart's sleeve as the horses approached the finish. The roar of the crowd muffled the announcer's voice as the horses crossed the finish line. Jerking her head up, Al, her face drained of color, sought Stuart's gaze. "Who won?"

"It's a photo finish," he said, looking into her fear-filled eyes.

The breath sagged out of Al. "Dear God," she whispered as she turned to look at the tote board where the words "photo finish" flashed. She caught her lower lip between her teeth. It didn't hide the quivering from Stuart. The nervous movement made him wonder just how much of her money rode on this race.

"The photos are in. It's—" The announcer's voice was lost in the cheer which rose from the crowd, but Al saw the results flash on the board.

Whirling around, she threw herself into Stuart's arms and planted a kiss full on his lips. "He did it! He won!" She kissed Stuart again, then danced a fast jig, unknowingly squashing her sandwich beneath her feet.

In a heartbeat she had her tickets in her hand and was flying up the aisle toward the betting windows, leaving Stuart staring after her. When she disappeared from sight, he dropped down in his chair. The woman was nuts. Plain and simple. And Lucky. Damn lucky, he added in frustration as he tore his own ticket stub in half and tossed it into the air, letting the breeze carry the useless paper where it would.

He bent over and picked up the program Al had dropped on the ground. Beside Ripcord's name was scribbled five hundred dollars. His jaw went slack as he quickly figured her take. The nut—that damn lucky nut—had just won over ten thousand dollars!

He wiped a hand down his face and looked again at her scribbling. Ten thousand dollars. His fingertips froze at his lips. And that harebrained woman was probably telling everyone within hearing distance about her luck.

You should go and help her, Stuart, protect her from anyone who might decide to take her money away from her. He ignored the little voice within him. Or at least he tried to. The woman wasn't his responsibility, he reasoned. What was it his stepfather always said? Something about God always taking care of children, animals and fools. In his mind, Al definitely fit in with the latter.

His reasoning didn't work. His conscience won out. Cursing under his breath, he pushed to his feet and went in search of Al. He found her weaving her way back through the crowd of people lined before the betting windows, victoriously waving a wad of bills above her head. The scene was exactly as he'd imagined...and worse.

A gnarled woman, standing in line with her purse clutched tightly at her waist, saw Stuart scowling at Al. "Do you know her?" she whispered, tipping her head discreetly toward Al.

"No. Well, sort of," he admitted regretfully.

"You'd better tell her to put that money in her purse quick before somebody decides to take it away from her." She nodded sagely, tightening her grip on her own purse. "It's been known to happen."

Stuart pulled his hands from his pockets, sighing heavily. "Yes, ma'am. I guess you're right." He approached Al and pulled her hand down, pinning it between their pressed sides as he ushered her through the crowd.

She tried to shake loose. "What are you doing?" she demanded.

"Just shut up and keep walking."

When she dug in her heels, refusing to take another step, he turned and glared at her. "I said keep walking."

"I'm not moving an inch until you tell me what's going on."

He released her wrist and cupped his hands at his hips. He jerked his head, indicating a group of people behind him and to his left. "See that guy over there?"

Rising on tiptoe to see over Stuart's shoulder, she asked, "Which guy?"

"The one in the yellow-and-green plaid jacket."

Al's gaze met that of a seedy-looking man wearing the flashy jacket Stuart had described and slacks of a different plaid. One of the man's shoulders rested negligently against the wall, the other was aimed at her. The man's gaze moved to Al's hand. Unconsciously she tightened her fingers around her roll of bills. "Yes, I see him."

"Well, aren't you just a little bit nervous?" he demanded irritably.

She shifted her gaze to Stuart's face. "No. Should I be?"

He rolled his eyes, then leveled them on her. "For God's sake! You're holding ten thousand dollars in your hand and carrying several thousand more in that suitcase you call a purse, and you're telling me you're not worried?''

Al laughed. ''Stuart, this is the Kentucky Derby! There are security guards everywhere.''

He folded his arms across his chest. ''Show me one.''

She glanced around, to her left, to her right, and finally behind her. Jerking her thumb over her shoulder, she proudly indicated a uniformed security guard. ''See! Right there by the gate.''

''A good thirty feet from where you are now standing. How long do you think it would take that security guard to get to you, if you needed him?''

Seeing the wisdom in his concern but not wanting to admit she was wrong, Al lifted a shoulder in a half-hearted shrug. Sheepishly she peeked through her bangs at Stuart's glowering face. ''Probably not in time, huh?''

''Probably not,'' he agreed.

She opened her purse and dropped her money inside, then looped her arm through Stuart's, startling him with her easy acquiescence. ''Does this mean you're going to be my bodyguard?'' she asked impishly.

His sigh was so heavy, it was audible even in the noisy crowd. ''Yes, I suppose it does.''

Stuart's concern for Al grew when they reached their seats. Word of her winnings had spread through the rows above and below them, and people were shouting their congratulations to Al. She accepted them with a curtsy and a wave.

Stuart started gathering up their belongings.

Puzzled when he pushed her purse back on her shoulder, Al asked, "What are you doing?"

"I'm getting you out of here. Where are you parked?"

"At Oxmoor Mall."

"Oxmoor Mall!" he echoed in disbelief. "That's on the other side of town! How did you get here?"

"The public bus. They have a shuttle that—"

"Forget it." He grabbed her elbow and guided her none too gently back up the aisle. "I'll drive you to your car."

She fought for balance as he hurried her along. "That's really not necessary. I'm sure I'll—"

"Trust me. It is." The tautness of his voice convinced her the man would brook no further arguments.

When they stepped through the gates fronting Churchill Downs, Al stopped, jerking Stuart to an abrupt halt at her side. She turned, shading her eyes with her hand as she looked back up at the twin spires behind her. She'd done it. Really done it! The money to save the farm was safe in her purse. Without warning, she whirled around and demanded, "Kiss me, quick!"

"What?" he asked in surprise.

"Kiss me! Daddy always said when you have a streak of luck you have to seal it up inside you with a kiss so it won't get away."

She tilted up her face, her eyelids shuttering closed over irises as blue as the May sky above them. The sun picked up the highlights in her hair, turning the mass of curls to spun gold. Before he realized he'd even moved, Stuart found his fingers threaded through the thick tresses above her right ear, exposing a pearl earring the size of a pea.

Pink lips, colored by nature, pursed invitingly just out of reach. Oh, what the hell, he thought recklessly. He bent his head and touched his mouth to hers. His lips had no sooner met hers when she threw her arms around his neck and her purse slapped him hard on the back. The whack on his back was nothing in comparison to the jolt his insides received when he felt her body mold to his.

Sweetness, innocence, a breath of spring. Thoughts and impressions piled up on one another faster than he could discern her taste.

The laughter of passersby slowly registered, and reluctantly Stuart pulled away. He was hard-pressed to decide which of them had been most affected by the kiss, as both of them were gulping for air, their gazes locked.

Everything within Al screamed for her to grab this man and hang on for dear life, lest he get away. One look at the worry lines deepening between his brows was all it took to silence those screams. Her arms still circling his neck, she squinched up her nose and gave him another fast peck. Stuffed shirts weren't Al McCord's style. No way!

She dropped her arms and adjusted her purse at her side. Smiling, she looped her arm through his and headed him toward the parking lot. "Now let me guess. You drive a four-door car. Probably gray. Right?"

Two

His car was a four-door, but more silver than gray. And loaded. It was all Al could do to keep from laughing.

Much to Stuart's annoyance, she entertained herself during the drive to Oxmoor Mall by fidgeting with the buttons and gadgets on the dashboard and door. The radio dial was changed from an easy listening station to one playing rock and roll. The passenger seat and headrest were adjusted to fit her smaller frame. The thermostat was turned to a cooler setting, and the window opened to let in volumes of fresh air.

Obviously, the woman wasn't one to be content with things as they were, Stuart thought irritably, but changed her environment to suit her own personal tastes.

When they reached the mall parking lot, Al pointed

out a fire engine-red Datsun. Stuart pulled to a stop behind it while she gathered her belongings. Plucking his jacket from the back of the seat, she started to climb out. She felt a tug from the opposite end of the jacket and tugged back.

"What do you think you're doing?" he asked in frustration.

She pointed to the mustard stain on the jacket's sleeve. "My fault entirely. I'll clean it and return it to you."

A mental picture of Al throwing his one-hundred percent linen, Italian-cut jacket in with a load of dirty towels made Stuart pull harder. "Please don't concern yourself. I'll have it dry-cleaned."

"No, really. It was my fault. I should have wiped my hands before I hugged you. Besides, it's the least I can do considering you acted as my bodyguard."

The reminder of her big win coupled with the memory of her throwing herself into his arms loosened Stuart's grip. The woman was nuts. He had to keep reminding himself of that fact. And he wasn't about to divulge his address to some crazy woman on the lame excuse of returning his jacket. Deciding that the price of the jacket would be small payment to be rid of her, he released his hold.

The sudden loss of tension had Al grabbing for the car door to keep from pitching over backward. After regaining her balance, she folded the jacket neatly over her arm, mimicking the care Stuart had taken when he had removed it and draped it over the seat. She gave him a saucy wink. "Don't worry, Stu baby. I'll take good care of it. Thanks for the lift." With a quick salute, she slammed the door and headed for her car.

Stu baby! Stuart tightened his grip on the steering wheel, every muscle in his body tensed in reaction to the woman. Yes, damn it, the price of the jacket was small payment to be rid of Al McCord.

Al breezed through the kitchen door and plunked her purse down on the butcher's block perched in the middle of the country kitchen. She upended the bag, dumping its entire contents on the wood surface scarred from years of use.

"Verdie!" She scooped up a handful of bills and called again. "Verdie! Come quick!"

Twenties, fifties, and hundreds sifted through her fingers. She scooped up another handful of bills just as the elderly woman shuffled into the kitchen.

When Verdie saw the money piled high on the block, she sailed her arms up in the air, then brought them down to rest on waves of gray hair, pin-curled high on her crown. "Lord have mercy! Did you rob a bank?" she asked breathlessly.

Al laughed and spun around the room, showering Verdie with a rain of greenbacks. "No, Verdie. I won it at the Derby."

"Alyssa Claire McCord! You stop that lying this instant and tell me where you got this money."

Al swept past Verdie, laughing as she dropped a kiss on a cheek as wrinkled as a prune. "It's the truth. I swear. Looks like the sun has finally decided to shine on Clairemore Farms once again."

Though her mouth remained pursed in disapproval,

the sternness in Verdie's eyes softened. She never had been able to remain mad at Al for long. A fact Al had taken advantage of ever since she had come to live in the Clairemores' home ten years ago.

"The sun never quit shining, honey," Verdie chided gently as she followed Al to the butcher's block. "It just passed behind a cloud for a while." Her eyes widened behind smudged bifocals as she got a better look at the money. "How much did you win?"

"I think twelve thousand, give or take a couple of hundred after the IRS got through. Can you believe it?" Al grabbed the old woman and danced around the table. "We're rich!"

Verdie twisted out of Al's arms and settled her shirtwaist dress over ample hips. "We nothing," she corrected, shaking a finger at Al. "*You're* rich. And if you're smart, you'll take that money along with one of the offers you've had for this farm and hightail it outta here."

Al wrinkled her nose at her grandparents' longtime housekeeper. "I can't do that, and you well know it." She ignored the frown building on Verdie's face and began to transfer the money from the butcher's block to the oak table in the breakfast nook.

"Now, Al. You know darned good and well there's no way you can make this farm pay for itself." Verdie trailed Al back and forth between the two tables. "You've done sold all your granddaddy's livestock, and Lord knows you're not a farmer, so you might as well take what you got and git."

Al brushed past Verdie and took a seat at the breakfast table. "You're wrong, Verdie. In fact, the most stupendous idea came to me while I was driving down the lane to the house." She began to deal the bills into stacks of fives, tens, twenties, fifties and hundreds.

"You know that stone barn that fronts our property on the highway?" Al didn't wait for an answer. She didn't need or require one. "It suddenly came to me what a perfect location that would be for an antique shop. I can pay the April note due the bank and still have plenty of money left to start a business. It wouldn't take much because the barn's in pretty good shape, and the tourist traffic the Thoroughbred farms draw should bring in some customers. With what we have on..."

Wearily, Verdie sank onto the oak pressed-back chair beside Al. She'd seen that determined gleam in Al's eyes often enough to know that nothing short of a steamroller would stop her once she set her mind to something. But with Al's granddaddy gone now, too, there wasn't anyone left to advise the child. Unless she considered that no-count mother of hers, and Verdie had quit counting on that worthless piece of humanity years ago.

She laid a blue-rivered hand atop Al's, stilling her sorting and silencing her plans. "You know I'm not one to meddle." At Al's incredulous look, Verdie added reluctantly, "Well, not much anyway. But since I'm all you have left, I feel it's my responsibility to advise you."

Seeing that she had Al's attention, Verdie settled back in her chair, her hands clasped righteously at her waist, content with her position as advisor. "Your granddaddy loved this place. Maybe too much. Some folks thought he should have sold Clairemore Farms years ago. Lord knows there've been enough offers since Louisville started growing out this direction. But he didn't sell, and there's nothing that can be done about that now. The point is, I don't think he'd expect you to try to hold on to this place, especially considering the mortgages he piled on it before he willed it to you."

Verdie saw the tears glistening in Al's eyes, knowing full well the reminder of the child's granddaddy was what put them there and not the mention of the wolves snapping at the back door, ready to foreclose on Clairemore Farms.

Al straightened the stack of hundreds while she blinked back the unwanted tears. Verdie Mae Johnson was privy to more than her share of the Clairmores' private affairs. She'd worked for the family for almost thirty years and had even been at the house waiting when Harley and Virginia Clairemore had brought their granddaughter home to live at Clairemore Farms after the death of Al's father in Dallas, Texas.

Clairemore Farms had been Al's home for ten years and had symbolized home for more years than that. The summers she had spent visiting her grandparents were some of her most pleasant memories—sharing the exalted spot in her heart with memories of her father.

Granted, Harley Clairemore had been obsessed with hanging on to the farm that had been in his family almost two hundred years. But Al understood that obsession. She also understood that by willing the farm to her instead of to his money-grabbing daughter, her granddaddy had expected her to try to keep the farm intact.

The weight of that responsibility was almost more than Al could bear.

To pay her granddaddy's medical bills and funeral expenses, she'd sold off the remaining herd of cattle. When Verdie had said she knew almost nothing about farming, she wasn't far from wrong. Al had no clue how to turn the farm into a profitable business, at least not in the sense it had been in the past when crops and livestock had paid the bills.

What she *did* know was antiques. And therein lay her only hope.

She lifted her gaze to meet that of the woman who had had as much a hand in raising her as her grandmother and granddaddy. "I think he did intend for me to try to save the farm, Verdie. If he hadn't, he would have left the farm to my mother."

When Verdie opened her mouth to argue the point, Al lifted a hand, silencing her. "But I want you to know that I'm doing this as much for myself as I am for him. Clairemore Farms is my home, too, the only secure spot I've ever known. For my sake as much as Granddaddy's, I have to at least try."

Verdie pressed arthritic hands to even stiffer knees as she pushed herself to her feet. "Girl, you got yourself a long row to hoe this time." With that last warning, she turned and shuffled from the room, leaving Al staring thoughtfully at the pile of money.

* * *

"How long do you think you'll be gone?" Stuart asked the man sitting opposite him behind the cluttered desk.

"A week, I hope. Two at the most." Morrey Yale unlocked his desk and pulled the bottom drawer open. A diamond glittered on the ring finger of his left hand as he flipped through the tight line of files. "You might drop in on your mother while I'm away. She's seemed a little blue lately."

Stuart's mouth curved in a disapproving frown. "She lives in a blue funk, if you ask me." The look Morrey shot him made Stuart offer, "Sorry, Morrey, but it's the truth. I don't know why you put up with her dramatics."

"I love her, that's why." He tossed a file across the desk to Stuart. "This is the file on that land acquisition we've been working on. Of the total six hundred and forty acres, we've managed to obtain options on all but an eighty-acre tract. I've talked to the old geezer who owns the place until I'm blue in the face. Why don't you have a go at him?" He bit back a smile, one eyebrow arching high on his forehead without a prayer of touching the silver hair combed to cover the ever increasing baldness on his head. "Maybe you can work that famous Greyson charm on the old man."

Stuart's face flushed an angry red. "That's a low blow, Morrey."

Rearing back in his chair, Morrey eyed Stuart covertly. "Speaking of your father, how is the old devil?"

Stuart stood and gathered the bulging file under his

arm. "Why don't you ask Mother?" he asked, his calm voice a sharp contrast to the thunderous look he aimed at his stepfather. "She would know better than I."

Disagreements between the two men were scant, and what few they had in one way or another centered on Stuart's divorced parents. As far as stepfathers went, Stuart couldn't have asked for a better one than Morrey Yale. He paused at the office door and turned back, already regretting the biting remark. "By the way, thanks for the Derby ticket."

Morrey offered him a conciliatory smile. "My pleasure. Did you win any money?"

Chuckling, Stuart replied, "Win? Hell, Morrey, I lost the jacket off my back."

"I think the saying is 'shirt off my back,' isn't it?"

"In this case, I mean literally the jacket off my back." Stuart waved as he stepped through the doorway, leaving Morrey to stare after him, a puzzled frown wrinkling his forehead.

When he reached his own office at the end of the hall, Stuart tossed the file on his credenza and dropped down on his chair. He spun around until he faced the wall of maps and framed pictures on his left. A shopping mall, three apartment complexes and an office building were depicted there both pictorially and geographically. He'd had a hand in the development of them all. Each one was a step closer to his goal of becoming a self-made millionaire by the age of thirty. Morrey's knowledge and willingness to take his stepson into his successful real estate development company had given Stuart an edge most young businessmen lacked. It was a kindness Stuart would never forget.

He glanced at the file resting on his desk, the one Morrey had given him. This undertaking was the biggest investment yet. A subdivision of small acreage tracts on Louisville's fast developing southwest corner. Prospect, Kentucky. Even the name of the small country town quickly being absorbed by Louisville seemed apt for this endeavor. If they managed to put the real estate deal together, his share of the profits alone would put him well over his goal.

A smile pulled at the corner of his mouth. When he made that first million, he could thumb his nose at the bastards who were waiting for him to fail.

As always, just thinking about the subdivision made his pulse race, like a thoroughbred pulling on the bit, ready to run. He opened up the file and flipped through the pages until he found Morrey's notes on the eighty acres still outstanding.

Morrey was a meticulous man. His notes proved it. Each visit was recorded with a date and the results of the interview. The dates varied, but the results were always the same. An unequivocal no. Stuart ran a blunt finger down the list, noting the dates. The last contact had been over six weeks ago.

He leaned across his desk and picked up the phone, then dropped it back onto its cradle. Saying "no" on the phone was a lot easier than saying "no" in person, and Stuart Greyson wasn't going to make this easy on—he pulled the file back open and searched out the old geezer's name. Harley Clairemore. *Well,*

Mr. Clairemore, Stuart thought smugly, *prepare yourself to hear an offer you can't refuse.*

Where Louisville stopped and Prospect, Kentucky, picked up was discernible by one lone sign which read Prospect, Kentucky, Population 3,000. If a person missed it, he'd never even realize he was leaving Louisville. The city had grown, pushing at the neighboring town's boundaries until they were nearly invisible, tied as they were by constantly growing residential subdivisions.

He passed through Prospect proper and continued north toward Oldham County. Through the mirrored sunglasses he wore in deference to the bright afternoon sunshine, Stuart found May in evidence on the countryside. The dogwood and the redbud trees were in full bloom, creating a blur of red, white and pink as he sped down State Highway 42. Below the trees and along the shoulders of the highway, wildflowers pushed their way through rock and clumps of grass, intent on glimpsing the sun.

Bordering both sides of the winding roadway, black creosote fences spliced the rolling land into pastures dotted with thoroughbreds. Kentucky was as famous for its thoroughbred horse farms as it was for its grass that rippled in the breeze like a blue sea.

In his mind, Stuart could already picture the stone pillars announcing the entrance to Greystone Estates, the subdivision he hoped to begin work on within the year. The land would be subdivided into two-, five- and ten-acre tracts. The plans incorporated a plot of land to be set aside for the private use of the property owners and which would include a stable, swimming pool, tennis courts and a picnic area by the lake.

The thought of the lake reminded him of his purpose in driving out to the countryside today. The lake lay within the eighty acres owned by Harley Clairemore and was integral in the plans for Greystone Estates.

Seeing the wrought-iron arch on which Clairemore Farms was scrolled, Stuart flipped on his directional signal and turned right, guiding his Lincoln Continental down the lane bordered on both sides by massive oaks. The trees' branches laced above him, creating a canopy of shade, a welcome respite from the sun's blinding rays.

In front of the two-story stone farmhouse, he braked the car to a stop and climbed out. A dog appeared out of nowhere, barking at Stuart's heels. He held out a hand and allowed the dog to sniff it. The barking ceased and the dog's tail wagged, his hips rocking eagerly with each swipe.

Confident the dog's bark was worse than his bite, Stuart bent and gave the animal a friendly scratch behind the ears. "Hello there, boy. Anybody at home?"

The dog rolled to his back, inviting Stuart to scratch his stomach, as well. He laughed and gave the dog a last brisk rub. "Sorry, old boy. Maybe next time."

He straightened and headed for the front porch, the dog trailing behind him. To the right of the heavy front door, centered with an oval-etched glass, Stuart found an antiquated hand-crank door bell. He gave it a hearty twist, then waited. Beyond the front door, he heard the distant whine of a vacuum cleaner. Knowing the bell couldn't be heard over the ruckus inside, he lifted a fist and gave the weathered wood a couple of good whacks. The noise inside stopped, and he heard heavy footsteps, moving in a lethargic shuffle toward the door.

The door opened, and a grumpy-looking woman stuck out her gray head. "What do you want?" she demanded irritably. The dog tried to slip inside, and the woman pushed the door to until only a narrow crack remained, almost snipping off the dog's nose. "Get outta' here, you old mangy mutt," she yelled in a voice reminiscent of a fishwife.

The dog slunk off the porch and down the steps with his tail tucked between his back legs.

Stuart decided he wouldn't be as easily dealt with. He offered a friendly smile and his hand. "Mrs. Clairemore?"

"Humph!" The woman opened the door wider as she gave Stuart's manicured hand a disapproving glance while she held her own work-roughened ones in a tight fist at her waist. "I ain't Mrs. Clairemore. She's been dead and gone for nigh on to three years." She bowed her head and added reverently, "God rest her soul." She snapped her head back up and narrowed her gaze suspiciously at Stuart. "The name's Verdie. Verdie Mae Johnson. I'm the Clairemores' housekeeper."

Seeing his hand still held aloft, Verdie reluctantly unfolded her hands and extended her right to meet his.

"Stuart Greyson, Ms. Johnson. I'm here to see Mr. Clairemore."

Verdie tugged her hand from the grasp of the smooth-talking stranger's and folded it back at her waist, not sure whether to trust the man or not. "He's dead, too. Gone about five weeks now."

This surprising bit of news struck Stuart speechless. Not knowing what to do or what to say, he dipped his head and studied the peeling paint on the porch floor. "I'm sorry to hear that, Ms. Johnson. I had hoped to talk with him about some business matters."

The business matters he mentioned, Verdie was sure, had to do with the land. He wouldn't be the first—nor probably the last—to come offering to buy the place from Al. She gave the man in front of her a quick once-over. He was a businessman, and a successful one, judging by the cut of his suit. She narrowed an eye to better see the expensive car in the drive beyond him. Yep, he was rich all right, and God knew Al could do with a little of that money.

The humble way in which he'd dipped his head when hearing of Harley Clairemore's decease convinced Verdie that he had not known that fact before hearing it from her own lips. More people than she cared to count had come sniffing around after Mr. Clairemore's death, hoping to steal the farm at a bargain price right out from under Al's unsuspecting nose. Al called them buzzards, and in Verdie's mind the description fit.

Deciding Stuart Greyson was a gentleman and didn't deserve being labeled with them lowlifes, Verdie offered what she hadn't to the others who had come around when Al was away from the house. "Then you'll be needing to talk to Mr. Clairemore's granddaughter. She's the one in charge now."

"And how might I contact her?"

Verdie jerked her head toward the lane. "Back up the lane, just before you reach the highway, there's a stone barn on the left. You'll find her there."

Stuart smiled and extended his hand once again, unknowingly settling himself further in Verdie's good graces. "Thank you for your help, Ms. Johnson. I'll drive down and talk with her."

His smile was enough to kick up the speed of even an old woman's heart. Verdie watched him drive away and smoothed an age-freckled hand across the wisps of hair that had escaped her pin curls. He would catch me looking such a mess, she thought. Making a tsking sound with her tongue at her own foolery, she closed the front door while she sent up a silent prayer that Al had the good sense to at least listen to the man's offer.

Inside the barn, rock and roll music blared from a jam box propped up on boxes heaped with an assortment of debris, nearly deafening Stuart. On the far side of the barn, a young woman worked. Her hips swayed to the music's fast beat beneath jeans cut just short of exposing a well-shaped cheek. A fringe of white and blue threads from the jeans' jagged hem brushed across her tanned thighs. The red bandanna she wore tied around her forehead like a sweatband didn't keep her overlong bangs from obstructing her vision. She gave them a careless swipe before bending her back to the wide-based broom in her hands.

Dust motes danced in the sunlight, arcing from windows on her right while a barn cat sat on a window ledge washing its paws with a pink-tipped tongue, sunning, undisturbed by the chaos around it.

"Good God!" The oath slipped from Stuart's lips before he could stop himself, but it appeared she hadn't heard. The music was so loud he wasn't really surprised.

From the barn's open doorway, he took another step inside, not quite trusting the sight before him. "Al?" he called, raising his voice slightly.

The cat lifted its head, gave him a cursory glance, then turned back to its preening. The woman continued to sweep, dancing her way across the wide barn, leaving a swirl of dust in her wake.

He cupped his hands to his mouth, reluctant to draw any nearer to the dirt she was kicking up with her broom and her feet, and called again, louder this time. "Al!"

She dropped the broom and whirled, her face registering surprise. When she saw Stuart, a smile slowly spread across her face. She hurried toward him, rubbing her palms against the seat of her cut-offs. "Hi, Stuart!" She rose on tiptoe and pecked a kiss on his cheek, her hands gripping his elbows for balance.

Sinking back down on her heels, she planted her palms at her hips and cocked her head to the side, disarming him with her smile. "I'll bet you came for your jacket didn't you?" Before he could reply, she shrugged and said, "The dry cleaners won't have it ready until tomorrow."

The sense of relief Stuart felt at discovering his jacket was at the dry cleaners and hadn't been thrown in with a load of dirty towels was quickly forgotten. It was really Al standing before him. Al McCord— the ditzy woman from the Derby—owned Clairemore Farms. While that mind-boggling fact settled in his brain, he unconsciously touched a hand to his cheek, remembering other kisses she had planted there. The woman dealt out kisses with the speed most women batted their lashes.

She grinned impishly. "Don't worry. I didn't get you dirty."

Embarrassed, Stuart pulled his hand from his cheek. Dragging his gaze from Al's teasing eyes, he glanced around the barn. It was bare except for the boxes heaped by the front door from where the music continued to blare. "Can you turn that thing down?"

"Sorry." She jogged to the door and flicked off the offensive radio. Silence fell heavily over the barn. The only sound remaining came from the tin roof overhead where the wind plucked at a melody of its own.

She lifted her arms and let them drop. "Well, what do you think?"

"Think of what?" he asked in confusion.

"My antique shop."

A sliver of apprehension worked its way down his spine. An antique shop? Her pronouncement played havoc with his own plans for the farm. He had envisioned using this barn as a temporary sales office when he and Morrey were ready to sell the tracts.

Before he could question her further, a car horn sounded outside. Al whirled, straining to see beyond the barn's door.

"Darn!" she muttered as she fitted her hands into angry fists at her hips.

"Who is it?" Stuart asked, crossing to stand behind her.

"The buzzards have arrived."

The comment drew his gaze from the white Cadillac pulling up out front to the wisps of curls on the back of Al's head. She'd mentioned the buzzards in passing at the racetrack, but he had intentionally avoided questioning her about the odd statement. Now he wished he had.

He tried to mask his curiosity as he asked, "Who are the buzzards?"

"The sleazy guys who keep dropping by trying to weasel the farm away from me."

A wave of guilt washed over Stuart.

"Stand back," she warned. "This isn't going to be a pretty sight."

"Al, sweetheart!" A thick-waisted man stepped through the door, grabbed Al's hand and pumped it up and down. "How are you doing?" he asked, his smile melting into a look of concern.

"Fine, Mr. Bandy. Just fine."

"Such a shock," he said, shaking his bald head sadly. "Why it seems like only yesterday when Harley and I shared a glass of lemonade out on the front porch while we talked over business matters."

"Yes it does, doesn't it?" Al smiled sweetly, but Stuart could see the flush of anger on her neck. He knew George Bandy, or at least he knew the man's reputation. Al had pegged him right. George Bandy was a buzzard, always looking to profit from someone else's misfortune.

As if he'd just noticed Stuart, George stuck out his hand. "I don't believe I've had the pleasure. George Bandy."

Stuart accepted the hand. "Stuart Greyson, Mr. Bandy."

Bandy frowned and scratched at his chin. "Greyson? Name's familiar. Have we met before?"

"No, I don't believe so." Stuart experienced a moment's unease as he waited for Brandy to place the name Greyson with that of Yale and Greyson Real Estate Investment Corporation.

Thankfully Al sidetracked the man before he made the connection. "I'm sorry you've come all this way for nothing, Mr. Bandy, but my answer is the same as my grandfather's. Clairemore Farms is not for sale."

To his credit, Bandy hid his disappointment well. "Now I didn't come out here to talk business, Al. Just dropped by to offer my sympathies." He pulled a fat cigar from his shirt pocket and stuck it in his mouth, quickly rolling it to one side. He clamped his teeth around the brown stub and hitched up his pants.

With a proprietary air that made Al grit her teeth, Bandy strutted around the barn, slapping a meaty hand on a wall, testing for soundness. "What are you planning to do with the place now that you've sold off all the livestock?''

It grated against her nerves to know the man knew so much of her business. "Oh, I don't know," she replied demurely. "I've given some thought to raising thoroughbreds. There's a lot of money to be made on horses."

Raising horses? Stuart thought in bewilderment. Not more than five minutes ago she'd told him she was going to open an antique shop! Realization dawned when he saw the mischievous glint in her eye. It was all he could do to keep from laughing. The woman might appear harebrained, but she certainly knew how to handle a shyster the likes of George Bandy.

"If you'll excuse us, Mr. Bandy, we were just leaving." Al turned her head toward Stuart and gave him a conspiratorial wink. "Stuart here is a pro when it comes to horses and he's going to share that knowledge with me, aren't you, Stuart?" She linked her arm through his and positioned herself by the door, waiting for George to leave.

Scowling, Bandy pushed a business card into her hand as he brushed past her. "When you get ready to sell, give me a call. I'll treat you right."

Under her breath, Al mumbled, "I'll just bet you will."

At the door to his dust-covered Cadillac, Bandy paused and turned. He jerked the cigar stub from his mouth and aimed it accusingly at Stuart. "I remember now. You're Morrey Yale's stepson." He chuckled then flicked the cigar stub over the car door to land

RUN FOR THE ROSES

in the dirt at Al's feet. "Looks like I've got me some competition, huh?" He chuckled again, then angled himself into the car, squeezing his generous stomach behind the steering wheel.

Her eyes narrowed on Bandy's car as it drove out of sight; Al ripped the man's business card into shreds, then tossed it into the air. Without moving her gaze from the road, she asked, "What did he mean by that?"

"By what?"

She cocked her head toward Stuart. "When he said he had some competition?"

Stuart shrugged then admitted reluctantly, "I'm afraid I'm one of the buzzards."

Al's eyes widened and her mouth dropped open. Stuart braced himself for the brunt of her anger to hit him full force.

Instead she burst out laughing. "You!" she asked still laughing. "I can't believe this!" She turned and snapped the padlock on the barn door before she faced him again. With her arms crossed at her waist, she looked up at him, a half smile lingering on her lips. "And what would you do with Clairemore Farms if I were to sell it to you?"

"Subdivide it into acreage tracts."

Though her smile remained in place, he saw the flash of pain in her eyes at his mention of dividing the farm. "It would be a first-class development," he hurried to assure her.

"First-class, second-class, doesn't matter to me. Clairemore Farms isn't for sale."

"Now or ever?"

Remembering the size of the mortgages stacked against her property, Al's smile faded. "For as long as I can hold on to it. Does that answer your question?"

"For now, but I must warn you, I don't give up easily."

She cocked her head and studied him. No, he wouldn't be a man to give up easily, she decided. The determined gleam in his eyes told her that. What was behind that determination? There were acres and acres of land for sale in Oldham County.

Curious to know why he wanted her land, she asked, "Why Clairemore Farms? I'm sure there are plenty of other owners who would be more than willing to sell you their land."

"True. But your farm holds one attraction the others don't. Location. It's far enough away from Louisville to appeal to those who prefer a rural setting but close enough to the city that those who chose to live here could still enjoy the city's benefits."

Al's mouth curved into a thoughtful frown. "Bandy has much the same idea."

"On paper maybe."

"Meaning?"

"Bandy is a second-rate developer. He does everything below cost and without thought to environment or aesthetics."

"And you do?"

Stuart folded his arms across his chest and eyed Al sardonically. "I don't put my name on anything I can't be proud of."

Amused by his proudful stance, Al replied, "No, I

don't guess you would.'' Without warning, she slipped her fingers between her lips and let out a piercing whistle. An answering bark sounded from the pasture at Stuart's left.

Al turned to Stuart and offered him a smile. ''How about a glass of lemonade?''

As it had that afternoon at the Derby, the sunlight panned the gold in her hair, drawing Stuart's attention away from the bewitchment of her smile only to lose himself in the teasing way her hair feathered against a rosy cheek. More often than he would like to admit, he had found his thoughts over the past few days drifting to the woman who had monopolized his time and endangered his sanity at the Derby.

Without thinking, he brushed the wispy curl away from her cheek but caught himself before he allowed his lips to follow the path of his fingers. He couldn't afford to let his emotions get involved in a business deal. Especially this one. He withdrew his hand and rolled his wrist, exposing the face of a gold watch and a white starched cuff with the initials SPG monogrammed in rich burgundy. ''Maybe another time. I've an appointment to make.''

''Stuart, Stuart,'' she chided gently. ''Don't you ever play?''

He ignored the comment. ''Can I give you a ride to your house?''

She shook her head as she squinted up at the sun, relishing its warmth. ''I'd rather walk. I've been inside all day. The fresh air will do me good.'' Waving to him, she turned and jogged off across the field, stopping once to grab up a clump of daisies growing wild beside the worn path. Stuart watched as she slipped several of the flowers behind her ear before he turned to his car.

Al stopped and glanced back over her shoulder. With her fingertips pressed at her ear to hold the daisies in place, she watched as Stuart slid behind the wheel of his car. Though distant, his movements were easily defined. With his face angled toward the rearview mirror, he combed his fingers through hair the wind had seen fit to muss. His hand then dropped to the knot of silk at his neck and snugged it up higher in the nest created by the starched points of his collar. Although his hands were no longer visible, Al knew their movements when she heard the powerful engine roar to life.

Brake lights flashed red, then added a narrow slash of white as Stuart carefully reversed before heading the car down the dirt road to the lane. A modest cloud of dust swelled behind the rear tires. Unlike Bandy, who had gunned his car over the deeply rutted road, Stuart handled his car with the same caution with which it appeared he handled his life.

A daisy slipped from behind her ear and fell to the ground. Without bothering to pick it up, she turned and headed for the house, her steps slower than before. Her dog met her halfway to the house. She dropped a hand to trail along Ranger's back as he trotted at her side but her mind remained on Stuart Greyson.

He was an ambitious man. The signs were all there, flashing like warning beacons for her to see. The cut of his clothes, the thread of impatience kept just out of sight, the inflexibility that kept him on a schedule he himself had set. She'd seen ambition in a man before and had seen the havoc it could wreak. Stuart Greyson was on a roller coaster to self-destruction, and Al knew it was up to her to throw on the brakes.

Verdie met Al at the back door. "Did you talk to that man?" she asked as she kicked out one foot to block Ranger's entrance.

Al rolled her eyes when reminded of her meeting with George Bandy. "Yes, I talked to the old buzzard. And I told him the same thing Granddaddy told him—no sale!"

Verdie watched Al climb the back stairs, her lips pursed tight in disapproval. *Old buzzard?* The girl had surely gone daft. "Damn fool child," Verdie mumbled sourly as she gathered up her purse. "Ought to take that nice man's money and run while she has the chance."

Three

Yawning sleepily, Stuart pushed his fingers through his hair as he stumbled to the front door. After punching in the buttons to disengage the alarm system, he leaned a palm against the door frame and wearily pulled open the door.

"Hi!" Al stood opposite him, grinning. The sun peeked over her shoulder in blushes of pink, blue and mauve, confirming what Stuart already suspected. It was just after dawn.

He dragged a hand down his face and looked again, moving his gaze from the top of her curly head to her feet. Yes, it was Al. If nothing else, the high-top red tennis shoes rimmed with socks the color of egg yolks were enough to convince him it was indeed the outlandish Al who stood at his door.

While Stuart was apparently making his assessment, Al was busy making one of her own. She'd awakened him. That was obvious. His eyes were heavy with sleep, and his hair was tousled. A silk robe the color of a rich, dark wine was tied haphazardly at his waist. Below its hem, navy pajama bottoms, piped in the same color as his robe, drooped to puddle around his bare feet. Without seeing the monogram, Al *knew* his initials rode on his pajama's shirt pocket.

Not waiting for an invitation, she breezed past him and shoved a plastic wrapped jacket against his chest. The dry cleaner's ticket scraped Stuart's hand as he grabbed for a hold on the slick bag. Wide-awake now and incensed by Al's nerve, he kicked the door closed with a bare foot as his gaze narrowed on her back.

He watched as she trailed a finger along the entry hall table's black lacquered finish, then pause to pick up a cut crystal bowl filled with potpourri. Holding it aloft, she searched out the manufacturer's etched name. She smiled, nodding her approval of his taste as she gently replaced it. Her smile wilted and her nose curled slightly as she peeked into the living room with its ultramodern decor. Stuart suspected the potpourri might be the only thing of which she approved.

"What do you think you're doing?" he demanded irritably.

Al cocked her head toward him. "Returning your jacket."

"How did you know my address?"

"The telephone directory."

Obviously pleased with her sleuthing, she rocked back on her heels and slipped her thumbs into the side openings of her cutoff overalls. The bib dipped dangerously low, exposing a flash of bare skin. A bright yellow tube top, the same color as her socks, peeked from beneath her arm. Stuart felt his breath slowly ease out of him. For a moment, he'd feared she wore nothing beneath the wide straps of the carpenter-style overalls.

His anger returned with his breath. "Consider it returned." He reached for the brass knob, prepared to show Al the door. Her voice stopped him before he could twist it open.

"Do you wear boxer shorts or jockey briefs?"

He pulled himself around to face her and found her gaze centered below his waist. Fighting the impulse to glance down to make sure he was decently covered, he cinched his robe tighter. "My underwear is no concern of yours."

She shrugged as if it didn't really matter. "Just curious." She closed the distance between them and adjusted the wrinkled folds of his robe's lapels. "Most stuffed shirts wear boxer shorts."

He brushed her hand away. "I suppose you have statistics to back up that remark? Never mind," he interjected before she could respond. He found he wasn't sure he wanted to hear if she could indeed support her ludicrous statement.

She glanced at her watch. "Better hurry, Stuart or we'll miss the best buys."

"What best buys?" he demanded, his voice rising in irritation.

"The ones at the auction we're going to."

"I don't remember agreeing to go to any auction. Besides, I have to work at the office today."

"Stuart, Stuart," she chided in that placating voice that was beginning to grate on his nerves. "You've got to learn to relax a little. Have some fun for a change."

"And I suppose an auction is your idea of a good time?"

"Well, sure it is. Now hurry up or we'll be late," she said, as she propelled him down the hall.

An auction at daybreak wasn't Stuart's idea of a good time at all, and besides that, he'd already concluded that whatever attraction he felt for Al McCord would have to be stifled. He had business to conduct with her and he made it a policy never to mix his business life and his personal life.

The acquisition of Clairemore Farms was essential to the culmination of his plans for the future, and when the farm sold—as he knew it ultimately would be—he intended for the deed to the property to rest in his hand and not in the hand of some swindler like George Bandy. And he intended for that to happen without anyone being able to point a finger at him later and say he'd used the Greyson charm to entice the land away from Al.

With that thought in mind, Stuart jerked to a stop and pulled his arm from Al's grasp. "I appreciate the invitation, but I make it a policy never to mix business and pleasure."

Honorable. Al quickly added that adjective to the list of characteristics she'd already credited to Stuart Greyson. And stubborn, she thought as she caught his elbow again and continued down the hall. "Then what's the problem? I've already told you the farm's not for sale."

Although he tried to find a hole in her argument, something to grasp and debate the point, Stuart found he couldn't. It was too early in the morning and his brain wasn't up to matching wits with a woman whose mind switched gears faster than a race car driver. Wearily, Stuart gave in. "Okay, I'll go. Give me a minute to change clothes."

He was halfway to the bedroom when he realized Al was still at his side. Jerking his arm free of her, he said tersely, "I can dress myself, thank you."

She backed away from his thunderous expression. "Sure. I'll just wait in the kitchen. How do you like your coffee? A little sugar to sweeten your disposition?" she asked, her eyes bright with mischief.

"Black," he growled before slamming the bedroom door in her face.

Al found the kitchen at the rear of the house and dug through cabinets until she found the coffee grounds. She perched herself on the tiled countertop while she waited for the coffee to drip into the pot.

Without trying to hide her disgust, she curled her nose as she glanced around the kitchen. It was as cold and uninviting as the rest of his house. Stainless steel, white tiled countertops and black-and-white tiled floor. Not a speck of color anywhere. She wondered how he could stand it.

She kicked out her feet and smiled at her bright red high tops. She loved color and filled her life with it. And if she had her way, a little of that color would spill onto Stuart and maybe in the process take a little of the starch out of his shirt.

The light flashed, indicating the coffee had perked. Al poured two cups and headed for the bedroom.

In the master bath, Stuart rubbed a towel across the mirror over the double-sink vanity. Steam fogged all but the circle he'd cleared in front of him. He lathered his face and lifted his razor for the first swipe.

"I knew it had to be boxer shorts."

At the sound of Al's voice, Stuart whirled, then cursed as the razor nicked his skin. A spot of blood appeared on his jaw, as bright a red as the color warming his cheeks.

Al laughed at his embarrassment. "Don't worry. I've seen a man in his underwear before." She set the coffee cups down and pulled a tissue from the brass container on the vanity. "Although my roommate wore briefs. A strictly platonic arrangement," she assured the stricken Stuart as she tore off a corner of the tissue and pressed it against the cut.

He caught her wrist and pulled her hand down to her side. Shrugging, she hopped onto the vanity, "Suit yourself. I was only trying to help."

He glared at her through narrowed eyes. "If you don't mind, I'd like to finish shaving."

"Go right ahead. I love to watch a man shave. If you want, I can even do it for you. At the end, when Granddaddy was too weak to do it for himself, I used to shave him."

The thought of the harebrained woman with a razor at his throat made Stuart shudder. "No, thanks. I'm capable of shaving myself." He jerked his robe from the brass hook on the back of the door and, in deference to his own modesty, shrugged it on.

Al retrieved her cup and sipped at the hot coffee while he shaved, scowling at his reflection in the every-widening circle of mirror. She liked his hands, she decided, as she watched his deft movements with the razor. Strong, capable hands. Hands that could make a woman whimper.

One wide palm smoothed down his cheek and across his chin, checking for smoothness. The fingers that molded his jawline were long and slender, his nails carefully manicured. Soft hair curled on the skin between his knuckles, matching that which curled on the span of chest exposed in the V of his robe. The V closed at the waist, then reopened to bare a flash of powder blue cotton shorts and a wider expanse of tanned thigh.

Al felt the bubble of warmth spiraling in her abdomen and recognized it for what it was. Desire. She'd felt it before—and hoped to again—but it didn't lessen her surprise to realize Stuart Greyson could plant it there. He definitely was not her style.

Water splashed up from the marble sink and splattered on her thigh, cooling her thoughts, as Stuart rinsed the remaining lather from his face. Hopping down, she plucked a towel from the rack and dried her thigh, then touched the towel to a dab of shaving cream on Stuart's left ear. "You missed a spot," she said coyly, then breezed through the door, calling back over her shoulder, "Five minutes, Stuart. I'll be in the kitchen."

Four minutes and thirty-five seconds later—Stuart

knew because he timed himself to make sure he gave Al no further excuse to return to his bedroom—he appeared in the kitchen, dressed, combed and ready.

She took one look at his crisp oxford-style shirt and cotton slacks and groaned. "Don't you own any jeans?"

He glanced down, his arms cocked at almost shoulder level, then back up at Al, frowning. "What's wrong with what I have on?"

She heaved a sigh and shook her head. "Nothing, Stuart. Absolutely nothing."

When they reached the driveway, Stuart almost turned and ran. A rusty, mud-splattered 1952 truck was parked in front of his house. He should have expected it from Al, yet he hadn't.

"She's a honey, isn't she?" Al patted the rounded hood like a mother would pat the head of a precocious child. "Here. You can drive."

A set of keys sailed through the air. Stuart caught them before they hit his chest. The passenger door slammed, and Al called out, "Hurry. We've wasted enough time already."

Swearing under his breath at his stupidity in agreeing to go along, Stuart climbed behind the wheel. He turned the key and stomped the starter located on the floorboard. "Where to?"

"Take the Indiana bridge, and I'll guide you from there." She settled back, both feet propped on the dashboard, one arm cocked half out the open window.

After a grinding of gears and several jerky starts, they were on their way. Gradually Stuart became accustomed to the lack of power steering and automatic transmission and began to enjoy the truck's demands on his strength and attention.

Due to the earliness of the day, Louisville's streets and expressways were nearly devoid of other traffic. As they passed through the downtown area, Al pointed out a tall building. "That's where I used to work."

"Where?" Stuart followed the direction of her finger with his gaze.

"In the art gallery on the first floor. I quit last week." She sighed wistfully. "I'll miss it, but Barnstormers is proving to be a full-time job."

"Barnstormers?" he echoed.

Al laughed, the sound as bright and cheerful as the sun gleaming on the windshield from the May sky above. "That's the name of my antique shop. Fitting, don't you think?"

He remembered her mentioning plans to open a shop but was at a loss as to how the name could be considered fitting. "How so?"

She turned a knee onto the seat and settled against the door, facing Stuart's profile. She found he'd lost the irritated look he'd worn since opening his front door and finding her on his stoop. His features were more relaxed. She smiled smugly. Her plan was working. "That's what I'll be doing. Storming barns, looking for antiques and collectibles to sell in my shop."

"Since you've quit your job, am I to assume you're planning to make your living through your shop?"

The note of skepticism in his voice didn't escape Al. She replied confidently, "More than a living. I'm going to save the farm."

Stuart was fully aware of the mortgages stacked against Al's property. Morrey's research into Clairemore Farms had been thorough. But Al didn't know he was privy to that information, which made him ask, "What do you mean, *save the farm*?"

"I inherited my family's farm. *And* the mortgages that go with it," she added wryly.

Stuart gave a quick glance that encompassed her from head to foot. "You don't look much like a farmer."

"I'm not."

"Then why do you want to hold on to the land if you don't intend to put it to use?"

For a moment Al was silent. When she spoke, her voice was so soft Stuart had to strain to hear it above the roar of the wind at his ear. "Because it's my home. The only one I've really ever known. For the most part, my grandparents raised me, but even before I moved in with them, Clairemore Farms always represented a place of security in my life. You know, like home." Al turned her face to the window and squinted up at the sun.

The attempt to hide her wavering emotions didn't fool Stuart for a moment, although it did surprise him. The woman had always appeared such a scatterbrain and so carefree, he hadn't thought she had a sentimental bone in her body. She had mentioned her grandparents before, and he couldn't help wondering why she had been raised by them because she had also mentioned a father—but never a mother, he remembered suddenly.

He wasn't one to pry into other people's lives, so

Stuart pushed aside the questions her comments had drawn and focused on the farm itself. "Do you really think you can pay off the mortgages with the profits from a small antique shop?"

She turned from the window and looked at him in disbelief. "Well, certainly. Otherwise I wouldn't be wasting my time."

A shrewd businessman with a degree from Harvard to back up his claim, Stuart knew Al didn't have a snowball's chance in hell of paying off the mortgages with the profits from an antique shop. The woman was illogical, scatterbrained and much too impulsive. None of those qualities spelled success in his mind. Luck was on her side—her winnings at the Derby proved that—but luck couldn't be counted on to pay the bills.

"Maybe you should have kept your job," he offered thoughtfully.

Al grinned. "Oh ye of little faith." She scooted to a sitting position as they crossed over the Ohio River. "The auction is just north of New Albany, off County Road 111."

A blast from the steamboat whistle of the *Belle of Louisville* had Al straining her neck out the passenger window to catch a glimpse of the boat moored on the Louisville side of the river. "Have you ever ridden on the *Belle of Louisville*?" she asked.

"Probably when I was kid. I don't remember."

"We'll have to go sometime. During the summer they have dinner dances on board that are a lot of fun."

He let that offer pass. He wasn't about to commit

himself to another outing with Al McCord. Business was one thing, his sanity quite another.

County Road 111 was a two-lane road that wound its way through the Indiana countryside. Trees, budded out green and full on either side of the roadway, were a contrast to the rich autumn colors they offered in the fall of the year to tourists who drove for miles just to see the sight. Farm houses sat back far from the road, while cattle and horses stretched their necks through barbed wire fences, grazing on new spring grass.

In deference to the beautiful countryside, Al grew quiet. From the corner of her eye, she watched Stuart. The wind blowing through the window at his side ruffled brown hair as rich and dark as coffee laced lightly with cream. She suspected his conservative nature never allowed him to let his hair grow much longer than that. For a moment, she tried to picture it longer, just an inch or two, but long enough to let a woman run her fingers through and get a grip.

She shook her head and the thought faded. No, she wouldn't let herself get involved with him in *that* way. She only intended to save him from himself, then she'd step out of the picture.

A sign announcing Estate Auction and a bold arrow pointing to the left caught Al's eye. "We're here," she said, pointing at the sign. "You can park in the pasture behind that blue truck."

When he'd pulled to a stop, Al hit the ground running, slamming the door of the truck behind her. Stuart had to jog to keep up. From her purse she pulled a notebook and pencil as she headed for the flatbed trailers piled high with assorted boxes and—in Stuart's estimation at least—junk.

After noting a number on a box, she jotted it down on her pad, then moved farther along, peering inside boxes and sifting through loose items scattered on the weathered planks of the trailer. Curious to see what had caught her interest, Stuart moved to the box and lifted the lid. Stuffed inside he found several pairs of dingy long-handled underwear. "Al, surely you don't intend to bid on this?" he asked in dismay as he dropped the box's flap.

She glanced up. "Why not?"

He rolled his eyes. "I don't think there's much of a market for dirty underwear."

Hiding a smile, she placed a finger to her lips, shushing him as she eased to his side. "Now don't tell anybody," she warned as she lifted the flap, "but look underneath."

He bent to look inside. Unimpressed by what he saw, he lifted a shoulder. "So?"

"This box is stuffed full of embroidered linens, crocheted tablecloths and doilies. If I can buy it at the right price, I'll make a fortune reselling this box alone."

He picked up a piece of cloth. Between his index finger and thumb dangled a crocheted doily, once white, but now faded a dirty yellow. Something told him Al's idea of a fortune and his were somewhat different. "Do you really think people will buy this junk?" he asked in distaste as he dropped the doily back into the box.

Quickly, Al covered up her find with the dingy underwear. "After a good soak in lemon juice and a day hanging in sunshine, it'll look like new. Trust me on this one," she added, patting Stuart's arm in a patronizing way as she breezed past him.

After registering at the auctioneer's table, Al picked up her number to use in bidding, then continued combing through the multitude of housewares, furniture, and sundry items spread across the yard between the empty farmhouse and the barn. Stuart followed at a safe distance. To him, this was sick. He couldn't imagine anything worse than pawing through some dead person's possessions like some pilfering warrior after a battle.

When Al stopped in front of a pile of discarded wood and began jotting down the number attached to it, Stuart felt compelled to interfere.

"Now, Al," he offered gently. "You don't need that pile of wood. Surely—"

She grabbed his arm and wheeled him around, silencing him as she quickly steered him in the opposite direction. Her cheeks were flushed and her eyes overbright. Stuart feared she was suffering from too much sun.

"I can't believe my luck!" she whispered in excitement. "Do you know what that pile of wood is?"

He glanced back over his shoulder. "No," he said warily. "What is it?"

"A Jefferson breakfront. Can you believe it?" she gasped, pressing a hand at her throat.

He had a vague idea what a breakfront was, and that pile of wood back there didn't resemble it at all.

"Al, I think you're mistaken. A breakfront is a large cabinet—"

She waved away his explanation. "I *know* what a breakfront is. But didn't you notice? The base is lying flat on the ground and all the doors have been taken off and piled on top. The drawers are busted but they're there, too. A little wood glue and they'll be as good as new." Nervously, she bit her lip as she glanced over Stuart's shoulder. "Gracious! I hope nobody else notices." She stole a cautious glance at the crowd milling about, sizing up her competition.

The bidding started on the farm equipment, drawing most of the crowd to the barn. But Al hadn't come to buy farm equipment. She stayed near the house and continued to sift through the boxes.

Not sharing Al's excitement in her "finds," Stuart sought the shade of a thick-trunked oak to watch the auctioneer in action. Neat rows of plows, tractors, trailers, and other farm equipment he couldn't identify were lined alongside the barn. The auctioneer stood on one of the flatbed trailers. His voice rang out from a portable microphone he held in his hand while spotters moved among the crowd, keeping up with the bids.

As pieces of machinery were placed on auction, then sold, the group shifted to follow the auctioneer to the next item for bid. The people crowding around the fast-talking man were an interesting mix. Farmers, wearing overalls and brightly colored caps, made up the bulk of the group. A few men in the somber dress of the Amish stood on the fringe of the circle. Another man, obviously a secondhand machinery dealer, smoked fat cigars and showed his interest in a particular item with the barest lift of a triple chin.

With the sun warming him, the comforting strength of the oak tree at his back and the heterogeneous group of people milling around him, Stuart soon forgot about the paperwork stacked high on his desk and began to relax. He would never admit it to Al, but he was glad she had insisted he come with her to the auction.

For years, he had worked with one goal in mind: to become a millionaire by the age of thirty. On paper, he'd already achieved that designation. But paper wasn't good enough. Not for Stuart Greyson. He wanted his million in cold, hard cash. Few men understood that obsession. Fewer still worked as diligently as Stuart to achieve that goal. The least of whom was his father, Phillip Greyson.

Phillip had never worked a day in his life. Fresh out of college, he'd married Jenny Blakely, a young debutante from one of Louisville's oldest and wealthiest families. He had married her for one reason and one reason only—her money. Not that she had cared. For she had been blinded to his faults by his charm and handsomeness, and she had willingly handed over her trust fund to him. After he'd gone through her inheritance, Phillip had turned to other women for that same support, leaving a heartbroken Jenny and a young son behind.

Phillip's reputation as Louisville's most notorious gigolo had earned Stuart more than his share of fights. As a teenager he had fought anyone who dared tease him about following in his father's footsteps. When it came time for college, he had chosen Harvard, hoping to put enough distance between himself and his father to escape the shadow of his father's reputation. Unfortunately he hadn't. But it was at Harvard that he realized fighting with his fists wasn't the way to prove the gossips wrong. Success was the key.

An amused smile quirked one side of Stuart's mouth. He'd worked hard, and damn it, he was nearly there.

From her position at the house, Al saw the smile that tipped one corner of Stuart's mouth. Grinning, she crossed to him and slipped her arm through his. "Bought anything?" she asked, tilting her head to one side and looking up at him.

His wandering thoughts chased away by the sight of Al, Stuart chuckled. "And what would I do with a 1957 John Deere tractor?"

"Mow your yard?"

Throwing back his head, Stuart roared, his laughter drawing Al's smile even higher. He should laugh more often, she decided. The effect was devastating. Lips, full and inviting, widened to push dimples into smooth, tanned cheeks while laugh lines deepened at the corner of his eye. And his eyes! Usually a deep smoky blue, when he laughed they sparkled with a brilliance that rivaled that of the blue depression glass in her grandmother's curved-glass china cabinet.

Al couldn't have resisted, even if she'd wanted to. She rose up on her toes and centered a kiss on his right dimple. Immediately the frown lines between Stuart's eyes returned.

Pulling back from her, he asked impatiently, "Do you always kiss people like that?"

She shrugged. "Only when they ask for it."

His look was incredulous. "I didn't ask for a kiss!"

Al smiled smugly. "Not in so many words, but that dimple of yours was all puckered up just begging to be kissed." Ignoring his growing frown, she glanced at her watch and knew that the auctioneer would be breaking soon for lunch. "Come on, Stuart, I'll buy you a sausage dog."

She headed for the trailer parked at the rear of the barn, its striped, canvas awning flapping in the breeze. Stuart followed at a slower pace. When he caught up with her, she was squirting mustard with a heavy hand. She shoved one of the sausage dogs into his hand, and cupped the other in her palm. With her soft drink, she gestured to a spot under a nearby tree.

Mustard dripped between Stuart's fingers and oozed down his hand as he held the messy sandwich at arm's length. Glaring at Al's back, he jerked a handful of napkins from the trailer's countertop, then followed her, cursing under his breath.

Sinking down beneath the tree, Al took the first bite. She closed her eyes and savored the tangy taste of grilled onions, mustard and smoked German sausage. "Isn't this delicious?" She licked a finger before adding, "I've cooked this a hundred times at home, but it never tastes quite the same as it does at an auction."

She saw his dubious look and urged, "Go on, Stuart. Give it a try. I promise you won't regret it."

He *was* hungry, he reasoned, as he looked at the

drippy mess. And the woman at the counter who had prepared it and the miniature kitchen behind her had looked sanitary enough, so he probably wouldn't get food poisoning. The tangy odor of mustard and onions curled just beneath his nose, making his mouth water. Without another thought, he sunk his teeth into the sandwich. His taste buds flared, his eyes closed, and he sucked in a breath through his nose, savoring each flavor that rested on his tongue. He dropped down beside Al and took another bite, oblivious to her spreading smile.

"Good, isn't it?" she asked as she pulled a napkin from his hand and touched it to his chin.

He could only nod as he closed his mouth over another bite. Satisfied, Al settled back against the trunk of the tree. Yes, there is hope for Stuart Greyson, she thought happily.

Hours later, Stuart slammed the truck's tailgate shut and slipped the metal hooks into place to ensure it stayed that way. The bed of the truck was jammed full of the wildest assortment of junk he had ever seen. Boxes filled with everything from lace doilies to black cast-iron skillets, a washstand that Al swore was oak underneath several layers of sea-green paint, an iron bed with a feather mattress, a kitchen cabinet, and the pile of wood she insisted on calling a Jefferson breakfront. For the lot of it, she had plunked down nearly three hundred dollars. Stuart wouldn't have given them a dime.

During the ride back to Louisville, Al chattered away about each of the items she had purchased, claiming that at the price she'd paid, she had stolen them. A robbery had occurred, Stuart thought with regret, but Al was the victim, not the thief.

The position of protector was new to Stuart, but he accepted it without blinking an eye. Someone needed to look out for Al, and it appeared he was the only one in line for the job. And besides, he reasoned silently, he intended to be there when she admitted defeat and agreed to sell the farm.

Without asking if the arrangement suited her, he drove to the farm, bypassing the exit on the expressway that led to his home. Together they unloaded her purchases in the barn. When the last box was lowered to the floor, Al's dog appeared at her side.

"Hi ya', Ranger." She knelt and wrapped an arm around the dog's neck. "Been out hunting again, haven't you, boy?" she asked as she pulled burrs from his long coat. The dog lifted a paw to Al's knee and licked her full on the mouth. Al laughed. Stuart wrinkled his nose in disgust.

Standing, Al kept one hand on Ranger's head and turned to Stuart. "Hungry?" Without waiting for his reply, she said, "I'm starving. Let's go up to the house and see what Verdie's left in the refrigerator for us to snack on."

She opened the passenger door of the truck and waited until Ranger jumped in before she climbed in beside him. When Stuart slid onto the seat, he was greeted by a cold wet nose...Ranger's.

At Stuart's grimace, Al tugged Ranger to her side of the seat. "Don't you like dogs, Stuart?"

"Not in my face."

"That's Ranger's way of saying hello. You'll get used to it."

Get used to it? Now why had she said that? He didn't intend to be around long enough to get used to *her*, much less her dog.

At the house, Stuart followed Al through the back door and into the kitchen. Ranger was forced to stay outside with the promise of a bone to come later.

Stuart couldn't have asked for a better opportunity to inspect the house than the one Al unknowingly offered him. His original plans for the property had included tearing down the two-story farmhouse, but now he wasn't so sure.

The kitchen was large as most country kitchens tended to be. One wall was lined with glass-fronted cabinets, displaying an assortment of dishes. Below the cabinets, a scarred, wooden countertop held a rack of spices, a glass canister set and a chipped porcelain sink. In the center of the room was perched an old butcher's block on which Al was busy piling food from the refrigerator.

An idea began to take shape, that of turning the home into some kind of clubhouse for the exclusive use of the property owners. It would require work, as the house was in obvious need of repairs, but the final results might well be worth it. In hopes of stealing a glimpse of more of the house, Stuart asked politely, "Do you mind if I wash up?"

Al waved at the door on her right. "Through there. The door on your left is a bathroom. If you need anything, just holler."

The hall floor he crossed was fashioned from dark

oak planks, and a faded rug braided from what looked to be fabric scraps, ran down its length. Above him on the left, a staircase rose to the second floor. The top of the banister gleamed a lighter shade from hands smoothing over it through the years. A mental picture of a young Al sliding down the banister, her feet flying out in front of her, formed and drew a chuckle from Stuart.

At the far end of the hallway loomed the front door with its oval-shaped etched glass. A double-wide arch to the right of the door led to what he assumed would be the living room. A matching archway on the left, he was sure, led to the formal dining room. Surprisingly, the house appealed to Stuart.

He opened the door beneath the staircase on his left and stepped into the bathroom, which he guessed had been added since the original construction of the house. Above an old pedestal sink hung a silvered mirror, oval and slightly askew.

Always conscientious of his appearance, he was shocked by the man who stared back at him. Dirt streaked his face, the part in his hair had all but disappeared and a blob of dried mustard stained the placket of his shirt.

And Stuart Greyson discovered he didn't give a damn.

He'd had a wonderful, relaxing afternoon with a perfectly congenial—if somewhat unconventional—companion, and had worked up quite an appetite. A smile built on his face. As he watched his lips curve upward, he realized how good it felt to smile. And it was all due to Al.

He twisted the faucet and splashed water on his face and scrubbed his arms to the elbows where his shirt was neatly cuffed. As he dried his hands with the guest towel, he could hear Al humming off-key in the kitchen. His smile broadened. *Al McCord.* What a name. What a woman! he added in amusement.

He rubbed the towel across his face and remembered the kiss Al had planted on his dimple at the auction. *You asked for it,* she had said. He chuckled as he replaced the towel. She was so spontaneous, so free of inhibition...so unlike anyone else he knew.

Still smiling, he returned to the kitchen and found Al at the sink, washing her hands, her back to him. Unable to resist the temptation, he caught her by the elbow and swung her around. Her hands flew to his chest, dripping water down his shirt, her eyes wide in surprise. Before she had a chance to speak, he pressed his lips against hers.

He'd meant to kiss her quickly—as she had done to him—and release her, but his lips seemed to have a mind of their own. When they met the warmth and softness of Al's, they tarried a bit too long. Her taste was sweeter than he remembered, and her touch, God, her touch. Everywhere their bodies met, from Al's lips meshed against his, to her fingertips resting on his chest, to her thighs pressed tightly against his, a slow heat burned beneath his skin.

Angling his face for a better fit, Stuart moved his lips across hers, tasting, savoring, exploring. The fingers she pressed against his chest curled, making fists in his shirt. A soft moan rumbled low in her throat.

When at last he withdrew, Al opened her eyes to meet his. The passionate glaze she found there shocked her. The thundering of her heart shocked her more. She backed from his embrace. "Ham or chicken?" she asked, struggling to control the trembling in her voice.

William, as the waiter asked opened her eyes to
over his. The passionate glaze she found ther
shocked him. The deuce, waiting, I think, shaken her by
think, she backed from his embrace. "Kim of
ensue?" she asked, gesturing, or could she have
thing in his voice

Four

Before she'd taken one full step back, Stuart had her
arms and was pulling her flush against him, his face
dipping low over hers. She opened her mouth to refuse him but before she could utter a sound, he
slipped his tongue between her lips, shocking her into
silence.

Her eyes wide in surprise, her lips pressed hard
against his, she watched his lashes drift down, shuttering the heat in his blue eyes. His kiss was raw,
passionate and demanding. It was all she could do to
breathe. With her knees threatening to buckle, she
curled her fingers into the fabric of his shirt and hung
on for dear life.

She couldn't remember the number of times she'd
kissed Stuart, though she did try to count. But those
hadn't been kisses, at least not in the same league as

this kiss or the one she'd received a moment ago. Hers had been expressions of excitement or welcome, delivered in her usual carefree manner. But *this*! Closing her eyes, she melted against his chest.

Her lips, at first firm in defense, softened beneath Stuart's. Somewhere in the midst of his passion-fogged mind, he sensed her surrender. Knowing full well he should stop this madness, he caught her cheeks between his hands and angled her face, seeking a deeper exploration. His teeth grated against hers as he plunged his tongue again and again into the sweetness of her mouth.

Al. Her name might be masculine, but her taste was pure femininity. And the feel of her! The soft feminine curves he traced beneath the baggy overalls shook him clear to his toes.

He caught her lower lip between his teeth and nipped playfully. "The name Al doesn't fit you, you know that? Alyssa suits you more."

His breath blew warm against her ear while slender threads of desire wove their way through her body, making her shiver. She had to stop him, Al thought wildly when his hands moved to cup her hips. Pushing her palms against his chest, she gained a few inches between their bodies. He continued to hold her in his embrace, refusing to let her go.

Defenseless against the heat flaming in his eyes, she dropped her forehead to his chin, bracing her hands at his chest until she could catch her breath. Slowly, she raised her gaze to meet his. "What was that for?"

He arched one eyebrow in question. "The kiss?"

She nodded.

He grinned, and the dimples Al had discovered earlier that day deepened. "You asked for it."

"I—" Realizing she was hearing her own words echoed back at her, she swallowed her denial. In the future she'd be more careful of what she asked! She turned her back on his engaging smile. "What would you like to eat?"

Puzzled by her sudden withdrawal, Stuart replied absently, "It doesn't matter." He followed her to the table, aware of the tenseness in her movements. It had to be the kiss, he decided. But the woman gave away kisses with the blink of an eye, so why was she so upset? Was it because *he* had initiated the kiss?

"Have I offended you?" he asked uncertainly.

"Yes!" She wheeled around and almost bumped into his chest. "I—uh—I," she stammered, backing up. "Well, maybe surprised would be a better word."

Stuart's frown deepened as he continued to trail her. "Why?"

Her rear end hit the edge of the table, and she realized she had run out of room. Hastily, she threw out an arm to prevent him from coming any closer. "I don't want to get involved with you, Stuart."

His jaw went slack. *She* didn't want to get involved with him? Hell, he didn't want to get involved with *her*! Rejection was an emotion he hadn't experienced often enough to learn how to deal with it, which put him on the defensive. "And just exactly what do you want, Al? *You're* the one who appeared at my door at daybreak and insisted I go to the auction with you."

Frowning, she turned to the table, picked up a plate and leaned across the table to set it opposite her. True, she had pursued him, but he had misunderstood her intentions. "I know. But I was trying to save you."

Stuart snapped his gaze from where it lingered on the tantalizing expanse of her thigh and flattened it on the back of her head. He planted his hands on his hips. "Save me! From whom?"

She turned, her look incredulous. "Why, from yourself."

"From myself? I don't need saving!"

"Of course you do. You're way too uptight." She caught him by the elbow and guided him to a chair. "Now sit and eat."

He jerked from her grasp and backed away. "I've suddenly lost my appetite." Grabbing the truck keys from the countertop, he headed for the back door. "I'll return your truck in the morning," he said, his voice as tight as the tendons standing out on his neck.

Ranger slipped through the open door just before Stuart slammed it behind him. Al winced as the dishes, shaken by the force of the slam, clinked in the glass-fronted cupboard. She heard the truck start and the grinding of gears before gravel spun beneath the tires as he sped away.

"Oh, my," she sighed as she dropped onto the chair she had pulled out for Stuart. She filled her hand with the comforting warmth of the dog's fur. "It appears I've wounded Mr. Greyson's male ego, Ranger."

For a moment she simply sat, staring thoughtfully into space, tapping a finger against her lips. Had her purpose in going to his house been only to save him? Or had she subconsciously wanted to see him again? The question was definitely worth pursuing. She remembered his kiss, and frissons of heat exploded low in her abdomen. Maybe he's right, she admitted, acknowledging her reaction to him. Maybe she *was* interested in more than just saving him from himself.

Hooking an arm around Ranger's neck, she glanced at the back door. Stuart Greyson wasn't at all the type of man who usually attracted her. But then life was full of surprises.

She laughed as she thought of his face flushed in anger when she'd told him she didn't want to get involved with him. Yes, she could handle her attraction for Stuart Greyson, but could he handle his attraction for her?

A bubble of laughter welled up in her throat. Chuckling, she plucked a slice of ham from the platter and dropped it into Ranger's waiting mouth, then picked up a fried chicken leg for herself and took a bite. *Yes, I might be just what Stuart Greyson needs.*

True to his word, Stuart returned the truck the next morning. When Al awoke, she found it parked on the drive behind the house. The fact that he hadn't bothered to let her know he'd returned it didn't faze her. She smiled as she poured herself a cup of coffee. Apparently she'd been right. Stuart Greyson couldn't handle his attraction for her. It was time to implement the second phase of her plan.

For two weeks Al allowed Stuart to simmer. While phase two—a period of restrained silence—was underway, she was busy working. She finished cleaning the barn, attended several more estate sales, and ran an advertisement in the paper announcing her willingness to accept antiques and crafts on consignment. The tedious job of stripping the paint from the seagreen washstand was going slowly but surely. After checking her bank balance, she also discovered she'd spent a lot more money than she'd anticipated to start up the antique shop.

Al worked hard, but she was wise enough to know that in order to maintain her momentum and her enthusiasm for her new job, she had to make time for play as well. Two weeks to the day after her argument with Stuart, she decided the time was right to test the waters again...and begin phase three.

Pleased with herself and the progress she had made, she headed her car in the direction of Oxmoor Mall, her favorite shopping center.

Stuart opened the briefcase packed with work he'd brought home from the office and settled down at the desk in his study. Sunlight streaming through the French doors behind him warmed his back as he flipped through the files that needed his review: a contract for the purchase of a shopping strip, three bids for the remodeling job of an apartment complex he owned and an option on some land Morrey was interested in. At the bottom of the stack rested the thick file on Greystone Estates.

The phone rang. Stuart dropped the files and stretched across his desk to pick up the receiver. "Greyson."

"Good morning! Busy?"

At the sound of his stepfather's chipper voice, Stuart reared back in his chair, a smile spreading on his face. "Welcome home, Morrey. Not yet. I just opened my briefcase. How was your trip?"

"Interesting and hopefully successful. I'll let you know when I hear from the Westermans. Did you make any progress with old man Clairemore?"

Stuart leaned forward and picked up the file Morrey had left him. "The old man died."

Morrey's quick intake of breath told Stuart what he had already suspected—that his stepfather had not been aware of Mr. Clairemore's decease. "I knew he had a bad heart, but—when did he die?"

"About two months ago. His granddaughter inherited the farm. I've met with her. She's not interested in selling."

"Damn! We need that eighty acres."

"I know. But don't worry, Morrey. I guarantee you that within three months I'll have that deed in my hands."

"You sound awfully sure of yourself."

"Not of myself. Of Al."

"Al? Who the hell is Al?"

"She's Clairemore's granddaughter."

"Sounds more like a grandson." Morrey chuckled, then sobered. "If we don't get that eighty acres within three months, we'll lose the options on the rest of the acreage."

Pensively, Stuart replied, "Yes, I know."

"If she isn't willing to sell, how do you intend to get your hands on the deed? Marry her?"

Although he knew Morrey made the comment in jest, it hit a little too close to home for Stuart's liking. "That's more my dad's style, Morrey, not mine."

"Sorry, son. I didn't mean that the way it sounded."

"Forget it." To change the subject to a less volatile one, Stuart asked, "Will you be in the office Monday morning?"

"Plan to be."

"I'll give you the details then."

"Fine. By the way," Morrey added quickly, "your mother wants you to come for lunch tomorrow."

Stuart frowned. He wasn't in the mood to deal with his mother. "Can't. Got some work I need to catch up on."

"She'll be disappointed."

"She'll get over it." Before his stepfather could argue the point, Stuart said, "See you Monday, Morrey," and hung up the phone.

He thumbed open the file marked Greystone Estates. The last notation dealing with the outstanding eighty acres was dated two weeks before and written in his own handwriting. Al McCord's name was listed as being the new owner of the property. He remembered well the afternoon he'd discovered she was the owner of the farm. She'd been hard at work, cleaning out the barn in preparation for her antique shop. He didn't wish failure on Al, yet he knew her failure would make him realize his own goal.

He templed his fingers beneath his chin as he thought of their last conversation, something he had purposefully avoided thinking about for the better part of two weeks. For three days he had given in to his anger and stormed around his office, venting his frustration on his employees. Another three days, and he had finally cooled off enough to realize his own damned pride had been the cause of his anger.

Saving him from himself, huh? With a rueful shake of his head, he tossed the file down on his desk. *She* was the one who needed saving, not him. After all, the woman thought she could pay off Clairemore Farms' debts with the profits from a little antique shop! He shook his head again, flipped open the file and pulled out the plat maps.

As always, the engineer's drawings of the proposed subdivision drew a satisfied smile. Greystone Estates was going to be a showplace; no one could deny him that. The sketches depicting the entrance with GREY-STONE ESTATES etched into native stone made his chest swell with pride. He was close to his goal, so close he could almost taste the sweet flavor of success.

The only obstacle that stood in his way was Clairemore Farms. He knew he should have approached Al with another offer for her land, yet he hadn't.

The reason was obvious enough. He didn't want to fall into the same category with the likes of George Bandy and he knew that was exactly where Al would place him—right at the top of her list of buzzards.

As had been the case ever since he had met her, Stuart found his thoughts drifting to Al. Her unruly mop of hair, her blue eyes that always sparkled as if she were amused by some private joke and her outrageous friendliness. Those characteristics shouldn't add up to attraction, yet they did. Why, he wasn't sure.

Maybe he'd give her a call. Maybe. But certainly not now, he reflected, as his gaze rested on the pile of work in front of him. Shaking his head to dismiss the tempting thought, he pushed the file to the bottom of the stack and picked up the thick contract that needed his review.

The doorbell rang just as he turned the last page. He stood and stretched, easing out the kinks in his back, then strode to the entryway.

When he opened the front door, he found Al standing on the stoop. His surprise at seeing her quickly turned to dread when he saw the brightly colored package she held in her hands.

"Hi." She smiled and extended the gift. "I brought a peace offering."

He felt like a fool. If a peace offering were needed, it should have come from him. After all, he had been the one who had lost his temper. Wishing he hadn't responded to the doorbell and thus avoided this awkward situation, he shoved his hands deep into the pockets of his slacks. "It isn't necessary."

"Then consider it a birthday present."

"My birthday's not until January."

Annoyed by his reluctance to accept the olive branch, Al shoved the present into his stomach, nearly knocking the breath out of him. Reflexively, he grabbed for it as she brushed by him. "Well, call it what you like. The gift's for you," she said impatiently.

Stuart smiled and found the upward stretch of his

lips a pleasurable experience after two weeks without Al to produce it. He closed the door and followed her to the kitchen. "Thanks, Al."

She climbed up on a bar stool, making herself at home. "You better open it before you say that. You might not thank me once you see your gift."

Taking the stool next to hers, Stuart began to peel off the brightly colored paper. "Let me guess. A pair of jockey briefs?"

She tried not to smile. "No. Although I did consider it."

He lifted the box lid and pushed back the tissue paper. Beneath the thin white paper lay a pair of jeans. He tossed back his head and laughed. The sound warmed Al's heart.

He took another look in the box, still chuckling. "You shouldn't have."

"I know." She eyed the expensive cut of the slacks that covered the thigh next to hers. "But I couldn't very well take you fishing dressed like you are."

Immediately, Stuart started backpedaling. "Now, Al. I don't like to fish. In fact, I hate fishing."

She just smiled as she pulled the jeans from the box.

"And besides," he added quickly, "I have a briefcase full of work I have to finish today and—" His argument froze on his lips when he felt his belt tugged from its loops. He shot off the stool and away from Al's prying hands.

The determined look in her eye was enough to convince him. "Give me ten minutes to change."

"Make it five."

* * *

The soft breeze drew ripples around the two red-and-white weighted corks where they bobbed lazily on the lake's smooth surface. A thin nylon line ran from the corks to the bank and the cane poles Al and Stuart held. Al sat beneath the thick branches of a sprawling oak, her pole propped between her raised knees. Drowsy from the warmth of the hot afternoon sun, she let her eyelids drift down to half-mast.

Beside Al, Stuart swatted irritably at a gnat buzzing at his ear. He stood and pulled his line from the water, checking to make sure the worm was still on the hook. After nearly an hour of fishing without so much as a nibble, he was quickly growing impatient.

"Are you sure there are fish in this lake?" he asked dubiously.

Al lifted an eyebrow and glanced in Stuart's direction. Honestly, the man was so uptight! He had checked his worm at least a dozen times in the last half hour. "I never said there were any fish here. I just said I was taking you fishing."

He wheeled to face her. "You mean to tell me there aren't any fish in this damn lake?"

She shrugged, and her eyelids drifted closed again. "There might be. I don't know for sure. I've never caught one."

Stuart dropped his pole and flopped down on the quilt Al had spread beneath the tree.

The splashing sound the pole made in the water jerked Al upright. Stuart sat not two feet away, his shoulders hunched forward and his arms draped over his raised knees. She could tell by the angry rise and fall of his shoulders that she'd done it again. She'd succeeded in making him mad. But her intent hadn't been to make him mad, only to make him relax.

She scooted until she sat behind him and began to massage his shoulders. He tensed beneath her touch. "Now, Stuart," she soothed. "I brought you out here to relax and have a little fun. And just look at you! You're wound up tighter than a spring. Relax," she urged as she dug her fingers into the muscles in his back.

"I *am* relaxed!" he muttered through clenched teeth.

"You are not." She pressed against a muscle twisted so tight it felt like a tire iron between her fingertips. "Just feel that," she demanded. "If that's what you call relaxed, then you're worse off than I thought." When he continued to ignore her, she dropped her hands to her sides in frustration, then pushed to her feet. "Well, if we're not going to fish, we might as well go swimming."

Still glaring at the lake, Stuart replied tersely, "We don't have swimsuits."

Behind him, Al peeled off her T-shirt and tossed the brightly colored garment over his shoulder and onto his lap. "Doesn't matter. There's nobody here but us anyway."

Stuart stared at the T-shirt as if it had dropped from outer space. The subsequent sound of a zipper grating made his breath catch in his throat. Surely she didn't intend to go skinny-dipping in broad daylight. The thought had hardly formed when a pair of cutoffs joined the T-shirt on his lap. Closing his eyes in dread, he knotted his fingers in the cutoffs still warm from her body. "Al, we can't—"

"Last one in is a rotten egg," she challenged as she raced past him.

Fully prepared to see a naked Al sprinting for the lake, Stuart slowly opened his eyes to find Al poised for a dive at the edge of the weathered pier—and wearing a hot pink bikini. She turned, and even at the distance he could see the laughter in her eyes.

"Scared you, didn't I? But don't worry, you can wear your boxer shorts. Or are you too chicken?" she jeered. With that last dare, she dived in.

Before her feet left the pier, Stuart was up and tugging off his jeans. A chicken, huh? He'd show her who was a chicken. He'd had about all he could take from this woman and her constant stabs at his "stuffiness" and his level of stress.

When she surfaced, he was beside her, water lapping at his bare chest. Without saying a word, he raised his hand to her head and, in one smooth movement, pushed her under again.

Al came up laughing and sputtering water. "Hey! That's not fair," she cried as she grabbed for his shoulders and hung on.

"Look who's talking fair. You're the one who got a head start for the water."

She grinned as she reached to circle his neck with her arms. "Yeah, but I had to do something to make you relax a little."

Through the thin fabric of the bikini, her breasts rubbed against his chest, and his muscles tensed in response. Forgetting his intent at evening the score, he wedged her hips against his. "Am I relaxed now?" he asked, his voice dropping to a husky whisper.

She ran the flat of her hand across his shoulders and down his back. Tilting her face up to his, she smiled a lazy smile. "You're getting there."

A trickle of water ran down her forehead and angled across her cheek. Stuart caught it with his tongue before it reached her chin. Tracing his way back up, he settled his mouth over hers. Her lips, warm from the sun, tasted of lake water. He pressed deeper and found the sweetness he sought.

"You have to be the strangest person I've ever met," he murmured against her lips.

Al's mouth curved against his in a smile. "Is that a compliment or an insult?"

He leaned his head back to look at her. "I'm not sure yet," he replied absently as he brushed a strand of wet hair from her cheek.

Before he could withdraw his hand, Al caught it in hers and pressed it against her lips. Her tongue drew a scorching circle on his palm, eliciting a groan from Stuart. One minute the woman was driving him crazy with her wild and impulsive actions, and the next, she was driving him crazy with her irresistible sexuality. Either way he looked at it, she was driving him crazy.

Sensing his confusion, Al chuckled, then pushed out of his arms to float on her back. "Well, let me know when you decide."

As he watched her drift away, Stuart felt an unexplainable sense of loss. Shaking off the uncomfortable sensation, he swam to catch up with her. They reached the bank at the same moment, and he laced his fingers through hers as they crossed to the shade tree.

Al dropped down on the blanket spread beneath it, and Stuart stretched out beside her, pillowing his hands beneath his head. "Isn't this the most delightful place in the world?" she asked on a breathy sigh.

Craning his neck, Stuart looked around. While he'd fished, he'd passed the time imagining the land subdivided and sprouting with homes. Now, he tried to see it through Al's eyes. *Delightful?* he asked himself. No, to him it was only land. Raw, full of potential, waiting for someone like himself to bring it to fruition.

Al watched the doubtful expression cross his face and let out a deep sigh. "You're hopeless, you know it?"

Closing his eyes, Stuart accepted her assessment without argument. On the subject of the farm, they'd never agree.

Al studied the billowy clouds overhead. "Have you ever played the cloud game?" she asked.

Stuart opened one eye to peer at the sky. "Can't say I have. How do you play?"

"You study the clouds and try and find shapes of animals or people or whatever. Look," she said, pointing at a fluffy cloud above them. "That one looks like a profile of Bob Hope."

He followed the line of her finger. "I don't see it."

She edged closer, her cheek nearly brushing against his as she gestured again. The scent of her sun-warmed body blended with that of the grass and the wildflowers crushed beneath them, blinded Stuart to all but her nearness.

"See? There's his forehead, his ski-slope nose and his chin." She glanced at Stuart and found his gaze centered on her. "You're not looking," she said, her tone one of reproof.

"Yes, I am. And believe me, the view is much prettier than Bob Hope's profile."

The compliment brought a warmth to Al's cheek. She knew she wasn't pretty. Her mother had told her that often enough when she was growing up. But hearing it from Stuart made her wish she was. Uncomfortable with his close perusal, she pressed her thumb into his cheek, forcing his face to turn toward the clouds. "Now do you see?" she asked.

"Yes, but I liked the other view better." He caught her hand in his and held her fingertips to his lips as he turned on his side to face her.

Still damp from the lake, her hair fanned around her face in a wild profusion of curls. But it was her mouth he focused on. Full and inviting, her lips curved in a whisper of a smile. With his fingers still locked around hers, he dipped his head until their mouths touched.

Her response was instantaneous. He felt the passion flash through her with lightning speed. Unable to resist, he drew her closer, shaping her body to fit snugly against his.

From behind him—closer than he'd like to think—Stuart heard a low growl. Al lifted her head and peered over his shoulder.

"Don't move," she warned in a low whisper.

Sure a wolf or a coyote was at his back, Stuart—his lips barely moving—whispered, "What is it?"

"Ranger."

His breath sagged out of him. "Is that all?" He started to pull Al to him again, but her hand clinched his wrist at the same moment the growl rumbled low again, closer than before. The warmth of the dog's breath raised the hairs on Stuart's neck.

Al's fingers tightened in warning and she repeated, "Don't move." She lifted her head to look at the dog behind him. "Easy, boy. It's just Stuart. See?" She moved a hand to Stuart's face and touched him lightly on the cheek. "He's our friend."

Slowly, Al stood and stepped over Stuart. Once she had a grip on the dog's collar, she said, "It's okay now. I've got him. He thought you were going to hurt me."

Warily, Stuart rolled to his back and looked up to find the dog, its teeth still bared in a snarl, standing above him. He feigned a smile for Ranger's benefit, but his words were directed at Al. "Hurt you? I'm going to *kill* you just as soon as you tie up that damn dog of yours."

Stuart sat at the kitchen table, nursing an icy glass of lemonade and waiting while Al showered and changed. The ceiling creaked as she moved about on the floor above. He glanced up and pictured her naked, fresh from a shower, her skin glowing a healthy pink.

He'd known passionate women before but not one of them had ever matched the passion that burned within Al. He'd tasted it, been tempted to pursue it, yet he hadn't. Instead of following her up the stairs to finish what they had started on the blanket beside the lake, he'd elected to remain in the kitchen, sipping lemonade.

What had held him back? he wondered thoughtfully as he listened to her muffled movements. Was it because she owned the farm he wanted? Or was it the woman herself? She was so different from any other woman he knew.

Without thinking, he stood, then quickly sat again when a low growl sounded in the quiet kitchen.

Ranger lay on a rug in front of the backdoor, his eyes guarded, yet watchful. Stuart frowned at him. The incident with the dog by the lake had added about ten years to his life and maybe a gray hair or two. At the moment, he couldn't decide whether to slap a muzzle on the mutt or throw him a bone.

Better throw him a bone, he decided with more than a little regret. The dog had saved him from making a big mistake. Al was tempting. Too tempting, he reflected in frustration. He had no business getting involved with her. *She* might consider their relationship purely a personal one, but to him, as long as the land stood between them, he had to consider business as well. And business and pleasure didn't mix. Not in his book.

So engrossed in his reverie, he didn't know Al had joined him until he felt her breath at his ear. "Penny for your thoughts," she teased before dropping into the chair next to his.

He forced a smile as he glanced at her. "They aren't worth even that."

"No? Well, then tell me your life story."

He shrugged and settled his hands around his glass. "Not much to tell there, either."

"Oh, come on," she encouraged. "Mother? Father? Sisters? Brothers? Surely you have family."

"A mother and stepfather, but no brothers or sisters."

"What about your father? Is he dead?"

The frown lines appeared between Stuart's eyes again, and she watched his jaw set in that now familiar clench. "No, although there have been times when I wished he were."

Al thought of the loss of her own father and felt a squeeze on her heart. "You don't mean that."

He lifted his head and eyed her for a moment. "You'd have to know my father."

At a loss to understand the resentment she heard in his voice, she reached for his hand and squeezed it between hers. "I didn't mean to pry."

He quickly withdrew his hand and returned it to the glass. The dismissive action surprised Al. During their time at the lake, she'd thought he had thawed a little toward her. A gentle thawing, to be sure, but a definite improvement over his past behavior.

Yet, now that she thought about it, he had seemed distant ever since they'd returned to the house. She glanced around the room, then looked suspiciously at Stuart. "Did something happen while I was gone?"

"No. Why?"

"I don't know, but you seem different somehow."

He shifted his gaze to Ranger. "Let's just say I was reminded of my priorities. Business before pleasure."

Al tossed up her hands. "So we're back to that, are we?" Slapping her hands down on the table, she leaned forward until her nose was bare inches from Stuart's. "I've said it before and I'll say it again. We *have* no business. Clairemore Farms is not for sale."

"At the present."

Frustrated by his refusal to accept her position, Al fell back against her seat. "You just don't believe I can save the farm, do you?"

Stuart shrugged as he swirled the lemonade around in his glass. "Looks doubtful to me."

Refusing to let his pessimism affect her, Al smiled sweetly and crossed her arms at her breasts. "Okay, so why don't you tell why it's so important for you to have this land."

"I have my reasons."

"Let's hear them. I think I have a right to know."

Stuart sat for a moment in thoughtful silence, toying with the wedge of lemon in his glass. His reasons were his alone. He'd never shared them with anyone. Not even Morrey. But maybe she was right. Maybe she did have a right to know. Perhaps then she'd understand his determination.

When he raised his head, his eyes were dark with the strength of his convictions. "Three years ago I set a goal for myself, to be a millionaire by the age of thirty. The profits from this subdivision will put me over my goal. I've worked for over a year putting together this deal. Your land is just one parcel within a full section. I have options on all of it—with the exception of Clairemore Farms.''

"Couldn't you just cut out Clairemore Farms and proceed as planned?''

He shook his head. "It's not that easy. Roads, easements, utilities—everything's been planned with your farm in the overall layout. I'd have to start over virtually from the beginning.''

"And that would cost you money?''

"Money and time.''

Al sat for a moment, deep in thought. Her reasons for keeping the farm were based on emotion. Analyzing Stuart's position on strictly an intellectual level, she could understand his determination to own the farm, but when she added his goal to become a millionaire, the picture became blurred. There was more here than met the eye. "Okay, looking at this from your point of view, I can see why you want the farm. But what I don't understand is why you feel this obsession for money.''

"Let's just say I have something to prove.''

"To whom?''

"The bastards waiting for me to fail.''

Al shook her head and pressed her hands to her temples. "I'm sorry, but you've lost me. Who are the bastards, and why are they waiting for you to fail?''

Stuart sighed deeply and dropped the lemon wedge back into his glass. "The bastards are the people who think I'm just like my dad.'' He shoved his glass from his hand and reared back in his chair. "Phillip Greyson. Louisville's most notorious gigolo. I'm surprised you haven't heard of him. I've lived under the shadow of his reputation all my life and the only way I can crawl out from under it is to succeed in my own right.''

''And because I own the land you want, you insist on keeping our relationship strictly on a business level?''

''Right.''

Her brow puckered in thought, Al picked up Stuart's glass and took a sip. She licked a stray piece of lemon pulp from the corner of her mouth and eyed Stuart covertly over the top of the glass. ''If I were to agree to sell you the land—if and when I decided to sell, that is—that would mean we could be friends until then, right?''

''I suppose.''

Al slammed the glass to the table and rose. ''Good! Then you have my promise. If and when I decide to sell, the farm is yours.'' She grabbed his hand and pulled him from his chair. ''Now that it's settled, come on and I'll show you what I've accomplished at the barn since you were here last.''

Friends. It was as simple as that. At least for Al. Stuart sighed deeply as he followed her out the door and across the yard. He only wished the situation were that simple for him.

Five

Judging by Al's attitude, the conversation in the kitchen might never have happened. As they walked toward the barn, she chatted away at Stuart's side, pointing out different landmarks and telling anecdotes of growing up on the farm.

The stories she told had Stuart smiling in spite of himself. He could see her as a young girl, running wild in the fields with Ranger, constantly getting into scrapes and causing mayhem in general. He thought of his own growing-up years, which were smothered by his protective mother, and envied Al the freedom he'd never known.

Al stopped to pick a daisy from a clump growing wild in the field and slipped it through a buttonhole on Stuart's shirt. The simple gesture left him speechless.

At the barn, Al paused just inside the door. Her hands on her hips, she asked Stuart, "Well? What do you think?"

The sight that greeted him obliterated all other thoughts. The sun, cast through sashes of stained glass suspended over the barn's windows, painted rainbows across the floor and around the large room. Colorfully patterned quilts hung between the windows, covering the otherwise bare walls of the stone barn.

Antiques divided the room into what looked like storefront windows: a living room, a dining room, a kitchen, a bedroom. As he walked through the maze, he recognized some of the pieces Al had bought at the auction he had attended with her.

He stopped and turned to find her standing behind him, smiling, obviously pleased with herself. Her enthusiasm was contagious. "I can't believe it!" He turned again to look at the items surrounding him. "How did you manage to accomplish all this in two weeks?"

Al laughed gaily. "I'm fast." She picked up an iron skillet from the top of a Franklin-style wood-burning stove. "Remember this?" she asked, turning the skillet for Stuart's inspection.

"Yes. Although, as I recall, the last time I saw it, it was definitely rust-colored, not black."

"A good scrubbing, a little cooking oil and thirty minutes in a hot oven to season it. I paid twenty-five cents for it and I've priced it at fifteen dollars. That should give me a profit of—" She paused, tapping a finger against her chin as she mentally calculated her margin of profit.

"About a six thousand per cent increase on your investment," Stuart offered absently, his forehead knitted in thought.

A wooden drying rack, each rung draped with intricately laced doilies and tablecloths, caught his eye. He picked up a tag and noted the price of one hundred and fifty dollars. If his memory served him well, the tablecloth had been in the box under the dirty long-handled underwear. Al had paid a dollar for the entire box.

A chuckle rumbled low in his chest.

"See, I told you," she said smugly.

Turning, he hooked an arm around her shoulders. "Al McCord, you're a cunning horse trader if ever I saw one."

Pride swelled her chest as she looked around the barn where she had worked so hard for the past two weeks. "You bet I am. And this is only the beginning."

As her gaze settled on a bare spot by the front door, her smile dipped into a disapproving frown. "I only wish I was as good a carpenter as I am a horse trader."

Puzzled, Stuart looked down at her. "Whatever for?"

She pointed to the bare spots. "I need a tall rack of some kind over there. I've contacted several local artists to take some of their work on consignment." She gestured helplessly at the stone walls. "These walls are not conducive to hanging pictures. I need a place to display the artists' work."

"I'm pretty handy with a hammer and saw."

Al twisted her head around and peered incredulously at him. "You?"

Offended by her doubtful look, he replied defensively, "Yes, me."

A smile began to grow on Al's face. "And you'd do that for me?"

The warm, appreciative look she bathed him with blinded Stuart to the fact that his offer of help was like passing out ammunition to the enemy. If her business was a success, it spelled failure for his own plans for the farm. He lifted a shoulder and let it drop while his mouth puckered up in a thoughtful frown. "I might, if the pay were right."

The sight of his lips reminded Al of the feel of them pressed against hers. Goose bumps rose on her arms while a slow bud of heat blossomed low in her abdomen. "Maybe we can come up with a trade."

"What kind of trade?"

"Ever heard of Yankee Dimes?"

"No, what are they?" he asked.

She eased closer and slipped her arms around his waist. "Pucker up and I'll show you."

Sunday morning Stuart woke early. He stretched his hands out toward his upholstered headboard and immediately groaned, the muscles in his arms tightening at the extended movement. Rubbing his left hand over his sore biceps, he recalled the cause of his discomfort: the unaccustomed use of a hammer and saw.

He rolled to his back, easing his hands to clasp cautiously over his chest. He closed his eyes and pictured the portable wall he had begun constructing for Al. He hadn't built anything with his own hands for years. But the skill had been there, waiting for him to tap it again.

Anxious to get back out to the farm to finish the unit, Stuart rolled out of bed. When his feet hit the floor, his thigh and calf muscles balked at supporting his weight, and he fell back on the mattress. The hours he'd spent squatting and bending while he constructed the frame for the portable wall had strained muscles he'd forgotten he had.

Remembering the massage Al had given him out by the lake, he wished she were here now to work out the soreness. The memory of her hands working at his tense muscles brought a contented sigh. She was something, that Al. He closed his eyes and pictured her lying beneath him on the quilt.

As the memory formed, he discovered a new ache, one he knew a remedy for. A cold shower. Groaning his frustration, he squinted one eye at the bedroom window where bright sunshine flooded in. He'd told Al he'd be back early to complete the wall and he still had a mountain of paperwork to finish. With that in mind, he eased from the bed and headed for the shower.

An hour later he parked his car at the back door of Al's home and climbed out, whistling happily between his teeth. He hadn't taken two steps when Ranger tore around the corner of the house.

This time Stuart stood his ground. The dog circled him, sniffing at his heels. "Well? Do I pass inspection?" Stuart asked impatiently.

In answer, Ranger dropped down on his haunches, his tongue lolling. Chuckling, Stuart lowered a hand to the dog's head and gave him a quick rub. "You're as unpredictable as your mistress, you know that, dog?"

The smell of freshly perked coffee filtered through the screen door. Stuart's nose flared at the inviting smell. "Al?" he called as he pulled open the door. When she didn't answer he called again, louder, "Al! It's me, Stuart."

He heard the sound of bare feet skipping down the rear staircase. Seconds later she appeared, wearing a thigh-length T-shirt with the words Take It Or Leave It scrawled across the front. Her hair was tousled and her eyelids were still heavy with sleep. To Stuart, she'd never looked more seductive.

"Good morning!" she said before giving him a quick kiss. "You're early." She started to pass by him, intent on reaching the coffeepot, but Stuart caught her elbow and twirled her around and into his arms.

Grinning boyishly, he murmured, "I'll take it," and then he crushed his lips against hers.

The breath seeped out of Al. Yesterday and the memory of his kisses had been only a dream until she felt the heat of his lips again, reassuring her of the passion she'd tasted there. She threw her arms around his neck and gave herself up to him.

When at last he withdrew, she rubbed her thumb across his bottom lip, then lifted her gaze to his, mischief sparking in her eyes. "No more Yankee dimes, Mr. Greyson, until the work is satisfactorily completed." With a toss of tangled curls, she turned her back on him and poured two cups of coffee. Handing Stuart one of the steaming cups, she said, "Follow me."

The sway of her hips as she walked was invitation enough. He followed her up the stairs and down the hall. She slipped through a doorway and he followed.

When he stepped into the sunny bedroom, he stopped short. A man stood before the bureau mirror, dressed only in sweatpants, towel-drying his hair. Al plunked a cup of coffee in front of the guy and turned to Stuart, motioning for him to join her. "Come on in. I want you to meet a friend of mine."

Stuart tore his gaze from the man smiling in the mirror, to the rumpled sheets on the bed and finally to Al. Slowly he backed from the room, the scowl building on his face as dark as that of a thundercloud. "No thanks. Personally, I've always thought three was a crowd."

Stuart pulled the nail from between his tightly clenched teeth and positioned it on the 2 x 2 brace. In what would normally take four or five solid swings of the hammer, he buried the nail in two. It was easy. All he had to do was imagine the nail was Al and the hammer, his fist.

Inching farther down the portable wall, he pulled another nail from his mouth and hammered it into place. This time he pictured the face of Al's guest on the nail's head and drove the nail into the raw wood with one angry whack.

The woman had nerve all right. He'd give her that.

Inviting him upstairs, knowing full well another man awaited her there. Hell, she was nuts! He'd made that discovery the first day he'd met her, but somewhere along the way, he'd lost sight of that fact.

He wouldn't forget it again, he vowed as he pounded another nail into the portable wall. As soon as he finished this project, he would return to the house and make a final offer for her land, then he was getting the hell away from this damned farm and the crazy woman who owned it.

He had no sooner decided this than he heard her calling him. He ignored her and continued to hammer away at the wall.

Al heard the pinging sound of the hammer and followed it. She found Stuart hunkered down on the balls of his feet behind the portable wall, hammering into place the braces that would hold it upright. Frown lines cut deep between his eyes and the muscles in his arms tensed and bulged with each angry lift and fall of the hammer he wielded in his hand.

She bit back a smile. He was jealous, though she was sure he would never admit it. Slowly she eased to his side. "Gosh! You've certainly got a lot done."

He grunted and scooted on the balls of his feet farther along the wall—and away from her.

"Are you mad about something, Stuart?" she asked innocently.

Without ever lifting his gaze, he replied tightly, "Nope."

"Sure do look mad. Want to talk about it?"

"Nope."

"Want to know his name?"

"Nope."

"Rhys Dillard."

Stuart's lips thinned to a firmer line. "I said I didn't want to know."

"He was my roommate. Remember? The one I told you about? The one who wears jockey briefs?"

He remembered her saying she had a roommate and that the guy had worn jockey briefs. A platonic relationship she'd said. Like hell, he thought caustically. There certainly wasn't anything platonic about the way she'd sashayed around the man, dressed in only a T-shirt.

Judging by the way she was hovering over him, waiting for his response, he knew she wanted to pursue the topic. He didn't. He continued to hammer away.

"Rhys dropped in last night after you left. He's an airline pilot and he's in town for a twenty-four hour layover. He'd planned to stay with his fiancée's parents, but they're having a family reunion and there wasn't room for Rhys there." She shrugged her shoulders. "So he came by here to spend the night." Al dropped down on her knees beside Stuart, angling her face for a better look at him. "He left a few minutes ago. Still mad?"

He leaned over to grab another handful of nails from the box at his feet, refusing to meet her gaze. "I said I wasn't mad."

Al lifted one eyebrow dubiously. "Could have fooled me."

Stuart threw down the hammer and whirled around, his face twisted in anger. "Damn it! I said I'm not mad, and I'm not. I don't give a damn *who* you entertain in your bedroom.''

"It wasn't *my* bedroom. It was the guest room. And yes, you do give a damn.''

Stuart heaved a frustrated breath then picked up the hammer again. He angled a nail at the wall and swung at it. He missed, and the hammer slammed into his thumb. Cursing, he leaped to his feet, curling the fingers of his opposite hand around his throbbing thumb.

Immediately, Al was at his side. "Oh, Stuart," she said in concern. "Are you hurt? Let me see.''

She reached for his hand, but he yanked it to his chest, cradling his thumb protectively. "Just leave me alone,'' he grated through clenched teeth. "Your damn wall's finished.'' Without another word, he turned his back on her and strode angrily away.

Jenny Yale rested her hand on her son's arm. "I'm so glad you changed your mind about joining us for lunch, Stuart.''

The soft whine in his mother's voice grated on Stuart's already frazzled nerves and made him regret his hasty decision to take Morrey up on his invitation for Sunday lunch. The only reason he had come was to get his mind off Al and her *guest*. But he couldn't tell that to his mother and Morrey. His mother would probably faint dead away, and Morrey would probe him with questions about his involvement with Clairemore's granddaughter.

Easing his arm from beneath the cloying weight of his mother's hand, he picked up his napkin and draped it across his lap. "I finished my paperwork sooner than I expected."

"You work too hard, darling." Jenny turned a mournful gaze to her husband. "Tell him he works too hard, Morrey."

Stealing a glance at his stepson's tense face, Morrey patted his wife's hand. "He's a big boy, Jenny. He doesn't need us to tell him how to spend his time." He passed a platter of roast beef to Stuart. "Help yourself, son. Our new cook has a way with roast beef that will make your mouth water."

Stuart took the offered platter and forked several thick slices of beef onto his plate. He winced when he transferred the platter to his left hand to set it down.

The action drew Morrey's gaze to Stuart's hand. "What happened to your thumb?"

Stuart frowned at the two bandages bounding his thumb. "I got in a fight with a hammer this morning and lost."

"Oh, my word!" Jenny's voice rose hysterically. "Have you seen a doctor?"

Stuart groaned inwardly. Leave it to his mother to think of a doctor. She spent more time in doctors' offices than she did at home, searching for cures to ailments that existed only in her mind. She'd be better off visiting a psychiatrist. "It's just a bruise, Mother. It'll heal on its own." He picked up his fork and took a bite of roast beef.

"Doing a little building again, Stuart?" Morrey asked conversationally.

The question drew a half smile as Stuart remembered the summers during his college years he'd spent working for Morrey's construction company. "Not really. I was building a portable wall for Al."

"Al?" Morrey echoed, one eyebrow arching high on his forehead. "You mean Clairemore's granddaughter?"

Before Stuart could reply, Jenny clutched her son's arm, her face suddenly flushed with excitement. "You're seeing someone? How wonderful! After that unfortunate incident with Melaney Burroughs, I feared you would remain a bachelor for the rest of your life."

At the mention of Melaney's name, Stuart stiffened. He hadn't thought about Melaney in years. He hadn't allowed himself to. Yet her face appeared in his mind's eye as if he'd seen her last only yesterday.

He shoved the memory aside. "I'm not *seeing* anyone, Mother. Al is just an acquaintance." The statement was true, but in his heart Stuart saw it for the lie it was. His feelings for Al had grown beyond that of simple friendship.

"Why are you building her a portable wall?"

Stuart's face warmed beneath the curious look Morrey was shooting him and the challenge behind his question. He knew Morrey was concerned about the procurement of the acreage, and even more so by Stuart's reluctance in making Al an offer for the property. God, he wished he'd stayed at home and avoided all these questions.

Reluctantly he replied, "She's opening this antique shop in that stone barn that fronts the highway. Some local artists are offering their work to her on a consignment basis, and she needed a place to display their art.''

Worry lines fanned across Morrey's brow. ''How is this going to affect our plans for the property?''

''It won't. In less than three months she has another note due at the bank. She's depending on the profits from the antique shop to pay it.''

''And?''

''And she'll never make it. There's no way a little antique shop can generate enough business to pay off a note that size.''

Monday morning Al skipped down the back staircase, whistling a sunny song. ''Good morning, Verdie.''

''That's yet to be seen,'' her housekeeper grumbled. Without turning from her position at the stove, she shoveled a pancake onto a plate, then turned to carry it to the table. She stopped short and nearly dropped the plate when she saw Al. Giving the young woman a quick once-over, she noted the dress, hose and heels, uncharacteristic apparel for Al. ''And what are you all gussied up for?''

Al poured herself a cup of coffee, then sat down at the table, nursing the cup's warmth between her hands. ''I have an appointment with Mr. Feeber at the bank.''

''You mean Scrooge himself?''

Al chuckled. ''One and the same.''

Verdie shoved the plate in front of Al, then sat opposite her. ''What do you suppose he wants?''

Al shrugged as she poured syrup with a heavy hand. "Beats me."

"You paid the note, didn't you?"

Al looked up at Verdie in surprise. "Of course I did."

"Then why does he want to see you?"

Al sighed. Verdie, the worrier. Always fretting over Al's problems as if they were her own. Without Verdie, Al sometimes wondered how she would have survived it all. She stretched a hand across the table and squeezed Verdie's in reassurance. "I'm sure it's nothing. They probably just have some more papers for me to sign or something. Nothing to worry about. You'll see."

Nothing to worry about, huh, Al remembered in disgust. Opposite her, Mr. Feeber sat frowning over a sheaf of papers stacked a mile high. He pursed his lips and looked at Al over the top of his half glasses. She swallowed hard and offered him a weak smile.

Pulling off his glasses, he reared back in his chair, looking for all the world like lord of the manor. "Your grandfather was a good man, Al. A good man," he repeated, "but a poor businessman." He gestured toward the papers. "His payment history is deplorable at best, and with him gone now, the bank is naturally concerned about the outstanding loan." He shook his head sadly. "As much as I hate to do it, I'm afraid I'm going to have to call the loan."

Al's fingers dug into the rich leather of the chair's arms as she jerked herself to the edge of the seat. "But why?" she cried. "I made the April note."

"Five weeks late," he reminded her dryly. He sat for a moment, letting her absorb that fact before he continued. "I understand you've sold off the livestock and quit your job. With no income coming in, how do you propose to make the August note?"

His superior attitude irked Al, but she fought for calm. Losing her temper wouldn't help her case any. "I'm opening an antique shop in the barn that fronts the highway. The profits from it will pay the note."

"Oh? And what experience have you had in the antique business?"

Although she wilted inside at his persistence, Al kept her head up and her shoulders square. "None. But I've always loved antiques and know quite a bit about them. I also managed the art gallery where I worked, so I'm familiar with handling the accounts."

"New businesses are risky under the best of circumstances," he replied doubtfully.

"I agree. But you have to remember, Mr. Feeber, unlike other new businesses, I have virtually no overhead. I paid cash for all the renovations needed to put the barn in shape and I paid cash for my inventory." And I spent more money doing so than I'd ever anticipated, she added glumly to herself.

"Inventory?" he echoed in surprise, obviously unaware that Al had taken her business venture this far.

"Yes, the shop is stocked and ready to open. In fact, I'm planning an Open House in a couple of weeks to introduce my business to the public." She smiled her most engaging smile. "You'll receive an invitation by mail. I hope you'll be able to attend."

"Well, I don't know...."

His evasiveness proved what Al had already suspected: the man had made his decision to call the note before he had even called her for an appointment. Her appearance at the bank was merely a formality. That knowledge made her blood run cold, but she pushed back her fear and concentrated on the problem.

After doing some quick figuring in her head, she played her last card. "Tell you what, Mr. Feeber. What if I give you half of the August payment now? You know, to show good faith. Then if I can't pay the balance when it's due, you can call the note. That'll give me almost three months to prove I can raise the money."

She saw his hesitation and whipped out her checkbook before he could come up with a new argument. "Twenty-five hundred dollars. That would be half the August payment. Right?"

Feeber let out a long sigh. "Yes. Twenty-five hundred is half."

Al wrote out the check, dropped it onto Mr. Feeber's desk, said a hasty goodbye and slipped out the door. Through sheer willpower, she kept her emotions at bay until she reached the hallway beyond. At the elevators, her knees turned to jelly, and she sagged back against the wall.

The elevator door opened. Stuart stepped inside and, using the end of the cardboard tube he'd just picked up from the architect's office, he pressed the button for the lobby. He leaned back and watched the numbers flash his descent. Six. Five. Four. Three. On two the elevator eased to a stop, and the door slid open.

When no one boarded, Stuart glanced up and saw Al leaning against the wall opposite him, looking dazed and lost, her face as a white as a sheet.

"Al?" The door started to close and Stuart slapped a hand against it to keep it open. Tossing the tube aside, he caught Al's hand and pulled her into the elevator. Her skin was like ice, and she was shaking like a leaf. "Al, what's wrong?" he asked in concern.

She lifted her gaze to meet his, her eyes wide, unblinking. "They want to call the loan on the farm."

The devastation in her voice ripped through Stuart. "Who does?"

"The bank. Mr. Feeber."

"Dear God." He dropped his hand, and the door shushed closed. A shudder shook Al's shoulders, and without thinking Stuart pulled her into his arms.

Turning her cheek against the familiar comfort of his chest, she said, "Oh, Stuart. What am I going to do?"

Before he could offer a reply, the elevator stopped on the first floor, and the doors slid open again, revealing a lobby full of people waiting to board. Stuart scooped his tube from the floor, then quickly guided Al out of the elevator and through the crowded lobby to the street beyond, shielding her from the curious glances being cast her way.

"Where are you parked?" he asked.

Al looked around for a moment as if unsure where she was. "Never mind," he said gently. "I'm parked right here." He opened the car door and urged Al onto the seat. Crossing to the driver's side, he tossed the tube into the back seat and climbed in beside her. "Now, tell me the whole story."

Her gaze centered on the windshield, Al drew in a shuddery breath, then slowly released it. "The bank wants to call the loan. They said because of Granddaddy's late payment history and the fact that the farm no longer produces any income, they have no choice."

Foreclosure was a possibility Stuart had wondered about himself but had never voiced to Al. Banks made decisions based on numbers, unlike Al who thought only with her heart. Just as the banks had done, he'd made similar business decisions, but as he looked at Al's pale face, he cursed Feeber's numbers and his callousness. "Did you tell him about your antique shop?"

"Yes. He wasn't impressed."

Stuart sat for a moment in silence, thinking. All along he'd considered Al's chances of saving the farm slim at best. The truth of the matter was, he'd continued his own plans for the farm, banking on her failure. But faced with the reality of her loss, he found no sense of victory. That thought alone surprised him. After his last visit to the farm and his confrontation with Al and her *guest*, he'd wisely decided to keep a safe distance from the woman—close enough to know when she was ready to sell, but far enough away to avoid involvement with her.

Unfortunately, at the moment, the same protective instinct he'd experienced at the Derby welled within him. This time he didn't even try to suppress it. Instead he twisted in the seat to face her. The dejected slump of her shoulders tore at his heart. "I don't suppose you have the money to pay off the loan?" he offered lamely.

Al snorted at the ludicrousness of his statement. "Hardly."

"When will they foreclose?"

"I have until August. I paid half of the note today, but if I can't make the rest of the loan payment, I'll either have to sell out or give the land to the bank."

"I don't mean to pry into your financial matters, but what are your chances of making it?"

"Without the profits from the antique shop? Zilch."

"Even if you were to cut expenses? Maybe let your housekeeper go, that kind of thing?"

Al looked at him as if he'd suddenly gone mad. "I could never fire Verdie. She's been with our family almost thirty years. I'm her only source of income. No." She shook her head, emphasizing her refusal to consider his proposition. "I would never do that to Verdie."

Frustrated by her unwillingness to consider the only options left open to her, Stuart tossed up his hands in defeat. "Well in that case, you might as well sell out now. Cut your losses before you lose it all."

She whipped her head around to glare at him, color slowly seeping back into her cheeks. "That's what you'd like, isn't it?" she demanded angrily. "For me to sell you the farm so you can start your precious subdivision. Well, it's not for sale, Stuart."

"For God's sake, Al. Think of what's at stake here.

If you continue to sink money into this antique shop, you're going to lose it *and* your farm. If you want to go into the antique business, why not take what money you can and start over some place else? There are plenty of good locations for your shop within the city. And if you don't want to work, with what you make off the sale of the farm, you wouldn't even have to."

The anger slowly drained from Al as she listened to his impassioned plea. Money, money, money. It was all the man thought about. She'd lived with people who were consumed by wealth: her mother who sought it for the pleasures it could buy, and her father who struggled to earn enough to keep her mother happy. She'd seen the destruction the obsession for *more* could wreak.

"You don't understand, do you?" she asked sadly. "The money means nothing to me. For that matter, the antique shop means nothing. It's simply a means to an end. I want the farm, Stuart. Not for its monetary value, but for its intrinsic value. It's my home. The only one I've ever really known, and I'll do anything to keep it."

Emotion clogged her throat and, unable to say more, she leaned across the seat and pressed her lips to his. Drawing back, she rested a hand lightly on his cheek. "I hope one day something or someone means that much to you. Maybe then you'll understand."

Stuart crossed his office and dropped the cardboard tube onto his desk's polished surface. Wearily, he peeled off his suit coat and draped it across the back of his chair.

The unexpected meeting with Al had sapped his energy, leaving him feeling drained and with the beginnings of a headache. Talking to the woman was like talking to a brick wall and just about as productive. He shook his head as he wondered why he even bothered. It wasn't as if she were his responsibility.

Pushing the confrontation from his mind, he dropped down in his chair and pulled the tube to his lap. Sliding a finger into the open end, he eased out the plat maps the architect had drawn for him. Greystone Estates. The project that had monopolized his time and his thoughts for almost a year.

An aerial view of the entire section made up the first page. Alive with the colors of summer, the land pulled at him. In his mind, he drew the boundaries: the Foster place, the Myers's old dairy farm, Hank Thompson's pasture land and lastly, Clairemore Farms. Added together, they formed Greystone Estates.

Beside the highway, which was captured at the top of the photograph, he could just make out the tin roof of Al's barn, and farther down the narrow lane, the shingled roof of her farmhouse. He carried his gaze farther down the page to the lake where he and Al had swum. One day, property owners would swim there. He'd build a new pier with a diving board and a place to dock rowboats.

He tried to imagine the setting as it would look a year from now with children playing in the water. But the only image that came to mind was Al standing on the pier, as she had the day they'd gone fishing, looking back at him, laughing.

He rubbed a hand across his eyes and focused again on the aerial photograph. He had to get her off his mind.

"Busy?"

At the sound of Morrey's voice, Stuart snapped his head up. "No. Come on in." He gestured toward the papers on his desk. "I was just looking over the architect's and the engineer's final rendering of Greystone Estates."

Morrey crossed the room and propped a hip on the edge of Stuart's desk. Angling the photograph for a better view, he studied the layout as he pulled a cigarette from his shirt pocket. "Impressive, isn't it?"

Stuart frowned at the picture. "I suppose so."

Flicking his thumb down the wheel of his lighter, Morrey studied his stepson's face. "Second thoughts?" he asked as he touched the flame to his cigarette.

Stuart lifted his head. "What?"

"Second thoughts. Are you having some?"

With a rueful shake of his head, Stuart reared back in his chair, propping his elbows on the chair's arms and templing his fingers beneath his chin. He hadn't had any...at least not until he'd met Al. "Maybe. I don't know."

"Want to talk about it?"

"What good would that do?"

"Always helps to talk."

Listening was one of Morrey's most valuable traits. Stuart knew, for through the years he had depended on his stepfather for just such support on more than one occasion. He sighed deeply. "It's Al. The bank will call the loan if she can't meet the August payment on time."

"It's what you wanted, isn't it?"

"Yes—I mean no!" Stuart threw up his hands. "Oh, hell. This is crazy. I want the land, yet I don't want Al to lose it." Leaning his elbows on his desk, he rubbed his hands down his face, then lifted his head to look at Morrey. "Does this make any sense at all?"

Morrey smiled knowingly. "More than you realize." He stood and clapped Stuart on the back. "There's a solution to every problem. You just have to be willing to dig until you find it...and live with it once you do." After offering that pearl of wisdom, he snuffed out his cigarette and left.

Still deep in thought, Stuart put a thumb against the thick pages of the prospectus and flicked through them. When he caught a glimpse of the plat maps, he held the previous pages between his fingertips and flipped them back, exposing the engineer's drawing.

Frowning, he laid a hand over Clairemore Farms and studied the remaining lines and measurements. His forehead creased into deep furrows. Pulling a paper and pad from his desk drawer, he began making notes.

Envelopes, addressed and ready to be mailed, were stacked high on the kitchen table. Verdie sat opposite Al, dragging stamps across a wet sponge, then slapping them onto the sealed envelopes Al pushed her way.

"How many of these durned things are there anyway?" Verdie asked peevishly.

"Two hundred."

Verdie flopped back against her chair, wiping her sticky fingers on a wet cloth. "I know I've stamped at least that many already."

"Almost." Al shoved another envelope at her, then drew a line through the last name on the guest list at her right.

Wearily, Verdie stretched across the table, snagged the envelope in her arthritic fingers and slapped a stamp on it. "Done! And don't be throwing any more at me 'cause I'm through!" She pushed to her feet and crossed to the half-empty coffeepot. "How many folks you think will come?" she asked as she poured herself another cup.

Her mind on other matters, Al replied absently, "Oh, I don't know. Probably about a hundred or so."

"And I suppose you're expecting me to feed 'em all, too, aren't you?"

Impulsively, Al drew another envelope from the box of blank ones. "Who better than you, Verdie? You're the best cook in Kentucky."

"Humph! Couldn't tell it by looking at you. Skinny as a rail, you are. You don't eat enough to keep a bird alive. *Now* what are you doing?" Verdie asked crossly as she watched Al scribble an address on the front of the envelope.

Al licked the flap and grimaced when the gummy substance came to life beneath her tongue. "The last one. I promise.'' She looked at the name she had penned and crossed her fingers, hoping he would come. As she stood, she tossed the envelope onto the stack. Arching her back, she groaned from the cramped position she had held for the past several hours. "Two weeks, Verdie. Think we'll be ready?"

One hand planted at her hip, Verdie replied tersely, "Well, if God can create the world in a week, then we sure as the dickens can put together a party in two."

Six

Nervously, Al glanced at the guests milling around the barn. For two weeks, she'd worked like a Trojan in preparation for this party. At least a hundred, if not more, had responded to her invitation. In addition to the local artists whose work she had displayed, she recognized a good number of interior decorators circulating among the narrow aisles, inspecting her merchandise.

Verdie bustled among them, dressed in what she referred to as her "funeral garb," a black gaberdine dress cinched around her full waist with a belt of the same fabric. She carried a platter of tiny biscuits filled with country ham in one hand and a platter of pecan tarts in the other. A table against the far wall held a wider assortment of hors d'oeuvres.

Behind a portable bar, Verdie's nephew Luke filled

glasses of champagne stacked on a silver tray. Al shuddered at the thought of how much this party had cost her. But it's worth it, she assured herself as she glanced around the room. Everyone seemed to be having a good time. A few guests had even approached her about purchasing some of the antiques and art displayed.

Although excited about the number of people who had responded to her Open House invitation, Al was somewhat disappointed that one person had chosen to ignore it. She hadn't heard from Stuart since the day she'd seen him at the bank.

"The hostess is supposed to mingle," a feminine voice whispered in her ear.

Al wheeled around, a smile building on her face. "Roxey!" She caught her friend's hands in hers and squeezed. "I'm so glad you could make it. And Seth." Al rose to her toes in order to plant a kiss on Roxey's husband's bearded cheek. "What did she do? Twist your arm?"

Seth laughed good-naturedly while Roxey patted her rounded stomach. "The baby isn't due for three months, yet the man won't let me out of his sight."

"Just protecting my investment," Seth said and gave Al a wink.

Slipping her arm through her husband's and hugging it to her side, Roxey smiled as she glanced around the barn. "You've done a good job, Al. I'm proud of you."

The note of encouragement in her friend's voice made Al wish that Roxey was the bank officer in charge of her loan instead of old, tightfisted Feeber.

Sighing wistfully, she said, "Tell me that again in August when I deliver my mortgage payment to Mr. Feeber."

Stuart stepped through the door and stood for a moment, looking over the crowd. Something brushed against his leg, and he glanced down. Ranger stood at his side, looking up at him with soulful eyes. Judging by the gleam of his fur, Stuart assumed the dog had been bathed and brushed in honor of the party.

As he shifted his gaze to scan the room, he dropped a hand to scratch the dog's neck. His fingers met soft satin. Curious, he dropped down on one knee to look at the dog's collar. The leather band the dog usually wore was gone, and a black bow tie rested in its place. "Very nice, Ranger. What are you—the bouncer?"

In answer, the dog whined low in his throat. Stuart chuckled as he gave Ranger a last brisk rub. "Yeah, me, too, boy." He slipped a finger between his neck and the bow tie that threatened to choke him and tried in vain to gain enough room to breathe. "Never could stand one of these monkey suits," he mumbled irritably to the dog as he stood again.

He stuffed his hands into the pockets of his slacks and glanced nervously around the room until his gaze rested on Al. At least he thought it was Al. Her hair was swept up into a loose chignon and tendrils curled at the nape of her neck. Antique lace, the same shade as her calf-length dress of cream-colored satin, rose high on her neck, brushing against the loose curls at her nape. She looked like a Victorian woman.

The sight of her made his mouth go dry...and drew

a wave of guilt. He hadn't wanted to respond to her invitation. In fact, up until about an hour ago, he had planned to spend a quiet evening at home, thereby avoiding another confrontation with Al.

It seemed the two of them couldn't be in the same room without one or the other losing their temper. Ranger growled low in his throat, and Stuart glanced down at the dog and frowned. Apparently the mutt's talents extended beyond that of guard dog. They included mind reading, as well. Reflecting back over his disagreement with Al, Stuart silently acknowledged that the only time he'd seen Al angry was at the bank, when he'd tried to talk her into selling out.

"Okay, so it's me who usually ends up mad," he admitted reluctantly to Ranger. Obviously satisfied with Stuart's admission, the dog sank back down and rested his nose on his paws.

Still frowning, Stuart turned back to the crowd. His gaze settled again on Al. As he watched her talk to the tall, bearded man, he knew his hesitancy in responding to her invitation carried further back than just the incident at the bank. Considering the ass he'd made of himself the last time he'd been at the farmhouse when she'd attempted to introduce him to her *guest*, he was surprised she'd even bothered to invite him to her Open House. He had acted like a fool—and a jealous one at that. That knowledge alone was enough to make him cringe. Learning that the man was engaged hadn't even tempered his anger. Jealousy was a whole new emotion for Stuart Greyson. He'd never cared who a woman spent her time with...until he'd met Al.

* * *

She knew the moment Stuart arrived. Even with the distance of the room between them, Al felt the overpowering sense of his presence. As Roxey chatted away at her side, she stole a glance over her friend's shoulder.

Stuart stood framed by the doorway, his hand resting on Ranger's head. She had tried to imagine him dressed in a tuxedo, but her dreams fell well short of reality. His shoulders seemed to fill the narrow doorway as he stood with his feet slightly spread. The starched, white shirt he wore was a shocking contrast to the bronzed skin of his neck and face. Her fingers itched to trail the narrow band of white at his throat to tangle in the thick hair at his nape.

At that moment, he glanced her way. Their gazes locked, and her heart skipped a beat. Roxey's voice faded, and the hum of other conversations in the room dulled. It was as if she and Stuart were alone in the barn. Unaware of Roxey and Seth's curious looks, she slowly turned her back on them and walked toward Stuart, drawn by a force she couldn't name.

As Stuart watched her make her way through the crowded room, his breath lodged in his throat. She was a vision. A dream. A woman who had the power to make him crawl. He hoped she never discovered that power.

When she stood before him, she rose up on her toes and lifted her lips to his cheek. The gesture was so natural. So much a part of Al. His eyelids shuttered closed as the scent of lilacs filled his senses and the velvety texture of her lips brushed his skin.

"I'm glad you came, Stuart," she whispered at his ear before she withdrew.

Forcing his eyes open, he met her smiling gaze. "Me, too," he admitted in a husky voice as he touched a finger to the cameo brooch clasped at her throat. A low growl erupted dangerously close to his thigh.

"Back off, Ranger—" he warned in a threatening voice "—or I'll hang you up by that damn bow tie you're wearing."

Al's jaw dropped open as she watched Ranger slink back to the door. "I can't believe it! You're the first person to ever intimidate Ranger—other than Verdie, of course." She turned her gaze back to Stuart. "Now who will protect me from you?"

He lifted a derisive brow. "Since when do you need protecting?"

Al chuckled. "You've got a point." She looped her arm through his. "Come on. I want you to meet my some of my friends."

Ignoring the gentle tug on his arm, Stuart stood his ground. "There's something I'd like to say first." He cleared his throat and pulled nervously at his collar. "The other day when I saw you at the bank...well, I'm sorry for the things I said. You didn't ask for my advice, and I shouldn't have offered it."

Touched by his apology, Al hugged his arm to her side. "You don't have to apologize. You were only trying to help. Now, come on, I—"

Stuart stopped her with a touch to her hand. "Wait. There's more. When I was at the farmhouse the last time...well...I was rude to your guest. I was way out of line.''

She cocked her head and looked at him, her eyes reflecting her disappointment. "Were you? I was hoping maybe you were a little bit jealous.''

Warily, Stuart stiffened. Had she been trying to make him jealous? he wondered. Other women had tried that ploy on him with lesser results. "As I said before," he reiterated tersely, "who you entertain in the privacy of your home is no business of mine.''

"Oh, Stuart. You make it all sound so sordid. Rhys is a good friend of mine. Almost like a brother.''

The explanation, coming from Al, was almost believable. But the vision of her prancing around half-dressed while the man towel-dried his hair still had the power to curdle his blood. "At any rate, I apologize for my rudeness.''

She centered a kiss on his cheek again and smiled, totally disarming him. "Apology accepted. Now, come on. I want you to meet some of my guests.''

This time he allowed her to drag him across the room, but when she stopped in front of the couple he'd seen her talking with when he first arrived, he felt an immediate uneasiness.

"Roxey, Seth, I'd like you to meet a friend of mine, Stuart Greyson. Stuart, this is my friend Roxey Dandridge, and her husband, Seth.''

Stuart shook Seth's hand. "Glad to meet you, Seth.'' He turned uneasily toward Roxey. "It's good to see you again, Roxey.''

Roxey accepted the hand Stuart extended to her. "You, too, Stuart.''

Al looked at Stuart in surprise. "You know Roxey?"

"Yes. She's handled a few loans for me in the past."

"And I wouldn't mind handling a few more," Roxey added, smiling. "How are the plans for the new subdivision going? Ready to discuss financing yet?"

Nervously, Stuart cleared his throat and stole a glance at Al. She was smiling and waving at a group across the room. Obviously, she hadn't heard Roxey's question. Fearing the mention of the subdivision would destroy their tentative truce, he replied evasively, "It's a little early, yet."

"Well, let me know. I'd like to discuss the—"

"Stuart, darling," a feminine voice drawled, interrupting Roxey and drawing Al's attention to the group.

Stuart stepped back to allow the woman to enter the circle of conversation. "Hello, Valerie."

"What are you doing here?" she asked in a sultry voice as she ran a crimson nail down the front placket of his shirt. "Are you thinking of redecorating your home in antiques?"

Easing her hand from his chest, Stuart replied, "Not anytime soon. Do you know everyone?"

The woman ignored both Roxey and Al and turned her attention to Seth. Smiling coyly, she said, "I don't think I've had the pleasure."

Roxey stepped to her husband's side and slipped her hand possessively around his arm. "This is my husband, Seth Dandridge. Seth, this is Valerie. She's a friend of my sister Monica.''

Placing his hand over Roxey's, Seth ignored the diamond-studded fingers extended to him and politely nodded a greeting instead. ''Glad to meet you.''

Although she would rather have strangled the vamp, in a subtle attempt to shift Valerie's attention away from Seth, Al gestured to the antiques and art filling the barn. ''I hope you've found something you can't live without, Valerie.''

The woman gave Al a measuring look, then lifted her gaze to Stuart's. She puckered her lips provocatively and drawled. ''I think I might have.''

Over the top of Valerie's head, Stuart caught a glimpse of Al's thunderous look. A storm was brewing, and although it pleased him to know he wasn't the only one to feel the stab of jealousy, he didn't want an ugly scene to ruin Al's Open House.

Before he could respond to the situation, Roxey spoke up. ''Valerie, I need your advice. Seth and I are decorating the nursery and we saw the most unusual cradle over there.'' She pointed to the far side of the room. ''Would you mind taking a look and giving us your professional opinion?''

''Well, certainly, Roxey. I'd be happy to advise you.'' Valerie squeezed Stuart's arm to her breast a little too suggestively for Al's liking, then let it drop before sidling up to Seth. ''Some people are simply helpless when it comes to decorating,'' she said as she looped her arm through his. ''But don't worry. I have a flair for choosing just the right...'' Her voice faded as she led Seth away, her hips swaying. Roxey

was left standing behind. After giving Stuart a conspiratorial wink, she turned and followed the two.

Stuart's breath eased out of him in a sigh of relief.
I owe you one, Roxey, he promised silently.

"That hussy!"

Surprised by the venom in Al's tone, Stuart turned
to her. Her gaze was narrowed on the graceful sway
of Valerie's hips. "Do I detect a little jealousy?" he
asked, biting back a smile.

She curled her nose in disgust. "There's nothing
there—" she said with a toss of her head in Valerie's
direction, "—to be jealous of." Twisting her head
around to frown at Stuart, she asked, "How do you
know that little feline anyway?"

"She decorated my house."

Al remembered the ultramodern decor of Stuart's
home and the severe lines and drab colors of its fur-
nishings. With the exception of the crystal bowl of
potpourri, there wasn't a degree of warmth or character to the place. "Well, I hope you didn't pay her
much," she said petulantly. "If you did, you got
ripped off."

When the door closed behind the last guest, Al
kicked off her shoes and sank down on a red velvet
Victorian loveseat. "I'm beat," she mumbled in a
weary voice.

Chuckling softly, Stuart sat down beside her. "You
earned it." Throughout the evening, he had watched
her work her way through the crowd, seeing to her
guests' needs, answering questions about merchandise, and smiling all the while. She was a natural

salesman and obviously knew her merchandise well. He picked up the clipboard from her lap and scanned the list of reserved items. "Looks like you made quite a few sales."

She dropped her head to rest on Stuart's shoulders. "I did, didn't I?" Yawning, she snuggled closer. "Wake me up when you leave."

Trays clattered to the floor, and Al jerked her head up just as Verdie let out a blue string of curses. Al called across the room, "Forget it, Verdie. I'll clean up the mess tomorrow."

Her housekeeper straightened, leaving the empty platters where they lay. "Don't have to tell me twice. No siree. Verdie Mae Johnson knows when to quit." She stooped and pulled her purse from beneath the hors d'oeuvre table. When she rose, she narrowed a gaze at Al. "And don't you touch them dishes. I'll clean 'em up in the morning when I come in." She switched her gaze to Stuart. It softened perceptibly. "And you get that girl up to the house and into her bed. She's bone tired, she is, working from dawn to dusk for the last two weeks getting ready for this shindig."

Stuart dipped his head to smile at Al, his gaze warm on her face. "Yes, ma'am. I'll do just that."

After Verdie left, Stuart helped Al turn out the lights and lock up. Due to the line of cars parked at the barn when he had arrived, he'd left his car at the house and walked the short distance to the barn.

Hand in hand, Stuart and Al headed back down the lane. Ranger—at last freed of his bow tie—trotted at their sides. Above them the moon peeked through the canopy of oak leaves, creating a web of moonlight beneath their feet. A soft breeze carried the scent of pine and magnolia.

Al lifted her face to the dark, velvety sky. In the distance a shooting star streaked across the blackness. "Money, money, money, money," she murmured until it faded out of sight.

Stuart stopped, pulling Al to a halt at his side. "What are you mumbling about?" he asked curiously.

She pointed up at the sky, her eyes filled with the dreams that spiraled through her mind. "If you make a wish on a falling star, it'll come true. I was wishing for money." She laughed as she hugged her arms beneath her breasts. "Believe me, I need it."

At the reminder of her financial circumstances, a frown furrowed Stuart's brow. "I know I said I wouldn't offer any more advice, Al, but is it really so important that you try to hang on to the farm? Wouldn't it be wiser to just sell out and move on?"

"Yes. Definitely wiser." She looked up at him and grinned, unwilling to let his pessimism dim her high spirits. "But then, I'm not known for my wisdom. Only my luck at the races."

Instead of making him laugh, her comment caused his frown to deepen. He could see how much it meant to Al to keep the farm. Yet he didn't want to see her hurt, and he knew she would be if she continued to pour her energy and her money into a losing proposition. She'd lose it all. It was just a matter of when, not if.

"Why don't I loan you the money to pay off the loan, Al?"

Her eyes widening in surprise, she looked up at him. "You'd really do that, wouldn't you, Stuart?"

Flustered by her trusting look, he dug his hands into his pockets and looked down at the ground, scraping his shoe across the loose rocks on the asphalt lane. He didn't know where the proposition had come from. The offer had slipped out without conscious thought. But upon reflection, he knew he was willing to make good his offer. "Yes, I mean it. I hate to see you throw all your energy and your money into this antique shop for nothing when—"

She caught him by the elbows, forcing him to meet her gaze. "But it's *not* for nothing, Stuart. It's going to work. Didn't you see all the interest I generated tonight? And I haven't even officially opened the doors yet. Just think what I can do once I open my business to the public!" Slipping her arms around his waist, she leaned back and smiled up at him. "But I appreciate your concern, Stuart. You're sweet to offer."

He pulled her against his chest and rested his chin atop her head. *Sweet?* He'd been called a lot of things in his lifetime—ruthless, calculating, driven—but never sweet. Could it be that Al had discovered a tenderness within himself that even he wasn't aware of?

Lifting her chin, he looked down at her. "If you need anything, ever, you only have to ask. Remember that, will you?"

Moisture pooled in Al's eyes. For as long as she

could remember it seemed she'd been on her own, fending for herself. Even when her grandparents had been alive, she'd had to assume the role of caretaker as much as that of granddaughter. She didn't begrudge them the sacrifices she had made to be with them the last years of their lives, for in return they had given her a home and love…a place and an emotion she had been robbed of at the time of her father's death.

With her gaze focused on Stuart, she whispered, "Yes, I'll remember."

Unable to resist any longer, he dipped his head, taking her lips in a kiss that cut straight to his soul. He rocked his mouth over hers, sealing her promise with the passionate heat of his lips.

Warmth, softness, femininity. She was all of those things. Yet she was strong, as well. Anyone who took on the responsibilities she had would have to be strong. But it wasn't her strength he was aware of as he held her. It was her vulnerability, the one quality he was sure she would deny. More than he wanted her farm, he wanted this woman. He wanted to protect her and make her his.

Hooking an arm behind her knees, he swept her into his arms and carried her the rest of the way to the house. When they reached the back door, Ranger sank down on the porch steps and rested his nose between his paws. When Stuart kicked the door closed behind him, the dog didn't so much as lift an ear.

At the top of the stairs, Stuart paused. "Which room is yours?"

Languidly, Al lifted a hand and pointed at the room to her left. He pushed the door open with his foot and crossed to the antique four-poster bed. At its side, he stopped and slowly lowered Al to her feet, sliding her body sensuously down the length of his.

In the moonlight filtering through the lace curtains at the window beside him, he saw the heightened color in her cheeks and the glimmer of expectancy in her blue eyes. He touched a finger to her cheekbone and traced an invisible line to her jaw, carefully noting each feature of her face. She was so beautiful. Why hadn't he realized that before now?

Fascinated by his discovery, he drew his finger along the curve of her jaw. At her chin he paused as he felt a shimmer of passion course through her. He knew her passion, had tasted it, yet was humbled by it. Almost reverently, he rode the swell of her strong chin until his finger dipped down to trace the graceful curve of her neck.

When his fingers touched the cameo, he slipped the brooch from its place at her throat and tossed it onto the nightstand beside the bed. One-by-one he released the pearl buttons that stretched from the dress's high, lace collar to her waist. Though her breathing quickened, she remained silent and unmoving, her gaze riveted on his face.

He eased the satin over her shoulders and the dress fell to pool at her bare feet. A whisper of lace covered the rounded fullness of her breasts and a triangular slash of that same lace veiled her femininity.

Slowly, Stuart raised his gaze to her face. "Alyssa," he whispered huskily, awed by the fragility and beauty of the woman before him. "No more Al. You're my Alyssa." His lips touched the curve of her throat.

Her head drifted back and she closed her eyes, reveling in the sensuous warmth of his lips at her throat. *Alyssa.* The name was foreign to her, yet when whispered through his lips it sounded so right. Years ago she had been nicknamed Al by her father and had been called that ever since. She had always thought it suited her. Until now. *My Alyssa.* The possessive quality of the endearment plucked at her heartstrings. Yes, she was his. At what point she had become Stuart's she wasn't sure. But that she was brought joy soaring from deep within her.

He raised his lips to cover hers while his fingers sought the clasp of her bra. When the scrap of lace dropped between them, he flung it aside, then slid his hands down her back until they rested on the thin band of lace covering her hips. Soon all that remained between them was Stuart's tuxedo. With Alyssa's help that, too, quickly disappeared. Her heart sought his, and, with their naked bodies pressed flush, she found the answering pulse of his heartbeat against her breast.

Scooping her up high in his arms, he bent to place her on the bed, then followed, bracing himself above her with his palms. "I want you, Alyssa McCord," he whispered, his face bare inches above hers.

She touched a finger to the dimple in his cheek, then raised her gaze to meet the passionate heat in his eyes. "And I want you."

Slowly he lowered himself on top of her, the muscles in his arms bulging with the strain to remain poised above her, until his lips touched her. Softly. Oh, so softly, his lips moved across hers, tasting, testing, biting, drawing her to him like a moth to light.

He matched the rhythm of his lips with his chest, rubbing against her breasts until her nipples rose in turgid peaks beneath him. Propelling himself up and away from her body, then back down purely by the strength of his arms, he sought the hardened peaks, taking one between his teeth and nipping lightly.

Passion became darkness, blinding Alyssa to all but the sensations pulsing through her body. "Oh, Stuart," she groaned. "Please..." Her breathless plea drifted away into nothingness as he moved his lips to her other breast, suckling, biting, driving her crazy with desire.

In the darkness, she found the smooth planes of his back and swept her hands upward until they rode the muscled pads of his shoulders, higher still until her fingers threaded through the short hair at the nape of his neck. More than ever before she yearned for some length to his conservatively cut hair. Something to cling to, to knot her fingers in and hang on. She was falling, sinking deeper and deeper, lower and lower, and there seemed to be nothing below her to break her fall.

She gasped when his tongue snaked down the valley between her breasts, trailing a wake of fire to her navel. Burning out of control, she clasped his face in her hands and lifted him, guiding him back to her lips. "I want you, Stuart. I need you now," she murmured against the moist heat of his mouth.

Rising slightly above her, he fitted himself between her thighs. The rhythm, begun at what now seemed hours ago, flowed to her hips, and slowly she arched her body to meet his in a sensual dance.

With each thrust of his body, they climbed higher and higher toward the light that beckoned like a siren from long ago.

"Alyssa..." Stuart's fingers tightened in her hair as he gazed deeply into her eyes. "You're mine, Alyssa," he whispered.

In a blinding flash of white, together they reached the peak, and plunged over the precipice, clinging to each other as their bodies pulsed with the pleasure of shared satisfaction.

Stuart collapsed against her, every muscle in his body gone lax, yet his heart continued to thunder against her breasts.

Combing her fingers through his damp hair, Al snuggled his head closer in the crook of her neck and answered softly, "Yes, I'm yours."

Al awoke to the sound of Verdie's off-key humming and the rattling of pans. Sunlight poured through the lace-covered windows, bathing the room in a mesh of cheery yellow. Al groaned and flopped over on her back, away from the bright light, throwing her arm out to her side. The thick thud of flesh hitting flesh made her jackknife upright.

Slowly, Stuart sat up beside her. "And good morning to you, too," he said, rubbing his jaw with one hand while holding the sheet at his waist with his other.

Pressing her fingers to her lips to stifle a giggle, Al replied, "Sorry."

A loud crash sounded downstairs.

Stuart bolted from the bed. "What in the hell was that?" he asked as he grabbed for his slacks.

"Uh-oh."

His pants half-on and half-off, Stuart twisted around to look at Al. "*Uh-oh*, what?"

"Uh-oh, Verdie's here."

Realization dawned, smoothing the features of Stuart's face as he glanced at the open bedroom door. He pulled his slacks and zipped the fly, then turned to Al. "What do we do now?" he whispered.

"I don't know what you're going to do, but I'm going back to sleep." With that, she pulled the sheet up over her head.

"Oh, no, you're not. I'm not facing the music alone." Stuart crawled across the mattress and grabbed the sheet, jerking it away from Al. The sight of her naked body, bathed in sunlight, pushed all thoughts of Verdie from his mind. He raked her body with his gaze, taking in the satiny smoothness of her skin, the pebbly texture of her nipples, and the triangular matt of hair shadowing her femininity.

The boldness of his gaze drew a blush to Al's cheeks. Deciding that the delicious curve of her lips was much too enticing, Stuart lowered himself over her, brushing his lips against hers. "You wouldn't make me face Verdie all by my myself, now would you, Al?" he murmured against her lips.

She laced her hands behind his neck. "Mmm-hmm."

Frustrated, he sagged against her, dipping his forehead against hers. "Please, Al. I've seen her wrath. She'll probably sic Ranger on me."

"Probably."

"And to think I was going to treat you to dinner tonight," he said, shaking his head sadly as he knelt at her side. "Oh, well...." He backed off the bed and pulled on his shirt.

Al watched him fit the studs of his ruffled shirt through the buttonholes. Narrowing her eyes suspiciously at him, she asked, "Where?"

"Café Metro. But if you don't want to go—"

She was out of bed and pulling on a robe before he could finish the statement.

Smiling smugly, he shrugged into his tuxedo jacket. He laced his fingers through hers and led her down the hallway. "I knew you wouldn't let me down."

"It was Café Metro," she said dryly. "I love the place."

As Al and Stuart stepped into the kitchen, Verdie was lifting a stack of dirty trays from the table. When she saw the two of them, her eyes bugged out and her jaw went slack. The trays slipped from her fingers and crashed to the floor at her feet.

Before the woman could gather her wits and give him the tongue lashing he was sure was coming, Stuart strode up to her and kissed her full on the lips. "Good morning, Verdie. Wish I could stay for breakfast, but I've got to get to the office." He walked to the back door, turned and gave Al a wink, then pushed open the door and let it slam behind him.

Seven

Impulsively, Al ran out the back door to the porch. "Stuart!" she called.

He stopped and turned. "What?" he asked.

Unsure what to say but knowing she wasn't ready for him to leave, Al pulled self-consciously at the folds of her robe. "You promised me dinner at Café Metro."

He crossed back to the porch, hiding a smile. With Al a step above him, she stood at almost eye level. He circled her waist with his hands. "Did I?" he teased.

Her mouth curved into a pout. "You know you did."

"Then I guess I'll have to make good that promise, won't I?" He brushed her lips with his.

That little bit of reassurance was all Al needed. She

threw her arms around his neck and melted against him. "It's Saturday. Are you sure you have to go into the office? Couldn't you play hooky just this once?"

The invitation was tempting. More tempting than Stuart cared to think about. But he had business to take care of and he was already late.

Regretfully, he caught her hands in his and pulled them from around his neck. "As much as I'd like to, Al, I can't." He pulled his wallet from his back pocket and pressed a business card into her hand. "I'll pick you up at seven-thirty. If something comes up before then, call me. If I'm not at the office, they'll know where to find me."

When she dipped her head to hide her disappointment, he placed a finger beneath her chin and forced her gaze back to meet his. "I promise, as soon as I get through, I'll be back. Okay?"

Though she would have rather pleaded with him to stay, Al forced a smile. "Sure. I understand." She gave him a quick kiss and stepped back into the kitchen...and smack into Verdie.

"Alyssa Claire McCord! Your granddaddy's probably rolling in his grave right this very minute. Entertaining men overnight in his house. Humph! You've got some explaining to do, girl. You better start talking, and I mean fast!"

Al cinched her bathrobe tighter at her waist and headed for the coffeepot. Not a morning person even on the best of days, she felt the need for a strong kick of caffeine in order to deal with her housekeeper's indignation.

Through the kitchen window she glimpsed Stuart

climbing into his car. The sight of him stripped Verdie's disapproval from her mind, and she paused, a wistful sigh escaping her. She leaned a hip against the counter and nursed the coffee cup's warmth between her hands as she watched his car move out onto the lane.

Verdie stepped over the trays scattered at her feet and followed Al to the sink. "Now don't think for a minute I'm going to let you get by—"

"Have you ever been in love, Verdie?" Al asked. Unaware that Verdie had even moved, Al was startled when her housekeeper caught her by the elbow and propelled her to the kitchen table.

After taking a seat opposite Al, Verdie clasped her hands on the tabletop. She fidgeted nervously in her chair for a moment, then collapsed against its back, sighing heavily. "Lordy, how I wish your grandmama was still alive. I don't know diddly squat about how to deal with this kind of thing."

Al giggled at Verdie's discomfort but sobered quickly when the woman pressed her lips together in agitation.

"Some knowledge is better than none though, and I suppose it's my moral obligation to advise you." Verdie plucked a handkerchief from the cuff of her sleeve and threaded it through her fingers, her gaze focused on the scrap of white. "Yes, I was in love once. Years ago. Saw him off to World War II, expecting to become his bride when he returned home." Her voice shook and she firmed her lips more determinedly before she spoke again. "He's buried over there—" she waved a negligent hand back over her shoulder "—somewhere in England." She pushed her glasses up, dabbed the wrinkled handkerchief to her eyes, then dropped the bifocals back into place.

Not knowing this secret in Verdie's past, Al blinked back her own wave of tears and leaned across the table to squeeze Verdie's hand. "I'm sorry. I didn't mean to dredge up old memories."

"Distant in years maybe, but never old. Nary a day goes by that I don't think about him. Forty-five years he's been gone, and this old heart still races every time he comes to mind."

Al knew about loss. She'd lost her father and her grandparents, but she couldn't imagine the loss of a lover. She tried to envision her life without Stuart and a shiver shook her shoulders. She'd known him less than two months, but already he was firmly implanted in her heart. And after last night... She lifted her gaze to Verdie's. "I love him, Verdie."

"You love him?"

"Yes."

"And does he love you?"

"I don't know."

Verdie's cheeks puffed as she blew out a long breath. Slowly, she eased herself up from the chair. "God help you then, girl. Love can be painful. I know that for a fact."

Somewhat bemused by her conversation with Verdie, Al spent the afternoon at the barn, cleaning up the mess from the party. Her efforts were hampered by the fact that she couldn't seem to concentrate on her work. Her thoughts kept drifting to Stuart and the night she'd spent in his arms.

Did he love her? she asked herself honestly as she rested her chin on the broom handle. She thought back over the things he'd said, little memories she'd tucked away without being aware she'd been doing it at the time. He had offered to loan her the money for the land. That was certainly a change from his usual request to buy her out. She shook her head and began to sweep again. No, that wasn't a sign of love. A kindness certainly, but not a declaration of love.

Reaching the barn door, she flung it open and swept out the debris. Sunlight bathed her face, making her squint. She turned her face up to the sun, closed her eyes and let its warmth envelop her. Hugging the broom to her breast, she remembered the heat of Stuart's body against hers. A wistful sigh escaped her lips, and she dropped down on the grass by the door, giving in to the memories.

His words played through her mind. *You're my Alyssa.* Was that a declaration of love? She wrinkled her nose at the thought and shook her head. No. More a statement of possession than love. And that would be more his style. She chuckled as she hugged her knees beneath her chin. She suspected that staking a claim on a possession would come much easier for Stuart Greyson than words of love.

The man was obviously obsessed by this goal of his to become a millionaire by the age of thirty. And although she respected his ambitious nature, she couldn't help feeling a little disappointed that he'd refused her suggestion at playing hooky with her and elected to go into the office to work instead.

A horn honked, and Al glanced at the lane and waved as Verdie passed by on her way home. Heavens! she thought in dismay as she scrambled to her feet. Where had the time gone? She glanced at her watch and saw that it was after five. Stuart had said he'd pick her up at seven-thirty, but if she hurried, she could dress and drive into town and save him the trouble of traveling all the way back out to the farm to pick her up. That decided, she locked up the barn and headed for the house at a fast jog.

Stuart carried the memory of Al's half-hearted smile with him to the office. It can't be helped, he assured himself. As badly as he'd been tempted to stay, he knew he had work that couldn't wait. Setting his jaw in determination, he sat down at his desk and reached for the pile of papers awaiting his attention, determined to complete it quickly and return to Al.

He flipped a file open, stared at it for a moment in disinterest, then tossed it aside and replaced it with the file on Greystone Estates. He located the notes he'd made the day he'd seen Al at the bank and began to study them. Before long, he was scribbling figures alongside those he'd already made.

Reaching for the phone, he punched in Joe Barber's number. "Joe? Stuart Greyson. I have a question for you. You know that property out in Oldham County that Morrey and I have been looking at?" At Joe's affirmative reply, Stuart continued, "What would it cost to dig a man-made lake on that property? You don't have to be exact. A ballpark figure is good enough.''

Stuart winced when the subcontractor named his price. Switching the telephone receiver to his left ear, he jotted down the amount, then stretched to flip open his calendar. "And a completion date?" After noting the day, he sighed wearily. "Thanks, Joe. I'll get back to you," he said, and replaced the receiver.

He reared back in his chair, his mouth puckered in a thoughtful frown. The figures were there before him: the architect's, the surveyor's, and the engineer's fees for the preparation of a new set of plans; the cost for the excavation of a man-made lake; the lawyer's fees for the transfer of title. He tossed his pencil down in disgust.

Without Clairemore Farms, he could kiss his chances of making a million before his thirtieth birthday goodbye. What with the loss of the farm's acreage for development, the land sacrificed for the new lake, and the cost of digging the lake itself, his margin of profit was narrowed considerably. And that was without even considering all the money he'd already invested in planning the subdivision. Money he might as well have struck a match to and burned.

But it can't be helped, he thought as he templed his fingers beneath his chin and stared at the columns of numbers. Al didn't want to sell her farm, and that was that.

He sighed in frustration. No, that wasn't exactly true. If her antique shop failed and she was forced to sell out, he could still purchase the land and develop the property as planned. Al had promised if and when she sold, she'd sell to him, and he knew she'd never go back on her word. That thought brought him no pleasure, for he knew Al would be devastated if she lost the farm.

Burying his face in his hands, he rubbed his eyes wearily. He either had to wait out Al or start over. The choice was his to make.

Seven hours later, he was no closer to a decision than when he'd first sat down at his desk. He felt as if he were chained there. Murphy's Law in action—everything that could possibly go wrong was going that way. The ringing telephone jarred him out of his thoughts.

Raking his fingers through his hair, he listened to the plumbing contractor's lame excuses for not having completed the repairs on an apartment complex that were supposed to have been finished by the previous Wednesday.

When he'd reached the limit of his patience, he yelled into the telephone receiver, "I don't give a damn if you have to hire five extra crews to finish the job. We have people waiting to move into those damn apartments. You have until midnight Monday. If your crews aren't finished and out of there, you're fired. Understand?" He slammed the phone down, cursing.

"Problem?"

At the sound of Morrey's voice, Stuart jerked his head up. He scowled as he waved his stepfather to the seat opposite his desk. "Nothing I can't handle." He made himself a note to check on the plumber's progress on Monday morning, then closed his appointment book and reared back in his chair. "What can I do for you?"

"Just dropped by to check on you. Missed you at the club this morning."

Stuart dropped his forehead to his open palm and groaned. Their weekly racquetball game. He'd forgotten all about it. "Sorry."

"No need to be." Morrey pulled out a cigarette and lit it. He studied his stepson through the thin spiral of smoke. "Rough night?"

Rubbing a hand across the stubble of whiskers on his chin, Stuart sighed. "Yeah, you could say that."

"Who's the woman?"

Immediately, Stuart stiffened. "Who said anything about a woman?"

Morrey blew out a stream of smoke, then lifted one shoulder in a careless shrug. "When a man comes into his office on a Saturday wearing a day's growth of beard and a tuxedo that looks like it's been slept in, a person is bound to suspect a woman."

Up until that moment, Stuart hadn't even been aware of how he was dressed. His one concern had been to finish his work and get back to Al. He glanced down at his rumpled tuxedo, then back to his stepfather. Chuckling, he replied, "Yeah, I guess a person would."

"Anybody I know?"

"Not personally, but you'll meet her soon enough. I was with Al."

Morrey's hand froze, his cigarette halfway to his mouth. Puckering his lips thoughtfully, he leaned across the desk and stubbed out the cigarette in the ashtray. "Sounds serious."

"Could be."

"Has she agreed to sell us the land?"

Thinking of his own doubts concerning the property, Stuart shifted uncomfortably in his chair. "No."

"What's the holdup?"

"She doesn't want to sell."

"Stuart, I don't think I need to remind you that we have a lot of money riding on this deal. If you don't think you can handle the negotiations, I'll—"

Abruptly Stuart stood, cutting off Morey's offer. "I can handle it. I just need a little more time, that's all."

A soft knock sounded at the door. Both men turned just as Al peeked in.

She smiled uncertainly. "Am I disturbing anything?"

For a moment Stuart froze, unable to move. How much of their conversation had she overheard? Judging by the fact that she hadn't thrown anything or started screaming about buzzards, he could only assume she had just arrived.

Nervously, Al cleared her throat. "Bad timing, huh? Oh, well, I'll see you later then."

Immediately, Morrey was out of his chair and across the room. "Please don't go. You aren't interrupting anything. In fact, I was just leaving." He caught her hand in his. "I'm Morrey Yale, Stuart's stepfather."

His friendly smile eased her discomfort somewhat. "It's nice to meet you. I'm Al McCord."

He chuckled as if at some private joke. "Yes, I know who you are. Stuart's told me quite a bit about you." He patted her hand between his, then released it. "Well, I guess I'd better be getting home before Jenny starts worrying about me." He stepped to the door. "See you two later."

When the door closed behind him, Al turned to Stuart. His face was a closed mask, unreadable. She'd hoped for excitement or at the least, maybe surprise. Already regretting her impulsive decision to meet him at his office, she hurried to explain. "I didn't mean to disturb you at work. It just seemed so ridiculous for you to drive out to the farm and then turn right around and drive back to the—" She stopped short. "Stuart Greyson!" she exclaimed as she took a step backward.

Here it comes, Stuart thought with regret. She *did* hear Morrey's and my conversation and now she's going to let me have it with both barrels. He braced himself for the attack.

"I'm proud of you!" she said in surprise.

Proud? He'd expected her to damn him to hell and back. Instead she'd said she was proud of him. Confused by the unexpected compliment and the pleased smile brightening her face, he asked warily, "Why?"

"Well, just look at you. Your hair's a mess, you need a shave and your clothes look like you slept in them. And you don't even have on a tie!"

Almost Morrey's exact words. The relief Stuart felt was quickly replaced with impatience. He'd worked hard all day so he could finish his obligations quickly and return to her. And now that she was with him, all she could talk about was his appearance. He stepped from behind his desk. "Shut up, Al," he said, his voice threatening.

Her eyes widened in surprise. "What did you say?"

"I said, shut up." He took a menacing step closer, and she backed away but came to an abrupt halt when her rear end hit the office door. Bracing one hand on either side of her face, Stuart dipped his head until his gaze was level with hers. "You better than anyone should know I didn't sleep in my suit."

A whisper of a smile played at her lips as she recognized the heat flaring in his eyes. "Seems like I do recall seeing your suit on the floor." She lifted her hands to his lapels. "Didn't your mother ever teach you to hang up your—"

He covered her mouth with his, silencing her. "You talk too much, you know that?" he murmured against her lips.

"So I've been told."

He nibbled his way to her ear, wanting more than anything to take her where they stood. "What time is it?"

She sighed as his tongue flicked over the sensitive skin behind her ear. "I think about six-thirty."

He molded his body to hers. "Our dinner reservation isn't until eight. Got any suggestions on how to spend the time?"

Over the next few weeks, how Al and Stuart would pass the time was never a concern as both were busy—Stuart at his office and Al with her antique shop. Even though they spent their days apart, the nights were theirs alone. By mutual agreement Clairemore Farms became Stuart's second home.

Both Al and Stuart knew they had won Verdie's acceptance—albeit grudgingly—of their arrangement when she began to set a place at the table for Stuart each morning. After breakfast they went their separate ways, Stuart to his office and Al to her antique shop.

Barnstormers was an even bigger success than Al first predicted. Tourists driving out to visit the nearby thoroughbred farms stopped in, lured by the colorful display of antiques and quilts Al positioned outside in full view of the highway.

Word quickly spread of her generous percentage splits on consignments, and people flocked in, wanting to sell an odd assortment of items they no longer had use for. Al decided luck was still on her side when Rosemary Wicker approached her about renting a space on a permanent basis. Needing help manning the shop as much as she needed revenue, Al offered a trade. The two agreed they would rotate days in the shop, thus giving Al the freedom to attend auctions to obtain the merchandise she needed to keep her inventory replenished, and also allowing her more time with Stuart, time she cherished more with each passing day...and night.

One morning Al awoke early. She snuggled closer to Stuart, relishing the familiar warmth of his body in her bed. Three weeks had passed since the first night he had slept there. She stifled a laugh as she remembered Stuart's alarm when Verdie had arrived at the house and he had coerced Al into going downstairs with him so he wouldn't have to face Verdie alone. She also remembered he'd never taken her to Café Metro as promised. After she'd surprised him by meeting him at the office instead of waiting for him to return to the farm, they had gone to his house and made love, totally forgetting about their eight o'clock dinner reservation.

Her soft laughter woke Stuart. "What's so funny?" he asked sleepily.

"Do you realize you've never fulfilled your promise to me?"

Puzzled, he asked, "What promise?"

"To take me to dinner at Café Metro."

He smiled and dropped a kiss on her forehead. "Darn. I'd hoped you'd forgotten."

"No way." He tightened his arm around her and she snuggled closer, her heart full with her love for him. Twining her fingers through the soft hair matting his chest, her thoughts grew pensive. "Stuart?"

"Hmm?"

"Have you ever been in love before?" She felt him stiffen and hurried to explain, "Not that I think you're in love now or anything. It's just that, well, I wondered if you've ever been in love before."

"Once."

Al propped herself up on her elbow in order to better see his face. His eyes were closed and those darn frown lines were back between his eyes. His guarded expression was almost enough to silence her questions. Almost. "When?"

"Does it matter?"

Dropping her gaze, she ran a finger distractedly

across his chest. "No, I guess not." After a moment she raised her gaze back to his face. "What happened?"

Beneath her fingertips, his chest rose and fell in an impatient sigh. "I discovered she didn't love me enough."

"How do you mean 'enough'?"

"Enough to trust me."

Getting information out of the man was like pulling teeth, but Al was determined. "Did you cheat on her or something?"

"Nothing quite so sordid," he replied dryly. "Her father wanted me to sign a prenuptial agreement to prevent me from squandering his daughter's money. I refused."

"You were engaged, then?"

"Yes."

"Why weren't you willing to sign it?"

An image of Melaney standing beside Mr. Burroughs, her eyes mirroring her father's distrust, formed in Stuart's mind. "If the agreement had been simply to appease Mr. Burroughs, I would have. Unfortunately, I discovered my fiancée shared her father's fears."

Al heard the hurt in his voice and knew he had not walked away unscathed. She remembered Stuart telling her about his father's reputation and suspected that was the justification behind Mr. Burrough's request, but it didn't explain his daughter's distrust. In Al's opinion, a woman should trust the man she loved with all her heart.

She took a deep breath and asked the one question

whose answer she feared hearing most. "Are you still in love with her?"

The silence that followed was deafening. After what seemed like forever, Stuart replied quietly, "No, I don't believe in love."

Al was nothing if not flexible. Stuart's announcement that he didn't believe in love had hurt at first. But only for a moment. She knew he cared for her and that was what she focused on. Love was something that would grow over time. So instead of allowing his pronouncement to devastate her, she simply stepped back and regrouped.

In the beginning she'd been determined to save him from himself, to show him there was more to life than work and the pursuit of the almighty dollar. She hadn't given up on that plan. She simply decided that in the process, somewhere along the way, she would convince Stuart that he loved her. She was willing to wait. In the meantime, she knew her love for him was enough.

She made this decision as she clamped the lock on Barnstormers, closing it up for the day. Business had been slow that afternoon, and she had decided to close earlier than usual in order to dress for dinner. Tonight Stuart was taking her to Café Metro. She laughed, thinking their conversation that morning had at least resulted in one good thing—Stuart was finally going to made good his promise.

Verdie met her at the back door of the house.

"Scrooge called."

Al missed the porch step and nearly fell at Verdie's

feet. She hadn't heard from Mr. Feeber since their interview at the bank. "What did he say?" she asked as she climbed the last steps and crossed into the kitchen.

Verdie harrumphed. "Nothing to me. Said he needed to talk to you."

Al glanced at the clock that hung above the stove. "It's too late to call him back today. The bank's already closed."

"Won't hurt the old goat to wait until tomorrow."

"True." Al walked to the back staircase, quickly sorting through the possibilities for Feeber's call. "I'm going to take a shower, Verdie. If Feeber should call back, come and get me."

Al showered and dressed in record time, thoughts of her banker's phone call dulling her excitement for the upcoming evening with Stuart.

Thirty minutes later, wearing a white linen dress intricately tatted with lace, she returned to the kitchen and moved to peer out the back door. "Verdie, have you seen Ranger?"

"Not since this morning."

Beneath her overlong bangs, a frown wrinkled Al's brow. "Me, neither. I think I'll drive down to the barn and see if I can find him."

Verdie shook a finger at her. "You're going to mess up that pretty dress traipsing around after that blame dog. Leave him be. He'll come home when he gets hungry."

"I know. But I'll feel better if I take a look before I leave."

Taking her granddaddy's truck, Al drove to the

barn and climbed out. She fixed her hands like a megaphone at her mouth and called, "Ran-ger!" Then she waited for a moment, listening for his answering bark. The sound of her own voice echoed back to her.

She scanned the area, looking for some sign of him. It wasn't like Ranger to stray away for this long. He loved to hunt and on more than one occasion had scared up a rabbit or two. He also had an unhealthy attraction for the highway. There was something about the gleam of a chrome hubcap in motion he couldn't seem to resist. Nervously, Al glanced in the direction of the road. The hum of an eighteen-wheeler caught her attention, and she watched it until it disappeared over the rise of a hill.

It was then she noticed the buzzards. About a mile up the road, they circled high overhead. Years ago her granddaddy had taught her about buzzards and how they searched for wounded animals and waited until the poor creatures died so they could pick the carcasses clean. That was why she'd nicknamed old George Bandy a buzzard—just like one of the birds of prey, Bandy circled, waiting to snatch the farm away from her.

A sick feeling welled up in her stomach as she watched the birds' slow arc. Drawn by their hypnotic flight, she climbed back into the truck and headed down the highway, her hands growing clammy on the steering wheel.

When she reached the spot where the buzzards circled, she parked the truck and jumped out. Vines and burrs scratched at her legs, and gnats buzzed at her ears as she climbed down the embankment, fighting

her way through the thick undergrowth in the gully
that ran alongside the highway. Halfway down, her
heel caught in a rabbit's burrow, and she sat down
hard, sliding the last few feet.

Before her, not twenty feet from the edge of the
highway, lay Ranger, his eyes open and staring va-
cantly. The dog's head was twisted at a distorted angle, and already his stomach had that bloated look of
death. Flies buzzed around his still form, and Al swallowed hard, trying to fight back the nausea that threatened to bring her to her knees.

She squeezed her eyes shut. *Oh, God, please no,*
she begged silently. Opening her eyes again, she
slowly crossed to the dog and knelt down beside him.
Her eyes burned with unshed tears as she stroked his
matted fur. "I'm so sorry, Ranger," she whispered
brokenly. "I shouldn't have let you run free." Gathering her hands together into a tight fist at her waist,
she stood, her gaze fixed on Ranger.

"I'll be back in a minute," she promised, then
turned her back on the dog and climbed back up the
hill to the truck. She drove to the barn and pulled one
of the colorful quilts from the wall. Tucking it under
her arm, she retraced her steps to the truck and drove
back, using the buzzards as her guide.

When she reached the spot where Ranger lay, she
unfolded the quilt and draped it over him. Scooping
the large dog up in her arms, she struggled beneath
his weight as she climbed back up the steep embankment to the highway.

Gently, tenderly, she laid Ranger on the bed of the
truck. "You always loved riding in this old truck,

didn't you, boy?'' she asked in a watery voice. She tucked the quilt more securely around the dog, then laid her cheek against the brightly colored fabric and her arm across the lumpy form beneath. "I love you, Ranger," she whispered.

Stuart pulled his Lincoln alongside Verdie's battered Chevrolet. As he switched off the ignition, he saw Verdie, her purse in hand, closing the back door of the house behind her. She paused on the narrow porch, tilted up her glasses and dabbed at her eyes before shuffling toward her car.

Stuart called, "Hi, Verdie. Where's Al?"

"With that fool dog. Breaking my heart, she is. Won't wait for my brother Junior to come take care of it for her. Says it's something she has to do herself." She swiped at her nose with the wadded handkerchief, then lifted her face to Stuart, exposing red-rimmed eyes magnified by her bifocals. "The child won't even cry." Verdie shook her head sadly, then turned to her car, murmuring, "Poor Al. So much loss heaped on her so young."

Puzzled by the woman's disjointed mumbling, Stuart called, "Wait a minute, Verdie." She stopped and turned to him, her hand on the door. "I don't understand," he said as he reached her side. "Why won't Al cry and what should she be crying over?"

"I done told you once," she replied impatiently. "It's Ranger! That damn fool dog got hisself killed out on the highway. Al found him and now she's out digging him a grave under that grove of pecan trees."

Before Verdie had fitted herself behind the wheel

of her antiquated Chevrolet, Stuart was running across the field toward the trees, his mind fixed on one thing. He had to get to Al.

When he reached the grove he saw her standing beneath one of the trees, a spade in her hand. The breeze whipped at her hair, ruffling it across her cheek. The hem of her dress was ripped and dangled low at a point behind her knee. Off to her left, a rolled-up quilt held the lumpy form of what he knew must be Ranger. The sound of the shovel hitting the hard-packed ground shot Stuart into motion.

He stopped behind her and placed a restraining hand on her shoulder. "Al? Here, let me do that."

She shook his hand from her shoulder and bent her back to the shovel again, never once looking at him. "No. I have to do it myself."

Taking her firmly by the arm, Stuart turned her around to face him. He pried the shovel from her fingers and tossed it to the ground. With both hands planted on her shoulders, he forced her chin up with his thumbs. At the sight of her face, a fissure ripped through his heart. Other than the two high spots of color on her cheeks, her face was as pale as a sheet. Her eyes were dry and expressionless.

"Oh God, Al," Stuart groaned as he pulled her into his arms. He held her stiff body against his, rubbing his hands up and down her back, trying to rub some warmth into her.

After a moment, she stepped from his embrace and turned her back on him. "Go away, Stuart. I don't want you here."

He reached out a hand to stop her. "Al, please. Let me do this for you."

She jerked away from his touch. "No! I have to do it." She picked up the shovel again and started to dig. "I don't want you here, Stuart. I don't need you."

Her harshly spoken words ripped through him, cutting him to the bone. *Why was she doing this? He wanted to help her. To spare her this pain.* As the spade chinked against the hard ground, Stuart set his jaw. If he had to do it forcefully, then by God he would.

Twisting the shovel from her hands, he threw it down, then scooped Al into his arms. Her fists beat at his chest as he strode from beneath the canopy of trees. She fought him every step of the way to the house and, when at last he reached the safety of the kitchen and lowered her to her feet, she turned on him like a wild woman. "Get out!" she screamed hysterically. "I want you out of my house and out of my life."

The intensity of her anger shocked him. He didn't know where it was coming from, but he knew he couldn't leave until he discovered its source. He stood his ground. "I'm not going anywhere until you calm down."

After a full minute filled with nothing but the sound of her agitated breathing, she lifted her chin a notch, her gaze level on his. "I'm calm now. You can go."

"Sorry, but I can't do that." He stepped in front of her, blocking all hope of escape. Locking his hands on her forearms, he held her firm in his grasp. "Let it out, Al. For God's sake, cry."

She squeezed her eyes shut and shook her head as she tried to pull away from him. "I can't. Please just let me go."

"You've got to. You can't keep it bottled up inside you like this." He watched in silence as the muscles in her face convulsed while she fought for control. Once pale, her complexion was now flushed a mottled red as she tried to force back her grief. In spite of her efforts, a tear squeezed from between her tightly shut eyelids, then another. "That's it, Al. Let it go," he soothed tenderly as he pulled her closer into his arms.

Gradually the fight eased out of her, and she covered her face with her hands. Sobs racked her slender shoulders. Hooking his arms around her, Stuart pressed his cheek against her hair, rocking her gently back and forth. "I've got you, baby. It's going to be all right now."

Once the dam opened, Al was powerless to hold back the flood. Tears streamed down her face, soaking Stuart's shirt beneath her cheek. Grief, suppressed for years behind a carefree facade, ripped through her and threatened to tear apart her soul. Her father's death, her mother's abandonment, the death of her grandparents. All the pain rose within her and joined forces with this newest loss, that of Ranger.

God, it hurts so bad! she cried silently, wanting to hide from all the unpleasant memories she had buried for so long. But the memories came unheeded. Her father who had smothered her with his love in an attempt to make up for the lack from her mother. Her grandparents who had given her a home and their unconditional love after her father's death. And lastly, Ranger, who had been her constant companion ever since she had arrived at Clairemore Farms ten years before.

As each memory formed then faded, Al was faced with her own inadequacy. She hadn't been able to save any of them. Not her father from suicide, not her grandparents from old age, and not Ranger from the fatal pull of the highway.

She gave in to the grief and let it consume her.

Not understanding the depth of her anguish, but knowing he had to care for her, Stuart picked her up in his arms and carried her upstairs. He sat her down on the edge of her bed and eased off her shoes. After removing her ruined dress, he gently guided Al beneath the covers.

From the linen closet, he plucked a washcloth and wet it at the sink in the bathroom before returning to Al. Her eyes were closed, and her even breathing told him she had cried herself into an exhausted sleep. He smoothed the cool cloth across her face, wiping away the smudges of dirt and the paths of her tears.

As he straightened, he glanced at the window. It was almost dusk. He knew he would have to hurry in order to bury Ranger before darkness descended. After tucking the covers up to Al's chin, he pressed his lips to each of her closed lids. "I'll be back, Al. Rest easy," he murmured softly.

Eight

Stuart shrugged out of his sports coat and draped it over a kitchen chair before turning to the sink. As the water pulsed over his hands, his thoughts returned to Al. He knew she and the dog had been close, but he suspected the display of grief he'd witnessed earlier was for more than just the loss of the animal. And the anger she had turned on him...he had no explanation for that.

Taking the bar of soap in his hands, he scrubbed his arms to the elbows and watched the dirt from Ranger's grave wash down the drain. He had buried Ranger, thus sparing Al the macabre task. But he knew a bigger chore awaited him—discovering the source of Al's misery.

After drying his hands, he climbed the rear staircase again. At the door to Al's room, he paused. She was lying on her side, her cheek resting on her open palm. In the waning light from the window, he saw the soft shadow of her lashes where they brushed against her cheek. She looked so innocent, so peaceful. The sight made his heart constrict in his chest.

As he watched from the doorway, her eyelashes fluttered, then slowly lifted, exposing sleep-filled blue eyes. Quietly, he crossed to the bed and sat down beside her.

"Feel better now?" he asked softly.

She squeezed her temples between the width of one hand, masking her eyes for a moment, then lowered her hand to cover Stuart's. "Yes. Thank you."

"No thanks needed."

"Yes, there is. And an apology, too." She sighed deeply, and a shiver shook her shoulders, a delayed reaction to the tears shed earlier. "I'm sorry I was so rude to you."

"It's understandable. You were hurting."

The compassion in his voice tore at her self-control. She fought to get a stronger grip on it. "That's no excuse." She scooted upright, tucking her arms around her bent knees. "I meant what I said, though. I don't want or need you anymore."

"But why?"

Taking a deep breath to still her shaky voice, Al replied, "I can't take the chance. It hurts too much to lose those you love."

Her declaration of love stunned Stuart, rendering him speechless. It was what he'd worried about, but refused to consider—Al's falling in love with him.

He knew about love and had sworn long ago he'd never fall prey to its charm again.

Al saw the alarm on his face and waved it away with a casual flip of her hand. "Go on, Stuart, get out. I don't want you anymore."

"If this is your way of obtaining some kind of a commitment from me, Al, you won't get one. I told you before, I don't believe in love."

She pushed at her bangs in frustration. "I'm not asking for anything except for you to leave."

"I'll go when you've explained to me what the hell is going on," he said, his voice rising in frustration.

"I love you, okay? And I don't want to lose you."

He purposely ignored the profession of love and focused instead on her second statement. "You aren't going to lose me, Al."

"Death doesn't offer any promises, Stuart, only one guarantee. You're going to die, and I don't want to be around when you do."

He surged to his feet and paced across the room, his anger rising, then wheeled to glare at her. "This is absurd! Of course I'm going to die, and so are you, but that doesn't stop me from wanting to be with you."

"Does me."

Stuart didn't like the sudden change in her voice. He watched her hop up from the bed and cross to her closet.

"Verdie says love is painful. I'm just sparing myself some of life's misery." She tugged a pair of jeans from a hanger and flung them to her bed. "It's been fun, Stuart. But the party's over."

The old Al was back. The one who hid her vulnerabilities behind a constant whirl of frenetic energy. And Stuart didn't like it one bit. "Like hell it is," he grated through tight lips. He strode across the room, caught her arm in his and whirled her around. Holding her against him with one arm, he turned her chin up, forcing her gaze to meet his. "Tell me you don't want me," he demanded angrily.

Al swallowed convulsively, then whispered, "I don't."

His fingers tightened on her chin. "That's a lie and you know it." He tilted her chin higher until her lips were a breath away from his. "And I can prove it," he threatened darkly. His lips crushed against hers, snapping her head back beneath the unexpected attack.

No! Don't do this to me, she begged silently. *I don't want to love you, I don't want to need you.* But his lips were there, demanding a response she was reluctant to give. The kiss raged on for what seemed to Al like hours. At some point, she wasn't sure when, she curled her fingers into his shirt and simply hung on.

Finally, he pulled away from her and demanded in a husky voice, "Now tell me you don't want me."

"I don't—"

His lips came down on hers again, cutting off her denial. His fingers found their way to her hair and tangled there, angling her face to fit his. With his mouth locked over hers, he backed her slowly toward the bed.

When the back of her knees hit the mattress, her

legs buckled and Al fell on top of the bed with Stuart on top of her, knocking the breath from her.

His own breathing ragged, he rolled to her side and placed his hand over her left breast. Beneath his fingers her heart pounded erratically. "Your heart says you do," he said and waited for her to deny it.

A tear slipped down her cheek. "But I don't want to."

He thumbed away the moisture. "You're a lot of things, Alyssa McCord, but you're no coward."

"That's what you think." She sniffed indelicately. "Every time I allow myself to love somebody or something, I lose them. My daddy, my grandparents, Ranger. I'll lose you, too." She lifted her grief-stricken gaze to his. "I don't think I could stand that."

"You won't lose me, Al."

"That's a promise you can't make."

Realizing her fear, Stuart replied patiently, "Death is a natural progression of life, Al. When you grow old, death happens. There's nothing you can do to stop it."

"My daddy wasn't old. He was only thirty-seven when he died."

"Thirty-seven?" Stuart echoed.

"He committed suicide."

The pain in her voice ripped through him. At last he understood what Verdie had meant when she'd said so much loss had been heaped on Al so young. He gathered her into his arms and tucked his chin over the top of her head, cradling her against his chest. "I'm sorry, Al. I didn't know."

"You don't have anything to be sorry about. I'm the one who let him down."

"Now wait a minute." Stuart sat up and pulled her to a sitting position, facing him, his hands locked tightly at her elbows. "You can't blame yourself for your father's suicide. Hell, you couldn't have been more than a child."

"I was twelve. But I was responsible. If I had loved him more, I could have saved him. I know I could." She took a deep shuddery breath. "My mother didn't love my father, only the things he could buy her. But he loved her. God, how he loved her. He worked like a demon to provide her with her every whim. Yet, the more money he made, the more she wanted."

"When I was twelve, things started going sour in his business. He'd made a couple of bad investments, plus there were rumblings the oil price was going to drop. He started staying at his office later and later to avoid telling my mother the truth." She shrugged her shoulders, her chin dipping to her chest as she toyed with the lace on the hem of her slip. "One afternoon he took a pistol, aimed the barrel at his temple and pulled the trigger."

She lifted her chin and looked Stuart square in the eye. "So now you can see why I can't allow myself to love you."

Cupping her face between his palms, he searched her eyes for some emotion. In the gleam of unshed tears he found the vulnerability he'd always suspected lay beneath her carefree veneer. "No. I only see that you've been carrying around a lot of unnecessary guilt." His voice softened as he added, "I'm not your father, Al."

She pushed his hand away and fell back against the mattress, swiping angrily at the tears that escaped to her cheeks. "No, but you're just like him. From the moment I met you, I could see that same streak of determination to succeed."

The muscles in Stuart's chest tightened as the truth of her statement hit him full force. Yes, he was determined to be a success all right. In achieving financial independence, he would prove to everyone he wasn't like his father.

But his need for money wasn't an unhealthy obsession, he assured himself. Unlike Al's father, he could handle failure as well as success. Yet as he looked down at Al, he realized that while succeeding was still important, success alone had suddenly lost its allure.

He laid a palm against her cheek. "The only thing I want right now is you."

Fresh tears welled in Al's eyes while a deep ache squeezed at her chest. He wanted her and that used to be enough, but now she was afraid to open her heart again and allow him in. Verdie was right, she thought sadly. Love is painful.

Death had separated her from those she'd loved. She closed her eyes and rubbed at her throbbing temple. But if she sent Stuart away, would it be any different than losing him to death? Separation was separation, after all, no matter what the means. Wearily, she dropped her hand to her side. It was so hard to think.

The futility of the gesture pulled at Stuart's heart. He picked up her hand and pressed her fingertips to his lips. "If I could spare you all the pain in life, Al, I would."

Touched by his words, she opened her eyes and met the warmth of his compassionate gaze. "Oh, Stuart," she said tearfully as she reached for him. "Just hold me. When you hold me I forget everything but the now."

"That's the way it will always be for us, Al. Only the now," he promised before his lips covered hers.

The phone rang, startling Al awake. Hoping to catch it before it woke Stuart, she stretched a hand across his chest and nabbed the receiver from the nightstand. "Hello." As she waited for a response, she squinted at the alarm clock. Her eyes widened in surprise. It was after nine o'clock.

From beside her came Stuart's groggy voice. "Who is it?" he asked.

Al rolled her eyes at him, then turned her attention to the party on the phone. She forced a cheerful and hopefully alert tone into her voice. "Good morning, Mr. Feeber. Yes, Verdie told me you called, but the bank had already closed by the time I received the message."

She listened for a moment, her shoulders sagging in resignation. She didn't need this aggravation. Not so soon after Ranger's death. "Yes, I appreciate your concern, Mr. Feeber, but everything is going just fine. Barnstormers is proving to be quite a success."

She paused again, listening. "No, sir, there

shouldn't be a problem with making the loan payment as promised. You can count on seeing me in your office bright and early on the first of August." She smiled sweetly, although her thoughts were anything but sweet, before replying to Feeber's last comment. "That's quite all right. I needed to get up anyway. Thank you for calling."

Forcing back the overwhelming desire to slam down the receiver, thereby doing permanent damage to the old skinflint's hearing, Al leaned across Stuart and flipped the receiver back onto its cradle. She promptly fell back against her pillow and crossed her arms angrily against her chest. "That man!" she cried indignantly. "Nothing I say will convince him he'll get his precious money on time!"

Later, at his office, Stuart stared out the window at the Louisville skyline, thinking over the events of the previous night. The reflection of his own face was superimposed over the scene. Dark smudges lay beneath his eyes and worry lines plowed across his forehead. Wearily he rubbed at the lines, knowing he'd earned every one.

Had Al been right in saying he was obsessed with the idea of success and the rewards it offered him? He frowned at his reflection, and the worry lines cut even deeper. All he wanted was respect—something denied him because of his father's reputation. Money, with all its power, would buy him that lost commodity.

The sun peeked from behind a thick thunderhead, nearly blinding him. He narrowed his eyes and studied the cloud's odd shape. When he realized what he was doing, he dropped his forehead against his palm, chuckling softly. Ever since Al had taught him the cloud game, he'd caught himself searching out bears and watermelons and profiles of Bob Hope amongst the clouds filling the sky outside his office window.

Al. A heavy sigh escaped him as her name came again to mind. Last night had been tough. Watching her grieve over Ranger, listening to the story of her father's death. Even after a good night's sleep, her face had still born a ghostly pallor, and her eyes had been puffy and red from the tears she'd shed. Personally, he didn't think he could bear to see her hurt anymore.

Yet, so much still lay before her. Feeber's call had reminded him of that. If something prevented Al from making the note and she lost the farm, could she handle that loss?

So much loss heaped on her so young. Verdie's words pushed into his mind, and his heart twisted in his chest. Last night, while he'd held Al, her slender shoulders racked by her heartbreaking sobs, he'd been given a glimpse of all she'd lost and all the pain she'd borne. She had no one left to depend on. No one to protect her...

Stuart's hands came down hard on the arms of the chair as he swirled it around. His jaw clenched tight, he picked up the phone and made three calls in quick succession. The first to Roxey Dandridge at the bank. The second to Joe Barber. The third to Pets Unlimited.

As soon as he completed the last call, Stuart

pressed the intercom button. "Morrey, could you come to my office for a minute? I have some changes I'd like to discuss with you."

"No problem. I'll be there in a minute."

Sinking back in his chair, Stuart heaved a deep sigh. Now that he'd made the decision and the wheels were in motion, he felt a huge sense of relief. All he had to do was convince his stepfather the decision he'd made was the right one.

Morrey strolled into Stuart's office and sank onto the chair opposite the desk. "What's up?"

"I need to talk to you about Greystone Estates."

One eyebrow arched knowingly, Morrey replied, "I expected as much."

"I've decided to cut out Clairemore Farms and proceed without its acreage in the overall plan." Stuart waited for Morrey's shocked response. It didn't come. "Well, don't you have anything to say?"

Morrey pulled a pack of cigarettes from his pocket, shook one out and slipped it between his lips. Shrugging, he touched a gold lighter to the cigarette's tip. "It's your deal. Has been since the beginning. Whatever you say, goes."

Rain beat against the farmhouse window, blurring the grove of trees that held Al transfixed. Somewhere beneath the trees lay Ranger's grave. Moisture filled her eyes, and she blinked back tears. She wouldn't cry. Not anymore. She'd shed enough tears last night to last a lifetime. Instead she tried to focus on pleasant memories of Ranger. As hard as she tried, the only image that surfaced was one of Ranger lying beside the highway, his eyes open and staring.

Sucking in a deep, shuddery breath, she turned her back on the gloomy scene and the images it drew and tried to think of something to occupy her, to take her mind off her grief. Unfortunately, the day stretched empty before her. The auction she had planned to attend had been canceled due to the rain, and Rosemary, with no customers to wait on, had decided to close up the shop early. And, as usual, Stuart was at work.

Sad and rather lonely, Al wandered through the house. Her journey carried her to the kitchen and the phone that hung on the wall beside the oak table. She dropped down on a chair and dialed Stuart's office number, hoping to persuade him to play hooky with her.

After completing the number, she raised the receiver to her ear. She listened for a moment, then pressed the disconnect button several times. All to no avail. The phone was dead.

As if on cue, thunder rattled the windows, and the dim room brightened momentarily as lightning streaked across the sky. Groaning in frustration, Al dropped the receiver back onto the wall unit. *Now what?* she wondered dejectedly.

While the telephone continued its persistent ringing from the opposite side of the door, Stuart attempted to fit the key into the lock and at the same time keep a grip on the ball of fur scrambling to free itself from beneath his arm.

Raindrops dripped from his soggy hair and down his collar. Cursing, he pushed open the door and ran to the phone, half sliding on the black-and-white tiled kitchen floor.

"Hello," he said, short of breath.

"'Bout time you decided to answer the blame phone."

He cradled the receiver between his ear and shoulder and sought a better grip on the ball of fur. "Sorry, Verdie. I just walked in. What can I do for you?"

"You can get out to the farm and check on Al, that's what! I've been calling and calling and nobody answers."

His hand stiffened on the receiver. *Al?* Had something happened to her? Ready to drop the phone and run, he had to force himself to listen.

"Phone could be out of order. Happens sometimes when it rains this hard. But Al said she was going to an auction out in Oldham County somewheres, and I heard on the news we're in a tornado watch." She added irritably, "And you know Al. She hasn't got the good sense to come in out of the rain. I won't rest easy 'til I know she's home."

"Don't worry, Verdie. I'm on my way."

Minutes later he was speeding along the rain-slicked road enroute to the farm. His imagination ran wild with all the disasters that might have befallen Al. The old truck she insisted on driving could have broken down, and she could be stranded somewhere, frightened and in need of help. Or worse, she might have been struck by lightning while trying to hitch-hike home.

Silently he cursed himself for going to the office instead of going to the auction with her.

Lightning streaked across the black sky, exposing trees bent almost in half by the strong wind blowing from the south. A clap of thunder all but muted the sound of raindrops beating against his windshield as he pulled up in front of the farmhouse. After switching off the headlights, he unbuttoned the top three buttons of his shirt and stuffed the ball of fur against his chest. He winced as a sharp claw dug into his bare skin. "Hang on, girl," he mumbled as he leaped from the car. "We're almost there."

Rain stung his face and arms as he bolted for the front porch. Through the etched glass he saw a light glowing from the rear of the house and heard the muted sound of a television. Thank God she's home, he thought in relief.

He tried the front door, but found it locked. Raising his fist to the thick door, he pounded and yelled, "Al! It's me. Stuart. Open up."

A lace panel, covering the narrow slat of glass to the right of the door, lifted then dropped. The door opened a crack, and a hand snaked out, nabbing Stuart by the arm and pulling him through the slender opening. The door slammed shut behind him.

Al was halfway down the hall before Stuart had a chance to say a word.

"Now wait just a damn minute!"

Al slid to a stop at the angry tone in his voice. She turned and looked at him. He stood in the dimly lit hallway with his feet spread, his hands planted at his hips. A puddle of water pooled at his feet. "What's wrong?" she asked innocently.

"Wrong? Nothing's wrong," he said, his voice heavy with sarcasm. "At least there isn't if you don't consider Verdie worrying half out of her mind or me driving through the threat of a tornado to make sure you're all right."

She retraced her steps, her head dipped low to hide her smile. When she reached him, she slipped her arm through the loop of his and rose up on her toes to give him a kiss. "I'm fine, Stuart. But thank you for your concern. I was just watching a horror movie. The phone's dead or I would've—"

A whimpering sound came from the front of Stuart's shirt. Al eyed the suspicious lump there, then touched her fingers to the wriggling mass. "I've always said you were a stuffed shirt, Stuart, but this is a bit much!" She rose to her toes and peeked over the neck opening of his shirt. When she saw the ball of fur scrambling up his chest, she sank back down on her feet. Her fingers trembled as she pressed them to her lips. Slowly she raised her gaze to Stuart's.

"A puppy?" she asked in a quivery voice.

"A puppy," he confirmed, still frowning.

"For me?"

He held onto the wriggling mass while he tugged his shirttail from the waist of his slacks and eased the puppy into view. "For you." He held it out to her. "She's not as big as Ranger, but she'll grow."

Al cuddled the puppy to her cheek, crooning softly. "Oh, Stuart..." She lifted her face, her eyes brimming, to meet his gaze. "She's perfect. And so are you," she added as she rose to press her lips against his. The puppy squirmed between them, licking at their joined chins. Al laughed. "What are we going to name her?"

Stuart shrugged, "That's up to you. She's your dog."

Holding the puppy aloft to study her, Al frowned. "I don't know," she said uncertainly. "A name's awfully important." The puppy clawed at the air, looking for something firm to plant its feet on. The sight drew memories of Ranger as a young pup. Smiling at the bittersweet memory, Al turned to Stuart, her eyes bright with tears. "How can I ever thank you?"

Her pleasure with the gift was thanks enough. Stuart pulled her against him, nuzzling his nose at her neck. "I'm sure you'll think of a way."

Laughing, Al pushed out of his arms. "As soon as I find a bed for this little darling, I'll see what I can come up with."

A wicker laundry basket was found, nested with a soft quilt, and placed in the kitchen by the stove. While Stuart watched, Al dug out an old alarm clock from the kitchen drawer, wound it and placed it under the quilt. The puppy snuggled up against the ticking sound, fooled into believing it was her mother's heartbeat.

Satisfied the puppy was comfortable, Al crossed to stand by Stuart and looped her arm through his. "Sweet, isn't she?" she whispered as she watched the puppy's eyelids grow heavy.

Stuart rubbed an absent hand across his chest as he, too, stared at the cuddly ball of fur. Wincing when his fingers met a particularly tender spot, he replied dryly, "Her claws aren't."

Puzzled, Al looked up at him. "Did she scratch you?"

"A little."

"Let me see." Al started unbuttoning his shirt. "Good heavens!" she cried when she saw the angry red welts marring his chest. "We need to clean these and put some antiseptic on them."

"It's nothing. Really."

Pulling a reluctant Stuart along, she headed for the rear staircase. "There's some ointment in my bathroom. You get your shirt off, and I'll get the first aid kit."

Dutifully, Stuart peeled off his shirt and hooked it over the bathroom door knob while Al rummaged through drawers. He glanced around for a place to sit, found none, and settled himself on the edge of the footed bathtub.

Al dropped the first aid kit at his feet, then crossed to the sink and soaped a washcloth. When she returned, her eyes were filled with concern. "I'll try not to hurt you," she promised as she knelt beside him.

She moved the cloth gently across his chest, carefully tracing each of the red marks. Beneath her hand, Stuart's chest and stomach muscles tightened in reaction. She paused, her fingertips resting on a particularly angry looking scratch. "Does that hurt?"

"A little."

"Here?" she asked, gently touching the welt.

"No. A little lower."

She moved her hand down a fraction. "There?" she asked.

"No. Lower."

Frowning slightly, Al eased her fingers to the last visible scratch. "Here?"

"No. Lower."

Confused, Al glanced up and saw the mischievous glint in his eye. She dropped her gaze, this time to his lap and the swell in his slacks. Chuckling, she tossed the cloth into the tub and leaned to wrap her arms around his waist, squeezing her body between his parted thighs. "I can fix that, too," she teased as she lifted her lips to his.

"You can, huh?" he murmured.

"Yep," she replied confidently. Rising to her feet, she caught Stuart's hand in hers. "Just follow me."

The sounds of the storm beating against the farmhouse echoed in the narrow hallway as they crossed to her bedroom. Without bothering with a light, Al moved to the bed, pulled back the comforter, then turned to stand before Stuart. A soft smile played at her lips as she silently met his gaze.

While thunder boomed against the dark sky, shaking the floor beneath her feet with its intensity, Al slipped her hands to his waist and worked his belt through its loops. With a casual flick of her wrist the slender strap of leather dropped to the floor.

Stuart's breath caught and lodged in his throat when her fingers returned to his waist. She found his slacks' front closure, loosened it, then eased down the zipper. With a gentle push, she sent the slacks sliding down his legs to puddle at his feet.

Her gaze still locked on his, she took his hand in hers and led him toward the bed. "Now, where was that hurt?" she asked in a voice as soft as silk.

With an impatient groan, Stuart leaned into her, bending her back on the bed. His lips found hers while his hands sought the buttons on her blouse. In his haste to dispense with the annoying barrier, a button flew free and skittered across the wooden floor, echoing loudly in the silent room. Quickly stripping the blouse from her, he tossed it aside and buried his face in the valley between her breasts.

The storm continued to rage outside the window, but it was no match for the turbulence Al had unleashed within Stuart. Catching the waist of her jeans in his hands, he tugged them down her hips, his lips following the movement to light fires across her stomach.

When the jeans hit the floor, his lips were at her knees. Taking his time, he worked his way back up to her neck, biting, suckling, teasing until her need equaled his own.

When at last he filled her, the storm had reached its height, matching their passion with a frenzy of its own. Thunder rattled the windows of the old farmhouse, masking the sound of the lovers while lightning streaked across the black sky, casting their joined bodies in an ethereal light.

Just as they reached the peak of pleasure, an explosion ripped through the night. Al's fingers dug into Stuart's shoulders as she attempted to claw her way from beneath him. "What was that?" she gasped.

Stuart pushed himself up on his elbows and glanced

toward the window, a frown wrinkling his brow. "I don't know," he replied uncertainly. Heaving himself up and away from Al, he crossed to the window and looked out.

"Oh, my God! It's the barn." He grabbed his pants from the floor and jerked them on, hopping on one foot as he reached to snatch the phone from the nightstand.

Al was up and out of the bed in a flash. Grabbing her blouse, she shrugged it on as she ran to the window.

In the distance, flames leaped against the black sky, illuminating the barn and the area around it. Smoke billowed from empty holes that had once housed the barn's windows. As she watched, another explosion rocked the floor beneath her feet. A sob rose in her throat as she wheeled from the nightmare scene and grabbed for the rest of her clothes.

Beside her, Stuart continued to frantically punch its numbers. "Forget it. The phone's dead," she cried as she pushed her feet into shoes and ran for the door. Stuart was one step behind her.

By the time they reached the barn, the tin roof had given way, collapsing within the barn's walls. Al stood and watched in silence as the flames licked higher and higher at the sky, her face reddened by the heat from the fire. Rain blended with her tears and streaked desolately down her face.

What was once a distant whine grew stronger until Stuart distinguished it as the volunteer fire department's siren. Within minutes, the area around the burning barn was filled with trucks, swarming men and the constant swirl of flashing red lights. Throughout it all, Al stood, her gaze riveted on the barn, watching as her dreams went up in smoke.

"We'll do a more extensive study in the morning, but it appears that lightning started the fire."

Stuart stood in the kitchen with his arm draped around a wet and shivering Al, listening to the fire marshal's assessment. "Would that explain the explosion we heard?" he asked.

The fire marshal pulled off his hat and dragged his fingers through his hair. "No. The explosions came from the workroom. Evidently, some combustible materials were stored there. Once the heat got to them—" he slapped a hand against the hard hat for effect "—boom! The whole place went up."

"My stripping supplies." Al glanced up at the fire marshal and explained, "The workroom is where I refinished furniture. I stored gallons of paint thinner, paint remover..." Her voice drifted off and she glanced down at the floor again, fighting for control.

The fire marshal looked at Stuart, cleared his throat, and said, "Well, I guess I'll get out of here and let you folks get some rest. We'll be back in the morning to finish our report."

Stuart walked the man to his truck. When he returned to the kitchen, Al stood where he'd left her, her shoulders drooping in defeat. He crossed to her and wrapped her in his arms. "Why don't you go on up to bed, Al? I'll lock up."

"No." She rubbed a weary hand across her eyes. "I couldn't sleep now anyway." She stepped from his embrace and moved to the coffeepot. "There's so much to do. In the morning I'll need to call my insurance agent and then I guess I'll have to call all the people who had merchandise on consignment."

After plugging in the coffee maker, she pulled a pad of paper and pen from the cabinet and started making notes. "The stone walls will have to be sand-blasted to get the smoke stains off them, but at least they're still standing. And Verdie's brother can probably handle putting a new roof on the barn."

At the sight of Al, rain soaked and smudged with soot, making plans to start over again, a lump rose in Stuart's throat. He sat down beside her and closed his hand over hers, stilling her writing. "Don't do this, Al."

She glanced up at him, her eyes mirroring her confusion. "Don't do what?" she asked.

"Don't put yourself through this again. It will cost you a fortune to put that barn back in shape."

Al pulled her hand from his and pressed her pen to the paper again, her voice firm with determination. "I don't have a choice. The note's due in less than a month, and I promised Feeber he'd get his money."

Nine

Al sat on the front porch with the puppy snuggled deep in her lap. Late-afternoon sunshine warmed the wood beneath her while a soft breeze pulled at her hair. Limbs lay scattered about the yard, torn from the massive oaks by last night's storm. Across the sun-dappled field, the smoke-stained shell of the barn stood desolate against the rich greens surrounding it.

Al, her hand smoothing down the soft fur on the puppy's back, sighed deeply as she stared at the rubble. She'd spent her entire day with the fire marshal and the insurance adjuster, combing through the charred remains. When the men had finally completed their inquiry, they'd left with the insurance adjuster promising to contact her as soon as he'd completed his report. Now all she could do was wait.

Determined not to allow her problems to spoil a

perfectly beautiful evening, Al forced her gaze from the barn and focused instead on the lake in the distance.

A cloud of dust rose on the lane that ran between the house and the lake, blocking her view of the peaceful scene. A smile quickly spread across her face as she recognized the gray Lincoln. Stuart. He'd promised he'd come by after work. She placed the sleeping puppy in its basket and ran to meet him.

When Stuart stepped from the car, Al threw herself into his arms. After kissing him soundly, she leaned back in his arms and smiled up at him. "Hi."

As he looked down at her, Stuart couldn't help but chuckle at his own foolishness. All day he'd worried about Al and how she would deal with the loss of the barn. He should have known better. Al never let anything get her down for long.

"Hi yourself." He glanced over her shoulder at the house. "Where's Verdie?"

"Gone." Tucking her arm through his, she walked with him toward the house.

"How'd your day go?" he asked.

"Busy!" She gave an impatient swipe at her bangs. "The fire marshal and the insurance adjuster spent almost the entire day combing through the debris. When they left they said I could start rebuilding as soon as I received the insurance adjuster's report."

They reached the porch, and Al sat down on the top step, grinning up at Stuart as she patted the space beside her. "But I don't want to think about that anymore. Let's sit outside for a while."

Stuart loosened the knot of his tie and unbuttoned

the top button of his shirt before dropping down beside her. Honoring her request not to discuss the fire, he nodded toward the puppy. "Named her yet?"

"Sort of." Al shook her head, laughing softly so as not to wake the sleeping animal. "To be honest, she named herself."

"How so?"

"Well, since I couldn't decide on a name, I kept calling her puppy. She must have liked the name, because she answers to it."

"Puppy." Stuart frowned slightly as he tested the name. One eyebrow arched high, he cocked his head toward Al. "Sounds like a stupid name to me."

Still laughing, Al inched closer until her body brushed against his. "You'll get used to it." Content now that Stuart was with her, she gazed out over the land that stretched between the house and the lake. "Isn't it beautiful?"

His gaze leveled on the burned barn beyond Al, Stuart frowned and dipped his head to look at her. "What's beautiful?"

"Here. This place." She slipped her arm through the crook of his and snuggled closer. "Just listen to that music." She closed her eyes and lifted her face to the evening breeze.

Stuart strained but heard nothing. "I don't hear anything."

"Sure you do—you just don't realize it. Listen close and you can hear the wind whispering secrets in the trees. For years songwriters have struggled to capture it, musicians have studied to imitate it and people have gotten all dressed up to sit in a stuffy concert hall to hear it. Crazy isn't it? The world is full of music. All you have to do is throw open a window to hear it."

Her eyes opened, and a soft smile spread across her face as she stared up at the gradually darkening sky. "And get a load of that sunset, Stuart. Reds and pinks and blues and violets. More vibrant than any painter's palette. Can you imagine accepting a copy when you can have the real thing?"

The real thing? There had been a time in Stuart's life not so many months before when he'd thought the only real thing in life was money. Al had taught him what a cheap imitation it was for happiness. Through her eyes, he was learning to appreciate life, to live it, and say to hell with the rest. With his gaze focused on her upturned face, he replied softly, "No, I can't."

Tenderly, he swept her bangs from her eyes. As she met his gaze, her expression was one of innocence, one of trust.

She caught his hand in hers and turned his palm against her cheek. "I love you," she murmured.

Those same three words rose in Stuart's throat, pushing to be released, yet he held them back. He'd spent too much time and effort in hardening himself against that emotion. Old habits—even learned ones—were hard to break. Abruptly he rose. "Why don't we drive into town and get a bite to eat?"

Al had seen the love reflected in his eyes before he had stood and turned his back to her. He loved her. She knew he did. Then why couldn't he say the words?

Pushing back the nagging doubts, she plucked the sleeping puppy from the basket and hugged it against her breast. Puppy was her proof of Stuart's love and of his understanding of her needs. For now that would be enough.

"Sounds great," she said as she rose to stand beside him. "Just give me a minute to change clothes."

The week following the fire at Barnstormers was a rough one for Al. The debris had to be sifted through and hauled away, and plans made for remodeling the barn. Stuart helped when he could, but for the most part, Al handled the job alone. The task was difficult, but Al preferred the filthy, backbreaking work to the other chore that fell to her: that of calling the individuals who'd left merchandise on consignment in her care. Those calls proved to be the hardest job of all.

Repeating the story of the fire was like reliving the horror of that night over and over again. For the most part, the contributors accepted her assurances that they'd be paid for their losses when Al received her settlement from the insurance company. But there were those who demanded immediate payment, which placed a strain on Al's already dwindling finances.

Thankfully, as he'd promised, the insurance agent arrived bright and early on the Monday of the second week following the fire, a settlement check in hand. After he left, Al grabbed her ledger and her calculator and sat down at the kitchen table. Her fingers fairly flying over the keys, she began the tedious task of balancing the accounts.

A path was worn between the coffeepot and the

kitchen table by the time she reached the last page of the ledger. Crossing her fingers and offering up a silent prayer, she pressed the total button. When the amount registered, her eyes widened and her mouth dropped open in shock.

Ripping the long tape from the machine, she moved her pencil down the column of numbers, checking the amounts against those listed in her ledger. When she reached the end of the tape, she dropped her pencil and picked up the check her insurance agent had given her.

The amount listed on the check fell well short of her expectations. The way she had it figured, there was enough money from the insurance company to reimburse the consignees for the merchandise lost due to the fire, to sandblast the stone walls and to put on a new roof. That left virtually nothing for new inventory. And without anything to sell, there wasn't a prayer of making profits to pay off the loan.

"Bad?"

Al glanced up to see Verdie watching her. Grimacing, she folded the adding machine tape and slipped it between the pages of the ledger. "Bad doesn't even come close to describing how hopeless this situation is." She closed the ledger and leaned back in her chair, ruffling her bangs as she pressed a hand to her forehead where the beginning of a headache throbbed. "I'm afraid this is the end, Verdie. It doesn't look as if I have any choice other than to sell the farm."

Her worried gaze fixed on Al's face, Verdie pulled

up a chair beside Al. "I've got a little money set aside. You're welcome to it."

The tears Al had suppressed all morning pooled in her eyes. She grasped Verdie's hand in hers and squeezed. "No, Verdie. I won't take your money."

"Your mother, then. Why don't you call and ask her for the money?"

Al shook her head as she released Verdie's hand. "No, I won't ask Mother. She wouldn't give it to me anyway."

Sighing deeply, Al glanced out the kitchen window and to the land beyond. "Granddaddy always used to say, when something's over, it's over, and there's no sense trying to hang on." She turned and gave Verdie a watery smile. "Clairemore Farms is no more. We've just got to admit that and go on."

Suddenly Verdie's face brightened. "Stuart's got a pretty good business head on his shoulders. Why don't you talk to him? Maybe he'll have an idea or two."

"No!" Al shook her head for added emphasis. "And you have to promise you won't mention this to him, either. This is my problem, not his, and I've got to work it out in my own way."

Stuart pushed open the door to the law firm, still wondering why Al had requested he meet her there. At breakfast she hadn't mentioned anything about a meeting with her attorney, much less a meeting with her attorney and *him*.

The message his secretary had relayed had been brief and frustrating in its lack of information: meet

Al at 10:30 at the law offices of Myers, Lacy and Myers. Nothing more.

The receptionist behind the desk Stuart offered him a friendly smile. "You must be Mr. Greyson. Mr. Lacy and Miss McCord are waiting for you in Mr. Lacy's office."

At that moment the door behind the secretary's desk opened, and a man stepped into the reception area. "Mr. Greyson?" At Stuart's nod, the man extended his hand. "Frank Lacy, Mr. Greyson. Come on in. Miss McCord is waiting in my office."

Just inside the door, Stuart stopped, surprised by the drastic change in illumination from the reception area to the dimly lit, paneled office of Frank Lacy. Heavy drapes covered the windows, creating an eerie darkness considering the earliness of the day. While he was waiting for his eyes to adjust to the change, Al stepped from the shadows and into the triangle of light cast through the open doorway.

She offered Stuart a polite smile. "Hello, Mr. Greyson."

Surprised by her formality as much as her coolness, Stuart repeated, "Mr. Greyson?" then narrowed an eye at her. "What in hell is going on here?"

She knotted her hands together at her waist in a nervous gesture totally out of character. "Well, you always said you liked to keep your business and personal lives separate." She shrugged, palms up, and offered him a lopsided smile. "This is definitely business."

Before Stuart could question her further, the door behind him closed, reminding him that he and Al were not alone. Frank Lacy's deep voice confirmed that fact. "If you'll have a seat, Mr. Greyson, I think I can explain."

While Al and Stuart seated themselves, Lacy took his place behind the desk.

"Miss McCord tells me she promised you first option on Clairmore Farms if she ever decided to sell."

Stunned as much by the lawyer's knowledge of his and Al's agreement as he was by the purpose of this meeting, Stuart swung around to face Al. She sat beside him, her hands folded tightly in her lap, her gaze riveted on the attorney's face.

His mind reeled with questions, but Stuart could only stare at Al, speechless, as the attorney droned on.

"Due to circumstances beyond her control, it appears Miss McCord will be forced to sell the farm."

Moisture pooled in Al's eyes, but her chin lifted and she blinked back the unwanted show of emotion. Stuart wanted to touch her, to reach out and draw her close, but he could see by the stiffness of her posture that any offers of comfort were unwelcome.

The attorney cleared his throat and arranged the papers before him into a neater stack. "Although she agreed to sell you the farm, Miss McCord tells me a value was never discussed. Until an amount can be settled on, I'm afraid I can't prepare the necessary legal documents to consummate the sale."

Put a value on the one thing Al loved above all else? The very idea was ludicrous in Stuart's opinion. He ignored the attorney and laid a hand on Al's arm, directing his response to her. "You don't have to sell the farm, Al. I'll give you the money—"

"No." She glanced down at her hands but still refused to look at Stuart. "You'd be doing that out of friendship, and where the farm is concerned, our relationship is strictly business."

His own words echoed back at him. He remembered the day he had last said them to Al. He also remembered how glibly she'd dealt with his objections to their entering into a personal relationship. Her offer to sell him the farm—when and if she decided to sell—was what had forged the way to their friendship.

But damn it! he thought angrily, that was before he got to know her, before he realized how much he cared for her. He couldn't buy the land now, knowing how much she'd suffer the loss.

Lacy cleared his throat. "As I was saying—"

Tearing his gaze from Al, Stuart turned to glare at the lawyer. "I don't want the damn farm." He stood barring any further discussion. "If you want to draw up the papers for a loan, I'll be more than happy to sign them." He turned to Al, and his voice dropped to a husky whisper. "But I won't be a party to Al losing her farm." With that he walked out of the office.

Al left the law offices of Myers, Lacy and Myers minus her heart. She'd left it on the walnut conference table along with the deed to Clairemore Farms.

Outside the fourteen-story building that housed her attorney's offices, Al paused and lifted her face to the sun, hoping to capture some of its warmth. But the chill she'd felt since Stuart left the office remained.

Why hadn't he been willing to buy the farm? she wondered. It was what he'd wanted all along. And why had he insisted on offering to loan her the money again? Hadn't she made it clear she wouldn't accept his money, that she had to do this on her own?

The questions only increased the hollow feeling in her stomach. She felt as if she'd been gut-shot. She honestly didn't know how it felt to be shot in the stomach, but she knew it couldn't be any worse than the pain she was experiencing at the moment.

She glanced at her watch and felt the first flutter of panic. *No time for regrets now, Al,* she silently lectured. *You have business to take care of and a plane to catch.* Quickly suppressing the panic, she squared her shoulders and headed for the bank at the opposite end of the street.

At least Feeber will have a good day, she thought ironically as she tightened her fingers on the check in her hand.

Stuart pulled at the back door, but found it locked. Frowning, he fitted his hands at the corner of his eyes and peered through the door's curtained window. Nothing. No movement, no noise, no light. Assuming he had probably beaten Al home, he reached up and snagged the house key from its hiding place above the porch eave and let himself in.

"Al?" he called as he moved to the back staircase. When his call met with silence, a sense of unease settled over him. Something wasn't right. The house was way too quiet. He crossed to the laundry room and looked in. Puppy's basket was beside the dryer as usual, but Puppy was gone. Stuart's unease quickly grew to a heart-stopping panic.

He raced for the rear staircase and took the steps two at a time. At the door to Al's bedroom he stopped, and looked around the room, his breath coming in deep grabbing gulps.

No clothes were scattered about, no shoes peeked from beneath the bed. Everything was as neat as a pin. Totally unlike Al.

He strode across the room. When he reached the closet, he wrenched open the door. A few empty hangers swung lazily on the rod.

Slowly, he backed away from the proof he'd sought.

Al was gone.

Exactly what the doctor ordered, Al thought as she curled her feet beneath her and sipped from the fluted glass of wine.

"I'm impressed, Rhys." She held the glass up to the light, admiring its clarity, then smiled at her long-time friend. "Real crystal. What happened to the old jelly glasses we used to drink from?"

Rhys groaned. "Marcia. She bought these and, just to be sure I wouldn't knuckle under to temptation, she broke all the jelly glasses."

Al chuckled and clinked her glass against Rhys's in a toast. "My kind of woman. You chose well, my friend."

"I did, didn't I?" Smiling smugly, he hooked his

sneakered toes under the edge of the coffee table and inched it closer. With his feet propped on the polished surface, he leaned back against the couch's deep cushions. The silence that stretched between the two was one of comfort.

"Why did you run away from home this time, Al?"

The unexpected question caught her totally off guard. "What makes you think I'm running away from home?" she asked hesitantly.

"Every time you show up on my doorstep unannounced, you're running from something. The first time I think you were thirteen. You'd broken one of your grandmother's family heirlooms, and you were afraid she was going to spank you. The most recent was last winter after you'd moved back home and found out your granddaddy only had two months to live." He stretched an arm along the back of the couch and slipped his hand beneath Al's hair to squeeze the tense muscles in her neck. "What is it this time, Al?"

She bowed her head, avoiding Rhys's probing look as she watched her fingers' slow movement around the rim of her glass. "You know me too well."

"About as well as you know me, so come clean. What's bothering you?"

An involuntary shudder shook Al's shoulders. "I had to sell the farm."

"Oh, Al." Rhys's hand slipped to her shoulder and he hugged her against his side. "I'm sorry. I know how much that place meant to you."

Al sniffed and offered Rhys a brave smile. "Yeah,

it was pretty special.'' The tears she'd suppressed for the better part of twenty-four hours surfaced and spilled over. ''But that's not the only reason,'' she admitted tearfully. ''It's Stuart.''

Rhys's features stiffened. ''If that guy's hurt you, I'll—''

Al patted his thigh in reassurance before swiping at the tears on her cheek. ''No, no. It's nothing like that. He loves me. He just can't admit it. I'm hoping that by putting some distance between us, he'll realize how much he needs me.''

''And if he doesn't?''

Al sucked in a long shuddery breath. ''I don't know.'' She lifted her tearstained face to Rhys and repeated softly, ''I just don't know.''

''Well, where the hell is she?'' Stuart demanded in an angry voice.

''You don't have to yell at me! I ain't deaf, you know.''

Stuart turned the receiver away from his mouth and heaved a frustrated sigh. He rubbed wearily at the tension in his neck and fought for calm before he pulled the receiver back to his mouth. ''I'm sorry, Verdie. I didn't mean to yell, but Al hasn't been at the farm all week and neither have you.''

''I've been home. Al gave me the week off.''

''Great! Now I know where you've been, but I still don't know where Al is.'' Stuart raked his fingers through his hair and forced a calmer note into his voice. ''Look, Verdie, if you won't tell me where Al is, will you at least tell me when she'll be back?''

"Day after tomorrow. I know because that's when the movers are coming to load her things."

"The movers! Where is she going?"

"I don't know, but she can't very well stay now that she's sold the farm. The old buzzard only gave her two weeks to vacate."

A sick feeling rose in Stuart's stomach. Al had sold the farm. He knew without asking who the new owner was. George Bandy. The reference to "buzzards" told him that.

Mumbling his thanks, Stuart replaced the phone and sank onto the edge of his desk. His fingers settled on the brass ashtray beside his knee. Obviously, Al had meant what she'd said when she told him she had to do this on her own without any help from him.

Damn! Why hadn't he stayed at the lawyer's office and tried to talk some sense into her? He'd been so sure that once he refused to buy her out she'd agree to his loan. He'd never once considered that she might turn to Bandy.

In an unusual display of temper, Stuart closed his fingers over the brass ashtray and hurled it against the door.

Moments later the door opened, and a white handkerchief fluttered before Morrey stuck his head inside the office. "Is it safe to enter?" he asked.

"Depends on what you consider safe," Stuart replied tersely as he stalked across the room in three ground-eating strides. He scooped the ashtray from the floor, and, as he passed by Morrey, he tossed the now dented clump of brass to his stepfather.

On reflex, Morrey grabbed for it before it hit the

floor again. Chuckling, he followed Stuart and set the ashtray back on the desk. "Something tells me Al is behind this temper tantrum."

"What was your first clue?"

"A rumor I heard today."

Frowning, Stuart glanced up from the papers he was shuffling on his desk. "What rumor?"

"Heard George Bandy is the new owner of Clairemore Farms."

"You heard right. Verdie just told me the same thing." Stuart dropped down in his chair and anchored his hands behind his head, studying his stepfather's face. "Now what do we do?"

"We?"

Slowly, Stuart pulled his hands from behind his head as he stared at his stepfather. "Yeah, we. You have as much at stake here as I do. If Bandy follows his usual pattern, he'll throw up some cheap subdivision that will decrease the market value of Greystone Estates."

"And that's all you're worried about, Greystone Estates?"

"Well, what else is there?"

Morrey shrugged and reached for the ever present pack of cigarettes. "I thought maybe Al's sudden departure might have you concerned."

Suddenly wary, Stuart asked, "How did you know she was gone?"

Morrey shrugged again, but this time he hid a smug smile behind a thin curl of smoke. "I've got my sources."

In his impatience, Stuart lurched to his feet, his

palms planted flat on his desk. "If you know where she is, Morrey, and you haven't told me, I'll—"

Startled by his stepson's anger, Morrey held out a hand to stop him. "Wait a minute. I didn't say I knew where she was, only that I knew she was gone. Tuesday, when I was taking your mother to the airport, I saw Al running to catch a flight. But I thought you knew. Hell, you've been practically living with her for the past month. Don't people in love usually share their plans with each other?"

Uncomfortable with the implications behind Morrey's question, Stuart dropped back down in his chair and dismissed Morrey's assumption with an impatient wave of his hand. "We're just friends, that's all. Al doesn't owe me any explanations."

"And if you believe that, you're a fool." Morrey flicked the teetering cone of ashes into the ashtray and settled back in his chair. "The woman loves you, even I can see that. And I think you love her, too."

"Well, you're wrong."

Morrey lifted a shoulder as if Stuart's opinion really didn't matter. "Could be. But I doubt it. The woman's had you tied up in knots ever since you met her. In my book, that spells love." Pushing his hands against the chair's arm, he stood. "You've been letting the past rule your life for a long time, son. Maybe it's time you grabbed the reins for a while."

Al pushed at the hard-packed ground with the tip of her tennis shoe. Sprigs of new grass were already pushing through the dirt, nature's way of signaling that life must go on. For some reason, Al didn't find that thought particularly comforting.

A week alone in Rhys's apartment while he'd been piloting his scheduled flights had given her the opportunity to absorb—and, yes, even accept—the unexpected upheaval in her life. She had returned to Clairemore Farms better prepared to handle the loss of her grandparents' home place. But she was no closer on a decision as to handle Stuart.

One by one the daisies she clasped in her hand slipped from her fingers and fell onto Ranger's grave. Obviously thinking this was a new game, Puppy leaped onto the pile of flowers, growling and pawing until she nabbed one of the thin stems between her teeth. Pleased with her accomplishment, she trotted to Al's side and dropped the flower at her mistress's feet, then sank down on her haunches and looked up at Al, panting.

Unable to hold back the tears any longer, Al scooped the puppy into her arms and nuzzled the animal to her neck as she sank down beside the grave. "I wish you could have known Ranger, Puppy. You'd have liked each other, I know."

The puppy licked at the moisture on Al's cheeks then barked, making Al laugh. "Okay, so maybe you wouldn't have gotten along at first, but eventually you'd have become friends." She settled the animal on her lap. "Just look at Stuart and me—" At the mention of Stuart's name, the puppy whined low in her throat and lifted soulful eyes to Al.

"I know," Al said softly as she scratched at the pup's ears. "You miss him, too, don't you?" She ran a finger down its velvety snout. "But I had to leave. He needed some space, some time to think." A soft sigh escaped her as she leaned back, supporting her weight on her hands. "Even though I know it was for the best, it was probably the hardest thing I've ever done." She glanced down at the puppy. "Absence makes the heart grow fonder, right?"

The dog cocked her head and looked quizzically at Al. Chuckling, Al ruffled the soft fur on the puppy's head. "Oh, what do you know about love anyway?"

"Not nearly enough."

At the sound of the deep male voice, Al jumped, then twisted around to peer behind her. Stuart stood at the edge of the pecan grove, not ten feet away. The sight of him stole her breath. As usual, he was impeccably dressed, from the high gleam on his shoes to the tie knotted snugly between the points of a crisp white shirt.

Quickly setting the puppy aside, Al scrambled to her feet and brushed the dirt and grass from the seat of her jeans. "Stuart! I didn't know you were there."

"Obviously not."

Remembering the conversation she'd been carrying on with her pet, Al felt her face warm under Stuart's steady gaze. "How'd you know where to find me?"

"Verdie. She said I'd probably find you here."

Reminded of her purpose in coming to the pecan grove, Al glanced back at the grave. "I came to say goodbye to Ranger."

"Were you going to say goodbye to me, as well?"

Al wheeled, her eyes wide with alarm. "Goodbye?" she echoed.

"Yes, goodbye. You are moving, aren't you?"

"Wel—well, yes," she stammered. "I sold the farm. But I'm not leaving Louisville," she hastened to add.

It was Stuart's turn for surprise. "You're not?"

"No!" She took two steps toward him, then stopped, unsure of the welcome she'd receive. "Louisville's my home. I wouldn't think of leaving here."

"But I thought..." Shaking his head, Stuart said, "Never mind what I thought. You're not leaving and that's what's important."

Throughout her stay at Rhys's apartment Al had struggled with how best to resolve her relationship with Stuart. He loved her. She was sure of that. But his inability to admit his love concerned her. Giving herself wholly to him without any reserve of emotion hadn't seemed to have affected him one way or the other.

By the time she left Rhys's, she'd finally accepted the fact that Stuart's reluctance to a commitment and his lack of trust was his problem, something he would have to come to terms with on his own...without any further help from her.

But now, as she watched Stuart carefully mask the relieved look he'd exposed when he'd heard she wasn't leaving Louisville, Al smiled inwardly. She knew what she was about to do wasn't fair. She also knew it wasn't at all what she had *planned* to do, but since when had she ever followed the expected path?

"*Why* is my staying important?" she asked, deliberately taking one more step toward him.

"Well—" Stuart glanced down at the ground and

worried a blade of grass with the toe of his shoe "—because."

Al crossed her arms beneath her breasts. "Come on, Stuart. You can do better than that."

He pulled nervously at his tie, which suddenly seemed too tight and successfully avoided Al's penetrating gaze.

"Did you miss me while I was gone?" she asked helpfully.

He cleared his throat, then dropped his hand wearily to his side. "Yes, I did."

"Good."

"Good?" he echoed in surprise, glancing up at her.

"Yes, good. I'd hoped you would."

Stuart narrowed an eye at her. "Why do I suddenly have the feeling I've been duped?"

Al took a step closer, her eyes bright with laughter. "When have I ever tricked you?"

His fingers ticking off the number of times, Stuart began to enumerate them. "The auction, the fishing expedition..."

Laughing, Al closed the last few feet of distance that remained between then and and threw herself into his arms. "Why don't you just say it? You love me, you know you do."

Life would always be easy with Al, Stuart could see that now. Catching her around the waist, he lifted her until her eyes were level with his. "I love you, Al McCord."

At last, the words she'd waited so long to hear. Tossing back her head, Al laughed up at the sky, then wrapped her arms around Stuart's neck, squeezing him to her. "And I love you, Stuart Greyson."

Something thick and bulky dug into her breasts as she hugged him. Wincing at the uncomfortable sensation, she pushed against Stuart's shoulders until he released her.

When her feet touched the ground, she tapped at the suspicious lump beneath his jacket with an almond-shaped nail. "Another puppy?" she teased.

Slipping a hand to his jacket's inside pocket, Stuart attempted to hide a smile. "No, not a puppy."

Her curiosity aroused, Al inched closer and tried to sneak a peek. "What is it, then?"

"A gift." At her excited look, he took a cautious step backward. "But before I give it to you, we need to talk."

Puzzled, Al looked up at him. "What about?"

"We can start with where you've been for the past week."

"Oh, that." Al waved away his question with an impatient flick of her wrist. "I went to spend a week with Rhys."

"Why?"

"So you would have time to miss me. Now what is my gift?" she asked reaching for the thick envelope.

Stuart lifted it above his head, just out of her grasp. "You didn't have to leave town to make me miss you. I miss you every time we're apart."

A slow smile built on Al's face. "You do?"

"Yes, I do."

"But you never said so."

"No. I don't suppose I did." Still holding the envelope above his head, Stuart wrapped his free arm around Al and pulled her up against him. "When I went out to the farm the night after our visit to your attorney and found you gone, it scared the hell out of me. I thought you'd left for good."

Smiling, Al touched a hand to his cheek. "I'm sorry. I didn't mean to scare you. I only wanted to give you time to realize you loved me."

Dropping his uplifted hand to join the other he had clasped at her back, Stuart closed his eyes and hugged her to him. "I love you. Never doubt that."

Knowing she'd never grow tired of hearing those words, she touched her lips to his and murmured, "I won't. I promise." Passion flickered, then flamed between them as Stuart caught her lower lip and drew on it.

Al placed a trembling hand against his chest to stop him. "I know what you're trying to do," she said as she backed from his embrace, wagging an accusing finger at him. "You're trying to make me forget about my present."

Chuckling, Stuart rubbed a finger against his lips. "No. But I might have if I'd thought of it." He tapped the envelope against his opposite hand for a moment, then, without a word of explanation, handed her the envelope.

Her fingers shaking, Al tore open the flap and pulled out a thick sheaf of papers. Frowning at the oddity of the gift, she slowly began to unfold the stiff pages.

Typed in bold print across the front page of the

document were the words WARRANTY DEED. Al jerked one hand to her mouth to stifle the cry of dismay that escaped as she scanned the page. Names and phrases jumped out at her. George Bandy. Stuart Phillip Greyson. Clairemore Farms. Paid in full. Her mind whirled, trying to tie all the pieces together. Clairemore Farms. Stuart owned Clairemore Farms. But he couldn't, she thought hysterically. She'd sold the property to Bandy.

She lifted tear filled eyes to meet Stuart's smiling ones. "But how?"

He shrugged a shoulder. "I bought it from Bandy."

Looking down at the sheaf of papers, she murmured, "You should have bought it from me when I offered it to you. I'll bet the old buzzard charged you an arm and a leg to get it back."

"Let's just say the million I'd hoped to make by my thirtieth birthday is a little further out of reach."

Reminded of his goal to be a millionaire, Al offered softly, "I'm sorry."

He shrugged away her apology. "I'm not. The purchase of the farm was a gamble, but one I'm hoping will pay off big."

The hope for a big payoff, in Al's mind, meant only one thing. Stuart still planned to subdivide Clairemore Farms. Saddened by the thought, she swept her gaze to the farmhouse in the distance, the symbol of home and security.

Stuart saw the sadness in her eyes and hoped to dispel it. "If I owned the farm, I thought that might be a stronger inducement for you to agree to marry me."

"Marry you!" Al wheeled to stare at him, her mouth dropped open in surprise.

"Yes, marry me." He gestured to the papers in her hand. "Maybe if you turn a few more pages you'll understand."

Her fingers trembling uncontrollably, Al flipped through the papers until she found yet another page with the heading WARRANTY DEED. Stuart Greyson's name appeared as owner conveying title to Alyssa Claire McCord.

Clairemore Farms. The land was hers again. Laughing and crying at the same time, she fell into his arms. "Oh, Stuart. You didn't have to buy the farm to get me to marry you. All you had to do was ask."

Smoothing her bangs back from her eyes, Stuart sought her gaze. "I know how much this place means to you. Over the last few months it's grown to mean a lot to me, too." He tipped her chin higher and held her there, firm in his grasp, his gaze fixed on hers. "I love you, Alyssa McCord."

Just before his lips brushed hers, a strong tug on his leg and a low growling sound made Stuart jerk back. "What the—" He looked down and found Puppy, her teeth buried in the hem of his slacks, snarling and pulling for all she was worth.

Chuckling, Stuart scooped the puppy from the ground. With the puppy tucked beneath one arm, he wrapped his free arm around Al and headed her toward the farmhouse which beckoned in the distance.

"Let's go home, Al."

*   *   *   *   *

American HEROES
AGAINST ALL ODDS

Please address questions and book requests to: Harlequin Reader Service U.S.: 3010 Walden Ave.,
P.O. Box 1325, Buffalo, NY 14269 CAN.: P.O. Box 609, Fort Erie, Ont. L2A 5X3   PAHGEN

Harlequin Romance®

Delightful

Affectionate

Romantic

Emotional

Tender

Original

Daring

Riveting

Enchanting

Adventurous

Moving

Harlequin Romance—the
series that has it all!

HROM-G

HARLEQUIN SUPERROMANCE®

...there's more to the story!

Superromance. A *big* satisfying read about unforget-
table characters. Each month we offer
four very different stories that range from family
drama to adventure and mystery, from highly emo-
tional stories to romantic comedies—and
much more! Stories about people you'll
believe in and care about. Stories too
compelling to put down....

Our authors are among today's *best* romance writ-
ers. You'll find familiar names and
talented newcomers. Many of them are
award winners—and you'll see why!

If you want the biggest and best
in romance fiction, you'll get it
from Superromance!

Available wherever Harlequin books are sold.

Look us up on-line at: http://www.romance.net

Mulberry Square Productions
presents

A Family Film by
Joe Camp

FOR THE LOVE OF BENJI

starring
Benji
Patsy Garrett
Cynthia Smith
Allen Fiuzat

special guest star
Ed Nelson

with
Art Vasil
Peter Bowles
Bridget Armstrong
Mihalis Lambrinos

Music by Euel Box

Director of Photography Don Reddy

Original Story by
Joe Camp and Ben Vaughn

Screenplay by Joe Camp

Executive Producer Joe Camp

Produced by Ben Vaughn

Directed by Joe Camp

Filmed in Panavision
Color by CFI
A Mulberry Square Production

For The Love Of Benji

A Novelization by I.F. Love

From the Family Film by
Joe Camp

BANTAM BOOKS
TORONTO · NEW YORK · LONDON

FOR THE LOVE OF BENJI
A Bantam Book | June 1977
2nd printing
3rd printing

ISBN 0–553–11230–9

Published simultaneously in the United States and Canada

Bantam Books are published by Bantam Books, Inc. Its trade-
mark, consisting of the words "Bantam Books" and the por-
trayal of a bantam, is registered in the United States Patent
Office and in other countries. Marca Registrada. Bantam
Books, Inc., 666 Fifth Avenue, New York, New York 10019.

PRINTED IN THE UNITED STATES OF AMERICA

For The Love Of Benji

I

Stelios parked his taxi and climbed out into the warm sunshine of Athens, Greece. He walked, scowling, along the noisy street toward a sidewalk café, chose a quiet table, and sat down to wait.

Soon a heavy man, wearing a food-stained apron and carrying several newspapers, entered the café. He dropped the newspapers in front of Stelios and handed him a large envelope.

"The whole world knows now," he said in a coarse voice.

Stelios glanced at the newspapers. One was Greek, one German, and one English, and they all had a picture of the same man on the front page. The headlines announced that a prominent energy scientist had disappeared in Greece.

Stelios opened the envelope and looked at the top sheet of paper. "Chandler Dietrich," he mumbled and nodded thoughtfully. Then he thumbed through several other papers, finally settling on an eight-by-ten photograph. "What's this?"

It was a picture of a woman, two children—a boy and a girl—and a dog, all staring brightly into the camera.

"The dog is the courier," the man said. "He'll be carrying the code."

"The dog! Why a dog?"

The man in the apron shrugged. "I have no idea. His name is Benji."

Stelios studied the picture again. It was a fairly small dog; a mixed breed of some kind with floppy ears and light-colored hair drooping around the eyes and off the jowls. "Who are the other people?"

"The kids' names are Paul and Cindy Chapman. They're ten and twelve years old. The woman's name is Mary Henderson. She's their governess. They'll all be changing planes in Athens tomorrow and going directly on to Crete."

Stelios sighed, taking a closer look at the brown dog. He wanted to make sure he would recognize him. There was a small tuft of white hair just behind the dog's nose, and his chest was streaked with white.

"Benji, huh?" Stelios mumbled. The man in the apron nodded. "Well, Benji, I hope you have a safe trip."

Perched on the ledge behind the back seat of the taxi, Benji couldn't have been happier as he watched the city of Houston disappear

4

behind him. He wagged his tail and turned to look over Mary's shoulder toward the front window. He could already see a big jet plane taking off from the airfield up ahead.

It had all started about a month earlier. Paul had brought home an armload of books about Greece to read for a school assignment. Everybody in the house began looking at the books, and Dr. Chapman suddenly suggested they all go there for a vacation.

"But what'll we do with Benji and Tiffany?" Paul asked immediately.

"Well, we can't take them along," Dr. Chapman replied. "Maybe we can find someone who will board them for three weeks."

To Paul and Cindy, who had loved Benji even when he was just a floppy-eared stray with no family of his own, the suggestion couldn't have been worse. Now that Dr. Chapman had given his permission for Benji and his lady friend Tiffany to live with Paul and Cindy, they couldn't bear the thought of leaving their pets for nearly a month.

Cindy gave such strong arguments for taking them along, that the doctor finally said, "Well, let me check with the travel agent. I'll see what kind of regulations they have about taking dogs to Greece."

The taxi made a sharp turn and Benji took another look through the windshield. They were coming into the crowded airport. Cars and taxis and buses moved slowly ahead of them.

"Now let's all stick together," Mary said. "I don't want some of us ending up in Hong Kong instead of Greece."

The taxi slowed down and Benji glanced out the back window again. Then he stiffened, his eyes fixed on a fluffy cat prancing along the walk in front of the terminal buildings. A woman wearing a fur coat was attached to the leash behind the cat, and both of them had their noses up in the air. Crowds of people were moving along the walk, with men pushing cartloads of luggage between them. Benji smiled to himself. He took one more glance at the cat and then held himself ready as the taxi pulled into a parking place.

"Benji!" Paul yelled as Benji bounded through the window onto the pavement.

Benji didn't respond. He had no intention of getting lost, but cats were arrogant animals, and if you didn't let them know you were around they always seemed to think they owned the place. He let out a threatening bark and scampered across to where the woman was talking to a skycap. He skidded to a stop and gave two more loud barks.

The cat gazed indifferently at him, definitely unimpressed. Benji looked puzzled, but not for long. He suddenly felt himself scooped off the pavement.

"I'm sorry, ma'am," Paul said to the lady,

and then they were bouncing along through the crowds toward the terminal doors. "Benji, you've got to cut that out if you want to travel with us!"

Benji gave Paul's hand a lick.

"Count the bags," Mary said. "Are they all here?"

"I counted them," Cindy answered. "Have you got the tickets?"

"The tickets? Oh, dear! They must be in my purse somewhere."

They all stopped and finally breathed a sigh of relief when Mary produced the tickets. She moved into the line at the counter and Paul and Cindy stood to the side with Benji and Tiffany. Four reservations for only three people caused some confusion until Mary explained that Dr. Chapman would be coming a week later, and the ticket clerk went off to check the computers.

"We're going to Greece," Mary said to the man standing behind her.

He was a tall, handsome man with a little gray hair at the temples. He smiled politely. "So am I."

"You are?" Mary said with surprise.

"That's the only place this airline goes."

"Oh," Mary said, "of course." She looked off behind the counter and then turned back to the man. "I'm sorry this is taking so long. Where in Greece are you going?"

"I'm going to Crete," the man said politely.

"Really? That's where we're going."

The man smiled. "It's a beautiful island. I've been there many times. I'll be happy to tell you the good places to go. My name is Chandler Dietrich, by the way."

Mary smiled and shook his hand. "I'm Mary Henderson, and this is Paul and Cynthia Chapman. And that's Benji and Tiffany."

Just then a pretty girl in an airline uniform came up and asked Cindy for the names of her dogs. Cindy told her, adding that they were going to Crete.

"Well, I'm sure you're going to have a very nice trip, Benji and Tiffany," the girl said. She carefully wrote their names on two tags.

"Are you sure they'll be all right?" Cindy asked.

"They'll be just fine. My cat travels this way all the time."

"Tiffany hasn't been feeling well," Cindy said. "She sort of has a condition."

"Well, we'll take good care of her. I promise you that."

The girl had the tags attached to the cages now and she put Tiffany gently inside hers and locked it up. Benji took a final look at Paul and Cindy and then allowed himself to be lifted from the counter and locked into the cage.

"See you in Crete," Paul called out to both

of them and they were placed on a conveyor belt.

The two dogs passed into a narrow corridor, and the noises of the front terminal suddenly disappeared. The dogs moved through a small hole and into a huge baggage room. Now Benji could hear the whine of jet engines and the clatter of machinery and trucks. He settled down and rested his chin on the bottom of the cage. Then he looked up quickly.

Dietrich, the man who had been in line behind Mary, was coming toward him, walking fast alongside the conveyor belt. He rested his hand on top of the cage and peered in. "Hi there, Benji boy," he said.

Benji gave him a panting smile of recognition, then he felt his cage being lifted from the conveyor belt and they were moving away. He wondered why the man hadn't taken Tiffany too.

They passed through a door into a room that was crowded with noisy machinery. Dietrich placed the cage on a counter and slid a steel pin into the lock. Benji wagged his tail. Perhaps he was going to be let out of the cage. But the door stayed shut.

Benji watched as Dietrich opened the top of a tiny bottle and poured some liquid onto his handkerchief.

"OK, Benji, now just relax. This won't take long and it won't hurt a bit."

Benji hesitated as the man opened the door. Then he tried to turn his head away as the man grabbed his neck and held the handkerchief tightly to his nose.

Benji had never smelled anything like it. The powerful vapor stung his nostrils and made him feel dizzy. He dug his paws into the bottom of the cage and twisted with all his strength, trying to wrench his head loose. But his legs seemed to buckle under him and suddenly his whole body went limp.

He was flat on the bottom of the cage now and everything in the room was floating around, going in and out of focus. Mr. Dietrich had brought something shiny from his pocket and Benji blinked woozily, trying to see what it was. Then he felt his paw lifted and the pad of his foot was pressed hard against the cold metal of the object.

"There you go, Benji. That wasn't so bad, was it?"

The man was holding a match to the piece of metal now. It flamed away into nothing. The cage door came shut again, the lock rattling back into place. Dietrich peered in and smiled. "Good boy, Benji. I'll see you in Crete in about twelve hours, huh?"

Benji felt himself being carried back through the door and bounced down onto the conveyor belt. Then Mr. Dietrich was gone and Benji was moving along the belt, his head resting between his paws, blinking woozily.

"Here's another dog," somebody said. Benji's cage was lifted again, and placed on a big baggage cart. A couple of minutes later the cart was towed out into the sunshine and Benji closed his eyes. All he wanted to do now was sleep.

II

The flight from Athens down to the island of Crete took less than half an hour, but the scenery was magnificent. The plane was only half full, so all of them except Mr. Dietrich had window seats and a good view.

The color of the water was amazing: a rich azure that turned to lacy white around the hundreds of islands. It was even prettier than the postcards and travel brochures they had studied back in Silver Creek. Then, as the plane approached the island of Crete, the little whitewashed villages along the coast looked no different from how they must have looked centuries earlier.

Mr. Dietrich seemed to know the island of Crete very well, and told them about the interesting archaeological sites there. But because they had now been traveling for well over twelve hours, Paul and Cindy slept through a good part of the history lesson. Now the famous island was directly beneath them and the plane turned and seemed to slow down almost to a

15

stop as they started the descent toward the airport.

The airport at Crete was small compared to the one in Athens, and the passengers had to walk several hundred yards to the terminal building.

"As soon as you're all settled and catch up on your sleep," Mr. Dietrich said to Mary, "I'm treating all three of you to the best meal you've ever had in your lives."

Mary hesitated, then said, "You really don't have to do that, Mr. Dietrich. I'm sure you have other important business to attend to."

Mr. Dietrich shook his head. "I won't have it any other way. I want you to see the best of Crete."

Mary smiled, not wanting to protest too vigorously.

"Will it be Greek food?" Paul asked.

"Very Greek."

"What's Greek food like?" Cindy asked suspiciously.

"I will promise you only one thing," Mr. Dietrich laughed. "There won't be any fried chicken on the menu."

Paul laughed, but Cindy thought fried chicken sounded pretty good right now.

A young man in an Olympic Airways uniform was just inside the door holding a blackboard with Mr. Dietrich's name chalked on it. Cindy was the only one who noticed.

"Mr. Dietrich, look at that!"

He glanced at the board and stopped abruptly. "Can you believe that? I guess there's no escaping. Why don't you all go on ahead to the baggage claim area. I'll be right there."

When they moved off Dietrich turned quickly to the man. "I'm Chandler Dietrich, young man," he said in fluent Greek.

The messenger searched his pockets and brought out a folded piece of paper. "A man left this message for you, sir. He said it was urgent."

Dietrich unfolded the paper and frowned as he studied the message. "Did he leave his name?"

"No, sir."

Dietrich nodded and handed him a tip. Then he moved into the terminal building, angling off toward the baggage area where Mary, Paul, and Cindy were watching the luggage come through on a conveyor belt.

"Is anything wrong?" Mary asked when she saw his dark look.

"Uh . . . no. No, not at all. I just have to make a phone call." He smiled to reassure them. "Look, why don't you and the kids wait for the luggage and the dogs . . ." He searched his pockets for his claim check. "And if you don't mind, watch for my bag too. It's a light tan, about so big."

"Sure," Paul said, "we'll find it."

"I'd appreciate it, Paul. I'll be back in a minute and then we'll all take a cab together so you won't have to fight the language problem."

"That'd be great," Mary smiled. "Thank you."

"Thank *you*," Dietrich said with a smile, and strode off.

He moved along to the last pay phone in the line and stopped, glancing casually at the OUT OF ORDER sign taped across it. He consulted the note again and paced impatiently near the phone for a half minute. Suddenly it rang. He quickly lifted the receiver, and said, "Dietrich."

A cold and menacing voice answered him. "Welcome to Crete, Mr. Dietrich. Do you have the coordinate code?"

"I have it. It's in a safe place."

"Good. You will find the map in an envelope taped under the shelf below the phone."

Dietrich bent forward and spotted the bulky envelope. He tore it loose and took the map from inside. "I have it."

"Very good. The project is getting out of hand, Mr. Dietrich, so waste no time. Signal if you need help. We will be watching you."

"I won't need any help," Dietrich said irritably, "and I don't need to be watched. I'm perfectly capable of handling this alone."

The phone clicked softly and Dietrich rattled the hook. "Hello?"

The man had hung up. Dietrich banged the receiver down and quickly slid the map into his inside coat pocket. Then he looked out at the people crisscrossing the terminal lobby. He recognized none of them, and there seemed to be no one watching him. Then he looked up sharply at the mezzanine.

There standing by another bank of pay phones was a dark, thick-necked Greek. His cold, penetrating eyes seemed to be gazing idly down at the crowds. It was Stelios.

Dietrich wondered if he was the man who had been assigned to watch him. Or was he the man who had just called him? Or was he just another passenger killing time between flights?

Mary and the kids all looked worried when Dietrich got back to the baggage area. They were the only ones still standing by the conveyor belt and Mary turned quickly when she saw him.

"Chandler! I'm so glad you're back. They're not here! All the luggage came, but there's no sign of Benji or Tiffany!"

"What?" Dietrich snapped. His eyes showed real concern. "Are you sure?"

"We've watched everything that came in," Paul said. "They're just not here."

Dietrich glanced around and found the customer service counter. "They must be here somewhere!" He moved quickly to the counter with Mary and the kids following close behind.

"Excuse me, there's supposed to be two dogs on the flight from Athens. Is it possible they haven't brought them in yet?"

19

"No," the man said. He glanced at the baggage area. "They would be coming through there, the same as the luggage. Are you sure they were loaded in Athens?"

Dietrich explained that they had come from Houston and then caught the first flight from Athens to Crete.

The man smiled. "Well, I'm sure they're all right. They probably missed the plane change in Athens." He glanced at Paul and Cindy. "Now please don't worry. I'll go call and find out for sure. And I promise they'll get the best of care, and be on the next flight."

"When is the next flight?" Mary asked.

"Tomorrow morning."

"Oh, my," Mary groaned. And the customer service man vanished around a corner. "I think I'll go with him," Dietrich said, glancing after the man, "just to be sure."

"Mr. Dietrich!" Mary called as he hurried off, "be sure to tell them they haven't had anything to eat or drink in almost twelve hours!"

"And that Tiffany has a condition!" Cindy added.

Mary sighed as they waited. "I guess we'd better gather up our bags."

"What if they don't find them?" Cindy asked as they moved back to the conveyor belt. "What if they're still in Houston?"

"I'm sure they must be in Athens, sweetheart. Don't worry. If they're not on the flight tomorrow we'll go back to Athens and get them."

"Anyway," Paul said trying to bolster Cindy's spirits, "they're probably having a big time at the Athens Airport. Benji knows how to take care of himself."

Twenty feet away, Stelios folded his newspaper, studied Mary, Paul, and Cindy for a quick moment, then moved casually from the ticket counter.

For the tenth time in the last hour, Benji's stomach growled and twisted, reminding him that he was hungry. Even a drink of water would help. The liquid Dietrich had held to his nose in Houston had made his mouth and throat feel dry as dust.

When he and Tiffany were unloaded from the plane, Benji expected to see Mary, Paul, and Cindy smiling at him, but all he had seen was another cart piled high with suitcases. Then they were towed off to a big room.

Their cages were side by side on a counter, and Benji could hear Tiffany's low whimper, but he had no way of seeing her. Perhaps that was just as well because Tiffany looked terrible. She had barked and whimpered until she was exhausted, and now her head rested between her paws as she gazed forlornly out at the stacks of bags and boxes.

Somewhere across the room a bell rang

. . . and continued ringing repeatedly. Peering between two stacks of suitcases, Benji saw a man in coveralls pick up the telephone.

The man nodded as he listened. Then he frowned and looked off into the room.

He left the receiver dangling and soon Benji saw him moving up the aisle, looking under counters and between suitcases. Benji came quickly to his feet and barked. Then his heart jumped. The man was looking directly at him, a big smile coming to his face.

The man held up a finger and said something Benji couldn't understand and then went back to the phone. Benji turned a quick circle in his cage, his tail wagging happily, and then he moaned and yelped at Tiffany.

She came to her feet and shook herself awake. Benji peered through the suitcases again and saw the man hang up the phone.

A minute later he was smiling and carrying a bowl of water as he came up the aisle. Benji barked excitedly. They were saved! The man grinned and said something to Tiffany. Then he set the water on the counter and said something in Greek to Benji.

Benji cocked his head, listening carefully. The man's voice sounded sympathetic, but Benji couldn't make any sense out of the words. Then the man frowned and pulled at the lock on Benji's cage. He muttered some more of the strange sounds and checked Tiffany's lock.

Benji's hopes suddenly plummeted as the

22

man moved off again, leaving the water just out-side Benji's cage.

Benji watched the man go past the tele-phone and disappear. Then he stared at the clear, cool liquid only six inches from his nose. Water had never looked quite so good to him. He could almost taste it. He moved his nose as close to the wire cage as he could and thrust his tongue through one of the holes.

It was hopeless—he was at least an inch short. He shifted, trying another hole, but he still couldn't reach. Benji sighed and stretched out, resting his chin on the bottom of the cage.

He turned his paw and frowned at it, see-ing nothing particularly unusual on the pad where Mr. Dietrich pressed the metal. There were some tiny marks; a little square of dots that was hardly visible. Benji licked his paw, tasting nothing. But the marks didn't come off. He licked at it again and then gave it up, resting his head on the bottom of the cage again.

Ten minutes passed and Benji finally closed his eyes. The man would come back, he told himself—he just had to be patient. He sighed heavily and waited another ten minutes. Then he heard a door swing open and got up instantly.

The man came up the aisle again, carrying a huge pair of clippers. Benji wagged his tail and barked. Tiffany also rose, panting heavily with anticipation.

The man laughed, talking to both of them

as he gripped the lock between the jaws of the clippers. With one movement he squeezed the handles together and the lock snapped and dropped to the counter. The man's face brightened and he laughed again as he reached for the clasp of the cage. Then he hesitated, muttering something as he looked off at the corner of the room.

The telephone was ringing again.

Benji gave the man a hopeful look, but it did no good. The man was moving away, shouting something at the telephone as he strode back down the aisle.

Benji watched the man lift the telephone receiver and start talking. He pushed his nose gently against the door of the cage. It moved!

Benji pushed again. Slowly he nudged the door open enough to squeeze his nose through, then his whole head. In his earnestness to open the door, he failed to notice the bowl of water now teetering precariously on the edge of the counter.

The crash of shattering pottery sounded like an explosion as the bowl hit the concrete floor.

What happened in the next two minutes happened so fast, Benji wasn't sure what to make of it. As quickly as the water dish shattered he heard a shout from the man at the telephone. And then the man was gone from the phone and striding up the aisle. Benji stood on the counter ready to dash. As the man approached, suddenly his foot slipped on the wet pavement and the cage and Benji and the man all tumbled to the floor in a tangled heap.

Benji scrambled to his feet and moved fast. The man was shouting angrily and then groaning as he got to his hands and knees. By then Benji was under a different counter twenty feet away, watching, not certain what to do next. Then a nearby door swung open and another man was peering in.

"I say, is this the baggage storage area?" he asked with a decidedly British accent. "Do you speak English?" the Britisher continued, not seeming to notice that the luggage man was still sprawled on the concrete floor.

"You see, I'm looking for a . . ."

Suddenly the luggage man shouted and gestured wildly toward Benji. Benji bolted for the door, running right between the Britisher's legs.

"My word—what was that?" he heard the man cry as Benji raced past a woman who shrieked, "Ronald, it's him! It's the dog!"

Benji didn't go far. After about fifty feet he skidded to a stop on the slippery floor and ducked quickly into an opening under a vacant ticket counter. Then he peered back around the corner.

The Britisher was sitting spread-legged on the floor, having been run down by the baggage man as he rushed after Benji. A woman ran toward him shouting, "It's the dog! Come on!" as she helped the Britisher to his feet.

She was a pretty woman with blond hair and dressed in a neat suit. But Benji decided not to take any chances as all three of them came racing toward him.

"Here, doggie! Don't be frightened, doggie!" the Englishman was calling out behind him.

Benji glanced back and then searched for an escape route. He saw several open doors, but they all looked suspicious. Then he saw one leading into a huge room with tables and a lot of people standing by opened luggage. He made a sharp turn and dashed around the left side of the room.

A man in a uniform turned sharply from the suitcases he was inspecting and shouted something, but Benji kept moving.

The baggage man raced through the door followed by the English couple. They circled around behind Benji. The Englishman smiled and said something to the man in uniform, looking off toward Benji.

"Come on, doggie!" the Englishman shouted.

When he reached the far side of the room Benji stopped and waited, catching his breath for a minute. There appeared to be no good escape route from the room. Then, with the three pursuers almost upon him, he barreled straight

26

across the middle of the room and out the door they had come in.

"Blast!" shouted the Englishman.

Benji glanced around some more as he trotted through the crowded lobby.

"Would you catch my little dog, please?" pleaded the Englishwoman, looking anxiously for help. Her voice sounded sweet and innocent, as if she were some little girl in distress trying to get her pet back.

Benji picked up a little speed and quickly spotted a narrow door standing half open. It was risky, but Benji decided he'd better take the chance.

Behind the door a narrow corridor ran for a hundred feet and then turned. If there was a closed door at the other end, he was going to be in big trouble. He moved faster, trying desperately to outrun the approaching footsteps behind him. Then as he turned the corner his heart jumped. Daylight! And lots of wide-open space.

Eight or ten huge jet airplanes were standing just outside the building, some of them with their engines screeching and whining. There were also a lot of men in coveralls, and three or four trucks crossing the area. Benji took it in with a glance and darted along under the first airplane, heading up the line toward the end of the building. A man shouted, but Benji paid no attention.

A man in a uniform stopped the English couple and was motioning them back toward the corridor. But the baggage man was still coming. Benji watched, catching his breath for a minute, not too worried about the one man catching him in all that open space. The English couple looked upset as the uniformed man shooed them back into the corridor. And the baggage man was puffing hard.

In the other direction, at the far end of the terminal building, a high iron fence ran along the side of the airport runway. But the bars of the fence were wide enough for Benji to easily squeeze through. He threw a final glance at the baggage man and darted across the runway, eased his way through the fence, and disappeared into the traffic beyond.

III

Benji had followed the traffic into downtown Athens, and he had never been in such a crowded place. The sidewalk was a moving tangle of legs and tramping feet, making it impossible to walk in a straight line. He trotted into the gutter now and then before he could find a few inches to slip back into the crowd.

The noise was even worse. Everybody in a car seemed to honk constantly, and in front of every store and shop people were laughing and talking and shouting at each other with their hands and arms waving in all directions. Like the man in the baggage room, their words sounded strange.

He had tried to find some food in a couple of trash cans. The first one had nothing but paper and dirt and splintered pieces of wood, and somebody shooed him out of it the second before he had a chance to get to the bottom of it. Then he had seen a bunch of people sitting at tables next to the sidewalk and his hopes had lifted a little. Most of them only had cups in front of them, or they were sipping some colored liquid out of little glasses. But he had moved among the tables until he sniffed something good, and then he sat down, his tail wagging frantically. The man had reached over and patted his head, and then the woman was smiling and taking something from her plate. But then another man was yelling from inside, rushing out at him and flapping his apron. Benji had ducked around to the other side of the table close to the woman, but the man with the apron followed him, his voice harsh and threatening. Benji knew he wasn't wanted. He hung his head and moved on.

The terrible part was all the water he saw on those tables next to the sidewalk. He had passed five or six such places, and almost every one had glasses and pitchers of water all over the place, and he had seen one of the waiters emptying glasses into the dirt under a potted plant. He stopped briefly, panting up at the man, hoping for just a few drops. But the man looked right past him, staring off at something across the street, and then returning to the café with the empty glasses.

Benji finally stopped walking. He climbed up onto a large windowsill which ran in front of a store window filled with toys. In both directions there were more buildings and more traffic and more people scurrying along the sidewalk. He looked around for a minute and finally dropped his chin in exhaustion. Back home in

Silver Creek, he had always known where to find a scrap of food or a cool drink of water. But here, wherever "here" was, he only knew that he was hungry and thirsty and suddenly very lonely.

Suddenly Benji snapped to attention, his eyes riveted on a young girl with blond hair who was getting out of a taxi. An older lady also emerged and took the younger girl by the arm. Benji barked loudly, leaped onto the sidewalk, and raced frantically down the street, determined not to lose them. He scurried past pedestrians, twisting around legs and jumping over feet. He skidded to a stop, as his last bark died in his throat.

It was not Cindy. The girl was staring down at him, blinking and backing away. The older lady standing next to her yelled at Benji and waved her arms for him to get away. Benji couldn't understand any of her words, but the meaning was clear. He turned and moved dejectedly on down the street.

It came suddenly, and Benji was so surprised he couldn't believe it for a minute. He had turned a corner and walked slowly along with pedestrians for another block, and then they had all stopped to wait for a traffic light. When he looked up, there it was across the street—a huge fountain with plumes of water shooting high in the air and dropping into a big pond. Benji blinked, then blinked again. His dry tongue quivered. It was the most beautiful thing he had ever seen.

The light changed and he moved along with the crowd, making sure no cars were turning the corner into them. When he finally reached the curb on the other side he broke into a full run, crossing the wide strip of concrete, then the grass, then he leaped up on the ledge at the side of the pond. He took a couple of steps, balancing himself, and then he was drinking, lapping greedily at the cool, delicious liquid.

It was the best water Benji had ever tasted. Even better than the water he and Tiffany used to share from the old birdbath in the Silver Creek park. Benji reached to lap up some more, but before his tongue could reach the water, he suddenly found himself airborne.

The two strong hands which had interrupted him belonged to a policeman who dropped him back down onto the sidewalk. The policeman spoke sternly to Benji and shook his finger in Benji's confused face. Benji took one long last look at the huge fountain. He'd only wanted a drink.

Benji moped along, dodging feet, circling around in the gutter to pass the more crowded spots. His stomach ached with hunger. He thought of Bill's café back in Silver Creek where he could always manage a handout, and he remembered his favorite trash can in the park. He had no idea where he was, but surely they must have trash cans. At the corner he turned up a narrower street and ducked into the alley that he knew must run behind the many cafés.

A hundred feet into the alley, Benji pulled up short. A huge truck had turned into the other end of the alley and seemed to be coming at full speed, its motor roaring and gears clashing, and it filled the whole width of space between the buildings. Benji edged to the side, but the truck's big tires were scraping along only inches from the brick wall. He backed away a couple steps, uncertain what to do. Then a deafening blast suddenly sounded through the narrow alley, and Benji was running, charging out of the alley as if he had been shot from a cannon.

He didn't stop or even slow down when he reached the street but sped across the bigger boulevard. With the sound of the truck's horn still ringing in his ears, he headed for the hills he had seen behind the city. For the time being, he had seen enough of downtown Athens.

He was dashing across weedy fields of what appeared to be a collection of very old stones and statues before he finally slowed down a little and took his bearings.

On the hill above him there were a lot of old buildings that looked as if they had been shaken to the ground by a big earthquake. A few columns were still standing, but for the most part they looked like piles of rubble, with a lot of statues and carved slabs of marble lying around. Benji finally stopped and caught his breath while he took another look at the city below.

He was no longer so certain now about getting something to eat. This place was a lot bigger than Silver Creek, and maybe the place was so big and had so many people there just weren't any scraps left over for dogs. For a minute Benji wondered if he would ever find Mary, Paul, and Cindy. Maybe he would end up starving to death far from home.

He sighed wearily and glanced around. It was possible, he supposed, that there might be something to eat in these fields.

He finally moved on, sniffing at a few of the statues and fallen slabs of marble. They smelled old. He climbed up some fallen rocks and went over a wall, suddenly finding himself in a graveyard. That too smelled old, and some of the gravestones were so worn that the lettering was almost invisible. Benji gave them a couple of sniffs and trotted along, working his way toward the higher ground at the back. Then he suddenly stopped, sniffing the air.

Did he smell meat? It seemed like it, and the smell came from directly ahead. But it was hard to believe that there could be anything to eat in a place like this. He sniffed again and trotted on, following the scent. Then he came to an abrupt halt, his heart leaping to his throat.

There was food—a big, juicy bone about a foot and a half long, with ragged chunks of delicious-looking meat hanging from all sides of it. There was also a pair of jaws working on it, and attached to the jaws was the biggest dog Benji had ever seen in his life.

Benji was only ten feet away, and surely the animal had noticed him. But he didn't seem to be paying any attention—or at least he wasn't worried about it. He was lying in a kind of nook, with stone walls on both sides of him, and another wall against the hillside behind. One of his huge paws was resting over the bone and his eyes were half closed, not paying any attention to much of anything as he gnawed and chomped away.

Benji would have settled for one tiny corner of the bone, or even one of the good-sized chunks of meat hanging from all sides of it. But he had very little experience with unfriendly dogs. If this dog proved to be unfriendly, he could probably break half of Benji's bones with one bite.

Benji glanced to the sides and to the top of the wall behind the dog. It might be safe up there. He took one more look at the bone and licked his chops. Then, keeping a wary eye on the big dog, he trotted off to the side and scampered up the hill.

He was ten or twelve feet above the animal when he reached the top of the wall behind the nook. He stood looking down at him for a minute and then gave a friendly woof and wagged his tail as if to say "Hello there." Then he wagged his tail, waiting for the dog to glance up.

Could he be deaf? More likely he just didn't care to waste his time with Benji. But what Benji lacked in size, he made up for in persistence. He tried again, making his woof a little louder this time.

There was still no answer, or any indication that the animal had heard him. Benji watched for a couple of more minutes and finally moved to the edge of the wall. From there he bounded down to a ledge only three or four feet above the other dog. He barked again.

He might as well have been talking to the wall. There was no question about it—the dog was not friendly. On the other hand, he didn't appear to be mean or vicious either. So what should he do now? The dog certainly wouldn't miss one or two little scraps from his bone. But Benji could hardly jump down there and just grab them. If the big dog knew how hungry he was, and that it was a matter of life and death, would he be more cooperative? Benji glanced restlessly at the top of the wall and back to the dog. He would make one more try, he decided, and moving to the front of the ledge, he jumped down beside the dog, landing as softly as he could. Then he froze, holding his breath for a minute.

The dog was looking at him, his huge head twisted, his jaws dripping saliva, staring at Benji with a faint frown on his face. From the look the dog was giving him, Benji might have been an ant or a water bug, and he was wondering if it was worth the bother to squash him under his paw. Benji opened his mouth and panted, hesitantly wagging his tail.

The big dog didn't appear to be impressed. Without so much as a grunt or a sniff, he returned his attention to the bone.

Benji snorted. If he weren't so hungry, he would have trotted off without a backward glance. But this close the bone smelled twice as good, and his stomach was gurgling and grumbling so loud he couldn't believe the big dog didn't hear it. Benji moved cautiously forward and dropped to his belly, inching alongside the dog's huge shoulder and then to within licking distance of the bone. For a full minute he lay there, watching, listening to the rough scraping of teeth and the hissing and snorting of the big animal's breathing. Finally he stretched out as far as he could reach and gingerly touched a morsel of meat with his tongue.

The bone was gone in the same instant. Without giving Benji a glance the big dog clamped his jaws over it, pulled himself up and turned completely around, plopping his tail right into Benji's face.

It was really very rude and Benji still didn't understand as he trotted back to town. After all, he would have never hesitated a minute to share his food with a stranger. In fact, that's exactly how he and Tiffany had met several years earlier. But that time she had been the one who was starving and Benji had shared his big, juicy bone with her. Dogs must be different over here.

On the way back, Benji kept to the narrower streets, making a quick check of trash cans, pausing only briefly at a couple of doors where there was the smell of food.

There was a strong scent coming from somewhere in the town and he let his nose be his guide, moving deeper into the narrow streets of the city. The scent was growing stronger and suddenly there it was.

He had never seen anything like it back home. In Silver Creek all the markets were inside of buildings, with hissing glass doors and signs and lights. But standing before him now was a whole block full of small open booths, every one of them displaying some kind of food. There were fresh fruits and vegetables and candies and breads and cakes and cookies. In other booths there were things in boxes and cans, while others were stacked high with fish. The smells were incredible, and Benji sat down and licked his chops as he looked the place over. From where he was sitting he could see three meat booths, every one of them packed with all kinds of delicious-looking chunks of meat. Meat was hanging from hooks and resting on counters and packed on shelves and some of the pieces were absolutely huge.

Benji's gaze finally settled on the closest booth. A customer was standing in front of it holding a long string of sausages, waving it around as he talked to the man behind the counter. It looked as if they were having an argument of some kind. But the sausages looked delicious, and Benji couldn't keep his eyes off them. He moved closer, making a broad circle through the crowd, and his eyes suddenly spotted some juicy-looking scraps beneath the counter.

He glanced at the arguing men and then carefully slipped under the counter and proceeded to help himself, completely ignoring the argument, which was growing steadily in both volume and intensity.

The customer seemed to underline each loud complaint with a wild gesture which appeared all the more dramatic because of the long string of sausages held tightly in his fist.

Benji suddenly looked up. The irate customer had accidentally dropped one end of the sausage string and it was now dangling right in front of Benji's face. A veritable feast. His heart was in his throat as he watched the sausages swing back and forth. Should he or shouldn't he? Of course he shouldn't but he was rapidly getting to the point where he couldn't help himself.

As the customer pounded the table top, the long string of sausages once again began to rotate slowly in front of Benji. He couldn't resist a sniff. They must be delicious! Benji glanced up at the customer, still embroiled in the heated conversation. Benji's stomach ached and his mouth watered. The temptation was just too great.

Like a flash, Benji leaped forward, snatched the sausages, and took off at full speed, the wind tearing past his face. Behind him, he heard an angry cry. Then a second and a third man were shouting and suddenly people in front of him were turning and looking as he sped by. The sausages were bounding along behind him, sometimes flying over his head and whipping back, but he didn't break his stride. He was out on a sidewalk making a sharp turn, scooting between the legs of a woman carrying a basket, then bounding off down a long sidewalk. The woman screamed and Benji heard the basket crash to the ground.

If he had looked back, he would have seen a very curious sight. The customer and the meat man were standing in the middle of the street laughing uproariously. It suddenly seemed quite humorous that a little dog like Benji could throw an entire market into such an uproar. In fact, the more they thought about it, the funnier it seemed. Soon, they were both bent over double with laughter and curious pedestrians were casting puzzled glances their way.

Suddenly a small sports car screeched to a halt right behind them. The driver looked off down the street, trying to spot Benji among the crowd.

"I'm almost positive it was him," he said. His companion insisted that they must continue looking. It was the British couple who had so recently chased him through the airport.

The big brown dog was in the same spot, still facing the wall and chewing on the same bone as when Benji had left him. Benji trotted up the slope and made himself comfortable. Then he bit casually into the first sausage as if it was just one more ordinary meal.

After a minute or so he heard the other dog quit gnawing on the bone and sniff the air. Then he saw the big head turn and the eyes glance from the sausages to himself. Benji paid no attention. He glanced off at the scenery while he chewed, and then he bit into his second sausage.

The big dog finally rose. The huge body came up and the big head and dripping jowls were towering over Benji for a moment as the animal turned and sat down, staring at the sausages now. Benji chewed for a few more seconds and then glanced up indifferently as if noticing the dog for the first time.

There seemed to be a slight frown on the dog's face as he stretched out again and stared. Benji chewed a little longer and finally gave

43

the animal a look of mild surprise as if suddenly realizing his friend might be interested in a bit of sausage to go along with his bone.

Benji didn't hesitate. He was a gracious, friendly, and generous dog, and unlike some others he had met, the last thing he would consider would be to hog all of the food for himself. As if it were the most ordinary thing in the world, he picked up the other end of the sausage string and dropped it on the ground very near the other dog.

The big animal stared at him for a minute as if he couldn't quite believe it and Benji smiled to himself as he went back to his end of the sausage string and resumed eating.

IV

The sun was shining brilliantly when Benji finally awakened the next morning. He stirred uneasily, his paw twitching; he was having vague dreams about Mr. Dietrich. Then he was whimpering, and suddenly he was awake, blinking across the graveyard and the ruins at the sun-drenched city of Athens.

He yawned, stretching his mouth wide, and looked around for his friend. There was no one in sight. The big brown dog had slept at the back of the nook, taking up almost the entire width between the two side walls, and Benji had curled up near his head. But now he was alone.

Benji moved out to the edge of the nook where he could see into the graveyard and on the hill behind. Other than some birds chirping and a rooster crowing somewhere in the distance, there was nobody around. He stretched his back legs and dug at a flea just behind his ear. Then he scampered up to the top of the hill to look off toward the city again and his eyes suddenly brightened.

Quite a distance away and moving up some

steps that led into the city, his big brown dog friend was loping along with the air of somebody just starting out on his day's business.

Benji moved fast, running down through the graveyard and over the wall into the ruins. He scampered through the statues and marble slabs and then up the steps where he had last seen the big dog. When he reached the sidewalk he stopped and looked quickly around.

The big dog was nowhere in sight. Shopkeepers were opening up for the day, greeting each other across the street; people were getting on buses, while others read newspapers as they walked along. Benji looked in every direction before he finally gave it up.

He was a little disappointed. He had hoped his new friend would show him around, but the big dog probably had more pressing affairs to take care of. Benji took one last look, then trotted off, glancing at faces and giving a quick check to side streets as he started his search.

There weren't many people sitting in the sidewalk cafés that hour, and the loitering waiters all gave him cold looks. So Benji moved on, heading down to the open marketplace where he had found the sausages.

Things seemed to be busier than ever. Truckloads of food were being unloaded and taken to the booths, and customers with net bags were crowding through the aisles between the stalls. Benji kept his distance for a few minutes studying the situation.

The proprietor of the meat booth with the sausages was out in front of his stall sweeping a pile of trash out of the aisle. Benji watched him and then moved toward one of the other meat booths, keeping an eye on the man with the broom. Halfway there, the man looked up and Benji trotted quickly to a position behind a stack of crated lettuce. When he peered out the man was sweeping again. Benji gave him a final glance and moved forward, enjoying the mouth-watering aromas.

The shout from behind him came like a bolt of lightning, and Benji's heart almost leaped from his chest. All Benji saw was a quick glimpse of the man from the sausage booth moving quickly toward him. The man had a grin on his face and was waving something in his hand. For a split second Benji thought it looked like a huge meaty bone, but he wasn't about to risk a closer look.

"Ela! Ela!" the man called after him. Benji took off at full speed down the edge of the crowded aisle.

He heard the man scream again, but he didn't look back. He swerved in and out of feet and around packing crates. He slipped and skidded as he tried to turn and avoid a man carrying a huge basket on his shoulder. There was a yell and a crash and Benji was suddenly in a sea of fresh oranges and the man was sprawled on his belly. He shook his fist at Benji and yelled violently.

Benji raced under the booths and up another aisle, going between legs, or around them, or anyplace he could see daylight. He had an ominous feeling he was in big trouble this time, and his escape wasn't going to be so easy.

He heard more things crash to the ground behind him and more people joined the shouting. He skidded to a halt and reversed his direction again. Two men were coming at him, both crouched low to prevent his getting past. Then he faced another crowd, some of the people yelling at him and some reaching out as he tried to get by.

Benji turned under a booth and scampered out into what seemed like a clear escape route into the open plaza. Suddenly something flashed by in front of his face. He was stopped cold, twisting and tangled in a heavy net. He groped at it, turning and trying to run the other way, but the efforts only made things worse. He looked up.

Towering above him were two very tall policemen. One was wagging his finger at him, and the other was speaking very harshly. Benji hung his head for a minute and then gave the man a panting smile, hoping for a similar response. The man only frowned and didn't lift the net.

The two policemen didn't seem to understand or put much trust in the friendly barks and tail wagging Benji gave them. They kept him tightly closed in the net until a van showed up. Then a uniformed man transferred him to a cage in the back of the van and he was driven away. Ten minutes later a man looked closely at his collar and made some notes, and he was placed in a big cage with a dozen other dogs barking and yelping all around him.

A man came with a bowl of water and put it in the cage. Benji enjoyed the drink, and wished for a little food to go with it. He joined in the barking for a while. Then he gave it up and put his head on the ground, watching the door at the back of the building. Things looked bad, he reflected. Now he was going to find out what they did with homeless dogs in Greece.

Mary held the telephone receiver down for a moment and then picked it up and dialed for the tenth time in the last half hour. She groaned inwardly as the voice answered in Greek.

"Do you happen to speak English?" she asked, speaking slowly and distinctly.

There was a silence at the other end, then the halting voice said, "One minutes, if you pliss."

Less than half of the places she had called were able to find anyone who could speak to her in English, and she'd had to hang up not knowing if they had Benji or not.

"Maybe we just ought to get in a taxicab and ride around looking for him," Paul said now as Mary waited.

"You might be right, Paul. But there are

51

only three more dog pounds listed in the book. We can . . ."

She turned quickly back to the phone as she heard someone pick up the receiver at the other end.

"May I help you, madam? I speak English."

Mary breathed a sigh or relief. "Yes . . . that is, I hope you can help us. You see, we're American tourists, and we brought two dogs to Greece, and when we transferred flights to go to Crete one of the dogs . . ."

"Is the dog's name Benji, madam?"

Mary almost dropped the phone. *"Yes,"* she cried, "Do you have him there? Do you know where he is? Is he all right?"

"He's fine. He was brought in about twenty minutes ago."

Paul and Cindy were both hovering over her now, their eyes shining. "They've found him," Mary quickly told them.

"We'll be over to get him right away," she told the man. "Are you sure he's all right?"

"Quite sure, madam. Don't worry."

"Oh, thank you so much. I'll . . . oh, dear . . . we'll be right over. Goodbye. And thank you."

Benji watched indifferently as the man came out of the office and walked along between the cages. Then he jumped quickly to his

52

feet and wagged his tail as the man smiled at him and unfastened the clasp on his cage.

"Well, Benji, you're going home." Benji barked, jumped up excitedly, and turned a quick circle as he headed toward the office with the man. When the door was opened he bolted through and then skidded to a stop.

"Well, hello, Benji. How are you, old chap?"

Is was the English couple!

It was a pleasant-looking place with deep carpets and nice furniture. A stairway at the side seemed to lead up to a second floor and there was a kitchen off to the other side.

"Well, Benji," the man said, smiling down at him, "you seem to be quite a prize. I quite imagine you are the most valuable dog in all of Greece right now."

Benji gave the tall Britisher a puzzled look and began sniffing his way around the room.

"Come over here, Benji," the woman said from the couch. "Let's have a look at you."

Benji moved reluctantly to the couch and let the woman lift him to her lap. She scratched his back for a minute and then unfastened his collar.

"What on earth are you doing?" the man asked. He was across the room at a small bar, mixing drinks.

The woman squinted closely at Benji's col-

53

lar, then pulled a magnifying glass from a drawer. "I am looking, darling. Of course, it would help if I knew what I was looking for."

The man laughed. "Sometimes you surprise me, Elizabeth. As pretty as you are, I never suspected you might also be intelligent."

"Why, thank you, Ronald."

"Did you really take that as a compliment? In that case, I'll take it back." The man brought a drink to the woman and smiled. "However, I will grant that your suggestion to check the dog pounds was unusually brilliant."

"Hmph. And I hope you realize that I won't be the only one to think of it." She put Benji's collar back on. "And with all the interest in Benji here, I suspect we'll soon be having visitors."

"I'm sure of it. It appears that our hideaway scientist has suddenly become a very important man."

"And very valuable." The woman smiled as she took a sip of her drink. "Let's just hope we get our share of the profits."

Benji felt his ear being lifted. The woman was peering into it was a magnifying glass, pulling the ear from one side to the other.

"Do you see anything?"

"Not a thing." Benji felt the ear drop and the woman frowned at him. "Benji, why can't you talk and give us a hint? You didn't swallow it, did you?"

Benji put his head down on her lap and looked off at the man. He still couldn't figure out if the two of them were friends. By the way they acted, they didn't seem to intend him any harm.

Benji closed his eyes, enjoying the back rub, then he jerked his head up as the doorbell suddenly rang.

The man smiled faintly and glanced at the door. "I say, it appears to be starting already." He put his drink on the table and quickly picked up Benji. "I'll take Mr. Popular upstairs and we'll make a few photographs. All right, Benji?" He glanced at the woman as he headed for the stairs. "Give me a moment to prepare, darling. Then get rid of them."

Benji glanced at the door, but it was quickly out of sight as they went up the stairs and into a bedroom. The man shut the door and put Benji down, hurrying off to a dresser. He brought out a fancy-looking camera and studied it for a minute. Then he crossed to a couch under a window. He pushed the window open wide and leaned out, the camera lifted to his eye.

"I'm sorry, they must be mistaken," the woman's voice echoed clearly up from the porch below. "We haven't been to the dog pound, and we don't have a dog."

"This is your name and address, isn't it?" a man's voice questioned. "Maybe your husband picked up the dog." The voice was deep and a

55

little harsh. Benji didn't recognize it at all.

"No, I'm afraid that is impossible," the woman answered. "You see, my husband hates dogs."

Ronald smiled when he heard that. "Don't you believe it, Benji," he said softly. "Some of my best friends are dogs."

Benji stared at the man and cocked his head, listening to the voices downstairs again.

"I see," the man at the door was saying. "Well, thank you very much."

The door clicked shut and Benji moved across the room and jumped up on the couch next to the Englishman.

"Now," the man said, squinting into his camera, "just turn around, please, so I can have a look at your face."

Out the window, Benji could see the man as he walked down the steps and opened the door of a station wagon. He was wearing an Olympic Airways uniform, and his car had an airline insignia on the door.

The man glanced back at the apartment house and the camera clicked again.

"Ahhh," the Englishman said, "thank you very much." It was a perfect picture. The man was a thick-necked Greek with cold dark eyes. It was Stelios.

"What do you think?" said the Englishman, dropping back on the couch. "Was the gentleman really from Olympic Airways?" He smiled and put a cover over the lens of the camera. "I wouldn't want to bet on it. But we have him nicely recorded. That should be worth something."

The man put the camera on the dresser and Benji trotted alongside as he went to the door.

"No, no. I'm afraid you'll have to stay here, Benji." The man smiled and opened the door only wide enough to squeeze through.

Benji watched it shut and then scratched at the bottom and barked. Why did he have to stay in the room? He scratched again and gave a loud bark.

The door opened, but only a few inches, with the man blocking Benji's escape. "Here, here," he said, "we'll have none of that."

Benji barked again.

"No," the man said. He reached down, turned him around, and gave him a whack on the rear. "Now you might just as well make yourself comfortable, because this is going to be your home for a while."

Benji watched the door close again.

Locked in the room, there was nothing he could do. Until somebody opened the door, or took him out for a walk, he might as well make the best of it. He glanced, sniffed a couple of things and finally jumped back on the couch. He found a soft pillow in the corner and curled up, gazing emptily down at the carpet. He finally sighed and closed his eyes.

As he drifted off to sleep he heard a car door slam, and moments later the doorbell rang.

"Yes?" the Englishwoman's voice said.

"How do you do?" It was a woman's voice. "I'm here about the dog you picked up at the pound today."

Benji's eyes popped open. Was he dreaming, or had he heard a familiar voice? No, he wasn't dreaming. It was Mary. Or at least it sounded like Mary. He jumped onto the windowsill and listened closely.

"I'm sorry," the Englishwoman was saying irritably. "Somebody seems to have made a stupid mistake, and I wish whoever it was would correct it."

Benji stretched out the window, straining to see below, but the porch roof and an awning made it impossible to see the apartment door.

"You're the second person to ask about this," the Englishwoman said, "but we do not have a dog. We have never had a dog, and we did not pick up a dog at the pound today."

Benji looked toward the street where a huge truck was making a loud racket as it climbed slowly up the hill. He could hardly hear the voices anymore.

". . . and my husband hates dogs, so you see . . ."

Benji jumped from the couch and ran to the door, scratching at it again. He barked a few times, but the noise of the truck was growing so loud he was certain no one could hear him. He raced back to the couch and bounded up with his front paws on the windowsill. Then his heart jumped and he almost tumbled out the

FOR THE LOVE OF BENJI

The New Adventure of America's *Most Huggable Hero*

The plotters meet.

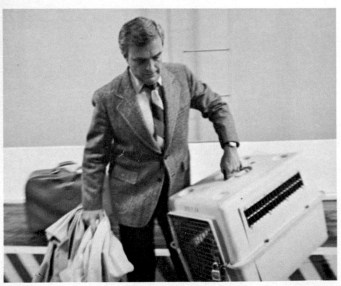

Chandler Dietrich makes his move.

Benji escapes.

Lost in Athens.

Looking for lunch.

Food at last!

The getaway.

Trapped!

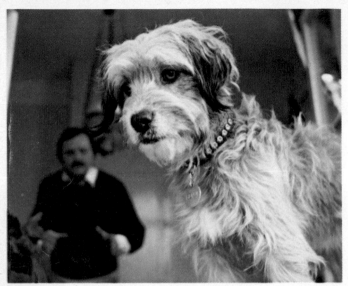

Looking for a way out.

Jumping to safety.

Chandler is close behind.

He captures Benji...

...But not for long.

Protected by a friend.

Reunited with the family...

But Chandler returns...

...And Tiffany.

...And gets Benji again.

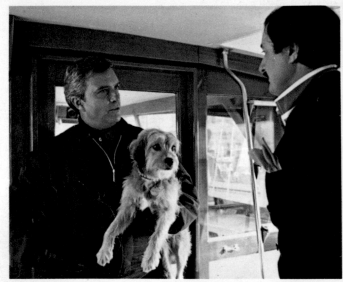

Benji waits for a chance to escape.

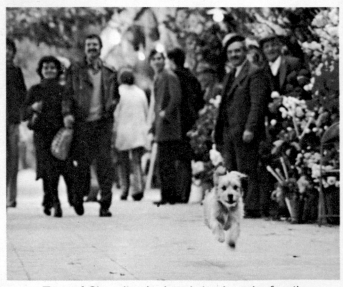

Free of Chandler, he heads back to the family.

Why is their hotel surrounded by police?

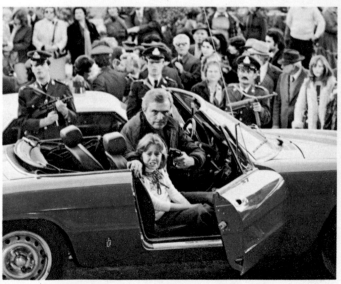

Chandler is holding Cindy hostage...

...While Mary and Paul look on anxiously.

It's a dangerous moment when
Benji comes to the rescue.

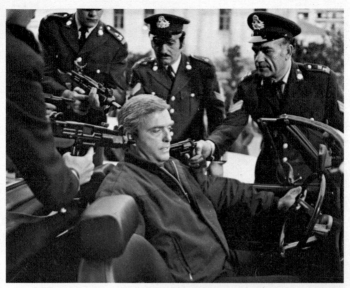

Chandler's dognapping days are over.

Now everyone can enjoy their vacation in
Greece—including the new father.

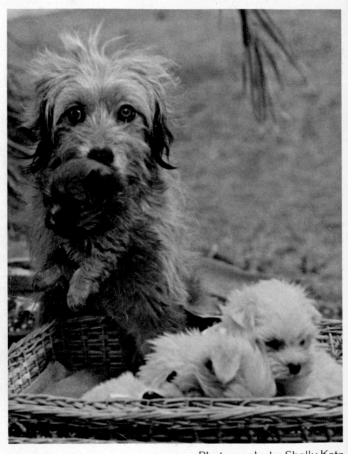

Photographs by Shelly Katz

window as he barked as loud and urgently as he could.

It was Mary! She was walking across the street to a taxi and the driver was holding the door open for her. Benji yelped frantically, his back feet on top of the couch and his front on the windowsill.

He saw the cab door shut and then the big truck was passing, the roar of its big diesel motor drowning out every other sound. But Benji continued barking, leaning far out the window as the taxi pulled out a little and the driver waited for the truck to go by. He barked and barked, putting all the urgency and desperation he could into his voice.

"Benji!" a voice behind him cried.

Benji looked back, almost losing his balance as he turned. Ronald, the Englishman, was just inside the door, moving toward him. He smiled uneasily and came closer. "Now, Benji, just take it easy."

Benji looked out at the street again. The taxi was pulling away from the curb, starting to move slowly up the hill. Benji barked again and again, hoping by some miracle Mary might look out the back window.

"Don't be afraid, Benji," the man behind him said as he came closer, "I'll get you down. Just don't move. That's a good boy."

Benji looked from the cab to the man and back at the cab again. It was halfway to the corner now and behind him the man was getting close. He looked down at the sloped awning eight feet below and hesitated.

"Benji!" the man cried out and lunged for him. Benji jumped.

The canvas awning sagged enough that it was like a net breaking his fall. But the slope was steep and Benji skidded and tumbled, unable to get his footing after he hit. Then he was over the edge, his legs groping at empty air for a minute before he crashed into a heavy shrub.

"Benji!" the Englishman shouted from the window, but Benji didn't bother looking back. He squirmed out of the shrub and was running at full speed when he hit the ground and dashed into the street.

Suddenly, there was a loud screech of tires and Benji swerved, just missing the front wheel of a small red sports car being driven recklessly by a distinguished-looking man in a dark suit. It was Chandler Dietrich. Benji bolted past the car and kept going, his legs flying and his feet hardly touching the pavement as he raced for the corner at the top of the hill.

Dietrich immediately threw the car into reverse, the gears grinding loudly. Before he could whip the car around he found himself in the middle of three other cars, all trying to go in the other direction. He groaned and beat his fist against the dash.

When Benji rounded the corner he could see the taxi picking up speed a block ahead of him. He ran faster, his eyes fixed on the back of the car, his heart pounding wildly.

The taxi was growing smaller and smaller, finally disappearing in the traffic as it sailed along the boulevard. Benji slowed to a trot and finally stopped.

He gazed forlornly at the street for a while and then moved to the sidewalk. He sat down and panted, watching the pedestrians go by.

At the end of the alley Benji stopped and surveyed the big cross street. Then he frowned, staring at a taxi waiting for a signal. He could just see the head of someone in the back seat. Could it be Mary? He moved quickly along the sidewalk. He ducked between two parked cars and got up on his hind legs, trying desperately to see into the back seat of the taxi.

The woman in the taxi looked at him through the window and blinked. It was not Mary. The cab moved on, pulling away with the rest of the traffic.

Benji saw a great deal of Athens that he hadn't seen before. There were several large parks in front of huge buildings, and he picked up a few of the tidbits that people were feeding to pigeons. But the people didn't seem to like the idea of his scaring the birds and taking their food, so he trotted on, watching the taxis and the people walking along the streets.

He had just rounded a corner and was enjoying the smells of a huge outdoor flower shop when he almost ran squarely into the two policemen. They were standing by the curb quietly talking and laughing. Benji made a sharp turn and ducked behind a big flowerpot. He stayed there for five minutes before he finally crept out and headed the other way, moving cautiously. He was glancing back to make certain the two men weren't following him when he suddenly banged into another pair of legs. He froze for an instant as he looked up. The legs belonged to a third policeman.

The man smiled and said something to him and then reached down as if to pet him. But since Benji's recent experiences with policemen had been none too pleasant, he didn't take any chances. Before the policeman's hand was anywhere close, Benji ducked and took off at full speed, tearing around the corner and disappearing up the first alley he came to.

As Benji rounded the corner he saw, across the street, a huge building with hundreds of windows. In front of it, a constant flow of taxis kept loading and unloading people. Benji stopped and took a closer look as three people emerged from the taxi nearest the door.

It was them! Benji was sure of it this time. He had a clear glimpse of Cindy carrying Tiffany, and then Paul and Mary following her through the revolving doors.

Benji moved quickly through the parked cars and watched for a break in traffic. Then he bolted across and raced at full speed toward the hotel door.

He didn't notice the man leaning into the window of the cab giving something to the driver until the man turned toward the hotel entrance. Both Benji and the man came to an abrupt stop.

It was Dietrich.

The man glanced at the revolving door through which Mary, Paul, and Cindy had just disappeared. Then an ever-so-slight smile spread across his lips and he began moving toward Benji. Benji looked nervously at the revolving door, then back to Dietrich.

"Come on, Benji," he said. He bent forward a little, holding his hand out. "Come on, boy, I'm not going to hurt you."

Benji remembered his first experience with Chandler Dietrich and moved a few steps back glancing at the door again. He barked at the man, trying to show he was not interested in his friendship. But Dietrich kept coming, moving a little faster now. Benji turned and trotted four or five steps away and looked back. Then Dietrich lunged for him and Benji was at the corner and across the street in seconds.

Dietrich stopped short of the corner and stood staring at Benji, a thoughtful look on his face. He smiled faintly and moved back toward the hotel door.

Benji heard the clank of a garbage can being opened. He stopped and peered up a long dark alley.

A round-faced man wearing an apron was singing and emptying smaller buckets of garbage into the big can. Benji stood still, watch-

67

ing quietly. Then the man saw him. He smiled and said something that sounded friendly, but Benji didn't move.

The man put the lid back on the can. Then he knelt down and smiled again, this time holding his hand out as he spoke. Benji still didn't move, although the man's smile was reassuring. Benji's stomach was starting to twist and grumble again.

Finally, he began to move slowly, glancing behind him once or twice, ready to run if he had to. As Benji got closer, the man suddenly rose and took a step forward. Benji quickly turned and retreated, watching the man carefully.

The man seemed to understand. He squatted down and held his hand out again, showing Benji an open palm. His voice sounded sympathetic and he spoke quietly.

Benji still wasn't too sure. He tensed as the man rose again. This time the man opened the big garbage can and came out with a tasty looking scrap of meat. He laughed and squatted again, holding it out to Benji.

This was more like it. Benji wagged his tail and moved cautiously forward. He stopped a few inches short of the meat and sniffed it. Then he couldn't resist; he stepped forward and took it, gulping it down.

The man talked quietly as he patted Benji's head. Benji wagged his tail and then hesitated as the man rose and opened the screen door at the back of the building. But the smells coming from inside were so delicious that Benji gave in easily. He wagged his tail and moved inside, glancing cautiously around.

It was a big kitchen, apparently at the back of a restaurant. Benji relaxed a little and gave the man a panting smile as he watched him get a big bowl from a cupboard. The man laughed and talked and put a handful of meat scraps in the bowl. Then he filled another bowl with water and placed them both on the floor.

It seemed like the best meal Benji had ever had and when he finished the first bowl the man filled it up again. Then he had a good drink of water.

The man wasn't watching him anymore. He was standing at a big stove, pouring something from one huge pot into another and stirring the whole thing. Benji sniffed around the kitchen a little and finally settled down in a corner.

The man smiled at him a couple times, but made no move to turn Benji out. That was fine with Benji. For the present he wanted nothing more than a safe, warm place to catch up on his sleep, and it looked like he had found it. He took a last look around and settled his head comfortably on the floor, closing his eyes with a weary sigh.

When Benji appeared to be comfortably asleep, the restaurant owner smiled pleasantly at him and moved to the wall phone in the corner of the kitchen.

He said something Benji didn't understand, and hung up the phone and walked through the door to the restaurant.

Benji looked up sharply as he heard the door swing shut. He glanced around the kitchen assuring himself that he was alone, and closed his eyes again. He thought dreamily about Mary and Paul and Cindy and imagined himself sitting with them on a lazy afternoon in Silver Creek. Then Benji slept soundly.

Benji lifted his head and blinked around. He heard a loud snarl. He stared at the dirty window above his head and instantly jumped to his feet.

A huge, black, vicious-looking dog was looking straight at Benji, his pointed teeth snapping against the window. And behind him, squinting and shading his eyes, was Chandler Dietrich.

The screen door creaked open and clicked softly shut again and there was the rustle of footsteps.

"I know you're in here, Benji boy," Dietrich said softly.

Dietrich paused to let his eyes adjust to the dimly lit room. He looked down to the spot where Benji had been sitting, but there was only an empty bowl. "Come on, Benji. You don't want me to bring that Doberman in here, do you?"

Dietrich walked toward the cupboard. His

arm brushed against a broom and it clattered to the floor.

"Come on, Benji. Be a good boy."

He threw open the closet door and quickly slammed it shut. "Why are you afraid of me, Benji? I've never hurt you. Don't you want to see your friends again?"

He paused again. There was no sign of Benji. "Come on Benji. Here, Benji," the voice continued in its soft singsong.

Dietrich cast a puzzled look around the room, then knelt to open the last door of the cupboard.

"Come on, Ben—!"

Like a gunshot, Benji sprang forward, crashing into Dietrich's face and knocking him backward.

Dietrich let out a cry and was on his back as Benji scampered over his legs, going directly for the screen door. Benji lifted his front paws in mid-flight and the door sprang open; he plummeted through it.

If the Doberman had been expecting him, Benji probably wouldn't have had a chance to get by. The big black dog was tied to a post just outside the door, and when Benji came flying out his head brushed by just under the Doberman's chin. By the time the big black animal had recovered from the surprise, Benji was halfway down the alley and taking the corner at full speed.

Benji ran for three blocks before he finally slowed down and took a glance behind. He could see no one following him, but he kept moving anyway.

Whenever there was a break in traffic he crossed the street, and then crossed again, hoping to leave the vicious black dog behind him for good.

It was getting dark now, and Benji finally headed back toward the ruins. It had been a long day and he couldn't keep moving forever.

The place looked as dark and lonely as ever. Moving through the ruins he circled a few statues and took a roundabout route getting to the wall and going up through the graveyard.

His friend, the big brown dog, wasn't there. An old, well-chewed bone lay in the corner of the nook. Benji sniffed at it, and then just to make sure about things he climbed up on the hill behind the nook and looked over the graveyard and the ruins below. There seemed to be nobody around, particularly no giant black dogs.

Benji went back down to the nook and made himself comfortable, his eyes fixed absently on the graveyard below. He thought of little Tiffany and wished they had never left Silver Creek. He finally sighed and gazed dully across the graveyard for a few minutes. Then he was fast asleep.

Benji's eyes popped open, and he froze, not daring to move. He was certain he had heard something. He came cautiously to his feet, watching, scanning the ruins beyond the wall. All the dark shapes and shadows now looked ominous, like people and dogs and animals holding themselves still, waiting for him to look the other way.

The graveyard looked even more frightening. Benji hadn't thought much about it when he walked through there in the daylight. But now he was certain he could see thin shadows moving around and hovering over gravestones. He stared, moving his gaze slowly across the dark shapes. Then his heart leaped into his throat and he jumped to the side as a small rock clattered to the ground just behind him.

He froze in his tracks and looked up. High on the wall, the silhouette of a big dog was clearly outlined against the sky and he could see the pale glint of white teeth. Benji looked quickly around, searching for Dietrich, but he could see no other distinct shadows.

Benji backed slowly, almost tiptoeing into a corner of the nook, just under the ledge. More gravel suddenly poured down from above and he tightened himself closer against the wall, pulling his tail close to his side.

There was a heavy *thunk* on the ledge above him. Then he saw the shape land on the ground just beside him. His muscles went limp with relief.

It was his friend. The big brown dog was turning slowly around, looking things over, giving the old bone a sniff. Benji panted and barked softly, saying hello, and stretched out on his stomach.

The dog swung his head over and nudged Benji, giving his face a half lick. He circled a couple of times and made himself comfortable.

Then Benji went back to sleep feeling much more secure with his friend at his side.

VI

At dawn, Benji returned to the hotel and watched the entrance most of the morning. He stayed across the street for awhile, keeping out of sight behind lampposts and telephone poles. He saw no one who looked like Mary, Paul, or Cindy, and nobody brought Tiffany out for a walk.

He considered the idea of marching up to the revolving door and just trotting inside. But there was a uniformed doorman constantly moving back and forth helping people out of cabs and calling other cabs for people coming out of the hotel. He waited, hoping the man would leave for a while. When he finally did, the man who took his place looked meaner than the first one.

Benji finally crossed the street. A narrow stretch of grass with bushes behind it ran along the front of the hotel, and he could lie near the bushes, half hidden from most of the people walking by. He spent another hour there, taking time out only to trot four blocks down the street to a big fountain and have himself a drink. When he got back things looked the

77

same. He finally rose and trotted a little closer to the door, quickly dropping to the ground when the doorman looked in his direction.

He waited as the man opened the cab doors and whistled for empty cabs to stop. Then, staying low to the ground, he scooched up another few feet. The man glanced in his direction, but didn't seem particularly interested.

Benji watched as a taxi with five people and a lot of suitcases stopped. The doorman opened the cab doors and then whistled for some bellhops to help with the luggage. They were all gathered around as the doorman shouted instructions. Benji trotted casually forward.

An empty section of the revolving door was coming slowly around. Benji watched carefully as a woman and two men pushed their way through the door, sending it into a rapid spin. They made it look so simple. Benji cocked his head, made one false start, then headed straight for the door.

"*Aaiieee!*" someone shouted behind him. Benji skidded to a stop.

The doorman frowned, stomped his foot loudly against the marble pavement, and started toward Benji.

Benji trotted a few steps and looked back. But the man was still watching him. He shouted again, suddenly moving quickly forward. Benji turned and ran.

As Benji sniffed at the screen door and peered inside the kitchen seemed to be empty. He barked and waited, then barked again. No one came.

The door was slightly ajar and Benji studied it for a minute. He scratched at it, but it didn't budge. He crawled close to it on his stomach, working at it with his nose. It finally opened enough to get a paw inside, and he squeezed through.

The cupboards were all closed again and three or four big pots were simmering on the stove. Benji tried the swinging door, scratching at it, then rising and pushing with all his weight. It opened just enough for Benji to squeeze through.

The inside part of the restaurant was also empty. The tables were all set with napkins and silver, but there were no customers. Benji trotted across the room and stopped in the open doorway to look around. There were tables everywhere . . . on the sidewalks, even *in* the street itself. But they were all empty. All except one across the street.

Benji's tail started wagging. It was his friend with the apron who had fed him the day before. He was talking to a second man, a large Greek with black hair and cold dark eyes. Benji didn't seem to remember him, maybe because the last time he had seen him, the man had been in an airlines uniform. It was Stelios.

Benji watched for a break in traffic, then

trotted across to the other curb, wagging his tail as he approached the table.

They didn't see him. The man with the apron was leaning across the table, talking in a low voice. The dark Greek was nodding and gazing off in the other direction, his eyes half closed. Benji sat down and barked.

Suddenly he was off the ground, his bark choked off by the tight grip around his chest.

It was Dietrich again, and he was acting most unfriendly. Benji squirmed and yelped, trying to push and scratch with his paws, but the man was squeezing the breath out of him.

"Don't get up, gentlemen," Dietrich said, "just stay put."

The two men at the table stared at Dietrich, who was pointing a black pistol at them. Stelios looked tense, his hands resting near the edge of the table as if he was ready to jump. "You know your identity is no longer a secret," Stelios said coldly. "Give me the dog and I'll try to see that you come out of this alive."

"That is very considerate of you," Dietrich answered, "but I'll take care of that myself." He was edging toward the street now, glancing back at the traffic.

"You're going to be very sorry, my friend!"

There were no cars coming now and Dietrich laughed. "Good day, gentlemen." And he backed across the street with Benji. When he reached the curb he turned and ran into the café.

Before he reached the kitchen door he turned sharply between the tables and ducked behind a curtained partition that hid a row of coffeepots. Then Benji felt the man's hand suddenly grip his mouth, clamping it shut.

Through the partition Benji could see the other two men come jogging across the street. They separated as they reached the curb. The man with the apron disappeared around the side of the building as Stelios moved cautiously to the door and peered in. Benji felt Dietrich's hand tighten painfully around his throat.

Benji watched, struggling to get some air. Stelios came quickly through the door, glancing around the empty tables. As he crossed to the kitchen door Dietrich squeezed himself and Benji tight around the wall. Stelios didn't look around. He stood at the kitchen door for a minute, listening. Then he pushed it open and disappeared. In the alley, Benji heard a noise that caused him to freeze; it was the vicious barking of Dietrich's huge dog.

Benji heard a chuckle from Dietrich as he headed for the door. His hand was still tight around Benji's nose. When they were out on the sidewalk and striding up the street, Benji struggled again, trying to get air.

"Sorry, Benji," Dietrich said and eased his grip a little. "Just a bit farther."

Dietrich walked a little slower now, trying not to attract attention. He turned a corner and headed toward the end of the alley.

Dietrich's red sports car was parked at a nearby curb. He shifted Benji to the other arm and groped in his pocket for the keys. Suddenly, there was a low snarling sound from behind him and Dietrich spun around. The huge black Doberman was galloping toward him at a terrifying speed, his eyes fixed on Benji.

"No, it's OK!" shouted Dietrich.

The angry red eyes and the glistening teeth kept coming. Benji struggled, trying to spring away from Dietrich.

"Stay!" Dietrich commanded. There was a note of fear in his voice as he backed away, edging along the side of the car. *"Stay!"* he shouted again.

The dog ignored him. His gaze was locked on Benji and he came even faster, then he leaped through the air. Benji struggled free as Dietrich threw up his arms to protect his face and they all crashed down onto the sidewalk.

Dietrich landed on his back and the Doberman skidded past, his legs splayed out in all directions. Benji tumbled over, miraculously landing on his feet and in a flash he was running at full speed back down the alley.

Benji had a head start but he knew he was in great danger. He threw a quick glance behind him as he rounded the first corner. The Doberman was coming, galloping along the parked cars and beginning to pick up speed. Benji crossed another street and headed into an alley.

He could hear the yelps and snarls coming closer, and as he rounded the next corner Benji skidded, almost losing his footing as he made a second sharp turn down three steps which led to a closed door. He quickly fell against the door, hiding himself below the narrow street.

A second later the Doberman flashed by. Benji leaped back to the street level and took off in the opposite direction.

He had picked up another head start but he knew it wouldn't last long. Benji sped on, beginning to feel a little tired. He eased his pace a notch, panting, trying to recover some breath. Then he suddenly slid to a stop as he passed a high board fence.

There was a small hole at the bottom of the fence. He turned and saw the Doberman bearing down on him. He lowered his head and in a flash was through the hole and under the fence.

The Doberman's snout came through the hole. The big animal snarled and bared his teeth and shoved his head through the hole. But that was as far as he could get. He backed away and the sharp teeth sank into the wood.

Benji paused at the end of the alley to glance back over his shoulder. He saw the Doberman's head and front paws appear at the top of the fence. He could hear the animal scratching desperately with the claws of his back feet and then he dropped from sight again. Benji stared as the Doberman tried again, straining every muscle in his black, sleek body. This time he made it.

Benji ran as fast as his tired legs would carry him through the ruins and finally paused at the top of the hill and looked back. His heart sank as he saw the big Doberman bounding down the steps into the ruins.

He took a different route through the cemetery, climbing the hill on the side of his hideout. When he reached the top of the wall, just above the nook, he peered down hoping to see his old friend stretched out on the ground.

The nook was empty. And down in the cemetery the Doberman was coming, following the same route Benji had taken. Benji was panting, ready to collapse from exhaustion. He watched the big animal for a minute; then he jumped down to the ledge and dropped to the floor of the nook. He slid under the ledge and looked up, waiting for the inevitable. He knew he could not run anymore.

A minute later the Doberman appeared. He was standing high on the wall above, panting easily as he looked down. He took his time now, knowing Benji was trapped. He bounded easily down to the ledge and then to the floor, flashing his ugly teeth at Benji.

Then suddenly he stiffened. His head jerked to one side and his look of satisfied anticipation melted into one of fear. For there, under the ledge with Benji, was the big brown dog. The *very big* brown dog. He pulled him-self up and began to move toward the Dober-man, teeth bared, totally confident. The Do-berman blinked and backed away until his rear bumped the wall behind him. Then, in a des-perate leap, he went up the ledge and over the wall.

The big brown dog turned to look at his small frightened little friend, but by now Ben-ji was far away, running . . . running through the narrow streets of Athens.

VII

Benji quietly circled around the two rosebushes, looking to see if the doorman was watching. Then he moved along more cautiously, crawling on his belly until he was within twenty feet of the door. He inched up the steps, pausing now and then to lift his head just high enough to look the situation over.

He saw several people going in and out, and then his ears popped up as he saw a door open off to the side. Two bellboys were coming through, pushing a big empty cart. Once they were out, the door swung shut and they rolled the cart off the curb.

The boys took suitcases from the roof of a big airport limousine and stacked them on the cart. A lot of people were getting out of the car and looking the hotel over while they moved toward the door. Benji watched and then looked at the bellboys again.

The cart was almost full now. One of the boys struggled to pull the last suitcase from the roof and finally wedged it into the top of the load. The doorman was bent forward talking to the driver of the limousine, and Benji glanced quickly at the revolving door. It was crowded with people waiting their turns to go through. He sighed and looked at the cart again.

It was coming toward the door now, one of the boys pulling and the other pushing from behind. Benji watched carefully. The bags were stacked high above the bellboys' heads. Benji glanced at the door and then off toward the limousine. The doorman was still bent forward talking to the driver. Suddenly Benji lifted his head. He scooched forward a little, never taking his eyes from the baggage cart.

The cart was about to pass within a few feet of him. Impulsively, Benji trotted across and fell easily into step with the cart. He walked as close to the center of the cart as he could, completely hidden from the doorman on the other side. The boy in front opened the door as they creaked slowly forward. Benji held his breath as they moved inside.

He passed a large plant, then a row of soft chairs with two or three people sitting in them. A man looked at him and smiled and then went back to reading his newspaper. Then the cart stopped and Benji stopped with it.

One of the bellboys walked over to the desk while the other one leaned on the luggage, staring out at nothing. Benji drew his head back and twisted himself around to face the other way. He could see several elevators and a glass door leading to a coffee shop. No sign of Mary, Paul, or Cindy. He glanced up and blinked.

The bellboy was staring down at him and

frowning as if he couldn't believe his eyes. Then he cried out and made a lunge for Benji.

The floor was slippery, but Benji got his feet going just in time. The boy half stumbled and then lit out after him. Benji kept going, racing across the slick marble floor. There were two bellboys chasing him now, both of them yelling.

Benji's feet hardly touched the ground as he headed for the broad stairway which descended steeply to the coffee shop. Benji took the stairs much quicker than the two bellboys, who stumbled down behind him.

Suddenly Benji heard a familiar voice cry out and his head whipped sharply around.

"Benji!"

It was Cindy, standing just outside the coffee shop, still holding the door open. "Mary! Paul! Benji is here!" she shouted behind her.

Benji couldn't recall ever having moved so fast. He wasn't too sure if he even took any steps. It seemed like he made one giant leap and flew twenty feet across the floor into Cindy's arms.

And then Paul and Mary were coming through the door and Benji was licking Cindy's face and then Paul's and then Mary's as they all crowded around him.

For a few minutes he didn't even notice the bellboys standing in the lobby watching. Mary, Paul, and Cindy were all grinning and talking at once, all of them hugging him and getting their faces licked. Then Mary's face suddenly became very serious and she turned to face the perspiring spectators.

"Thank you very much," she said as if she were dismissing servants, "You may go now."

Tiffany had never looked more beautiful. She was freshly groomed, every hair meticulously in place. Benji couldn't resist a happy bark as he trotted across the hotel room. He gave her nose a gentle nudge and licked her face affectionately.

Cindy laughed and Mary wondered aloud how Benji had ever managed to find *them* when they had looked all over Athens without finding *him*. Mary walked over to close the open door which led to the hall when she stopped abruptly and stepped back from the door.

A man with a heavy jacket was standing in front of her. Benji came instantly to his feet when he got a look at him. It was Stelios.

"Yes?" Mary said, surprised.

The man didn't answer immediately. He moved a couple of feet into the room and his narrowed eyes quickly found Benji. Then he looked at Cindy and Mary and glanced suspiciously at the bathroom door.

"I need to borrow your dog for a few days," he said gruffly. "The brown one on the couch there."

It was neither a question nor a polite request. With his grim face and the cold hard eyes the man looked like he was accustomed to issuing orders and having them obeyed without question.

Paul and Cindy flashed a puzzled look at Mary. "I beg your pardon," she said.

"The dog," the man said. "I need to borrow him for a few days."

Mary blinked incredulously at him. "I don't understand. Who are you, and what are you talking about?"

The man looked slightly uneasy, as if he was suddenly aware that his rough manner had startled everybody. He glanced at Benji again and shook his head. "Belive me, it's at least partly for the dog's own safety, lady. He'll be returned unharmed in a day or two."

"I still don't know what you are talking about," Mary said. She gave the man a hard stare.

"All right, lady . . ." The man reached for his back pocket.

Several things happened at that moment. Chandler Dietrich suddenly appeared behind the man and Benji barked as quickly as he saw him. Mary noticed him too, and with a look of relief she said, "Oh, Chandler, I'm . . ."

At that moment the Greek whirled around, and Dietrich struck him hard with the butt of his pistol.

"Chandler!" Mary cried out as the man crashed to the floor.

Benji was barking; partly at Dietrich and partly from surprise. He sat very close to Cindy, looking from Dietrich to the man on the floor.

Paul moved toward Mary and she reached protectively as she gaped at Dietrich. "Chandler, why on earth did you do a thing like that?! What in heaven's name is going on?"

"It's all right, Mary," Dietrich said. He took a quick look at the fallen man and moved across the room. "Now don't worry. Everything's going to be all right, I promise." He put his pistol in Mary's hand. "Just keep this pointed toward him and call the police. OK?"

Mary gaped at the pistol and back at Dietrich. "It most certainly is not OK! I don't like guns, and I want to know what this is all about, Chandler!"

Dietrich had moved back to the man and was going through his pockets. "I can't say right now." He found a wallet and stood up as he glanced through the contents. "I'm sorry, Mary," he said as he stuck the wallet in his jacket pocket. "I just can't tell you anything about it right now. Please trust me."

"Trust you for what?"

Dietrich hesitated. "It has to do with Benji. I have to take him for a couple of days."

"Why?" Cindy asked. "What's he done?"

"He hasn't done anything, Cindy, and I'll take good care of him. I promise."

"If he hasn't done anything, why do you want to take him?" Paul asked.

"And why did that man want to take him?" Mary added.

Dietrich chewed his lip for a minute and

then paced across the room to the window. "Mary," he finally said, "I work for the United States government, and Benji is the key to a very important situation. It's my fault he's involved in all this, and I'm sorry. I had no idea it would become this complicated." He shrugged. "But it has, and I'm afraid that's all I can say."

"Is Benji a spy?" Paul asked.

Dietrich gave a short laugh. "No, he's not a spy, Paul. But he is very important to the United States government right now."

"Hey, that's neat. You mean he'll be famous?"

"It is not neat," Cindy said.

Benji cocked his head, looking from one to the other.

"No, you're right, Cindy," Dietrich said. "It's not neat. But he is important. And necessary. OK?"

"What did he do?" Cindy asked, still not convinced. "Why is he important?"

Dietrich took a deep breath and sighed. "Honey, I just can't tell you right now. I'll explain the whole thing when I bring him back. OK?"

Paul and Mary looked doubtful, but Dietrich smiled at Cindy and waited for an answer. She looked glumly at Benji and finally nodded.

"Good girl," Dietrich said. "And I'm sorry, Mary."

"That's OK—I guess. Just take good care of him."

"I will. Now hurry and call the police. And if the man wakes up be sure to keep the gun on him."

"But I don't know anything about guns," Mary protested.

"All you have to know is to keep it pointed at him. He won't bother you."

Benji didn't like any part of what was going on. He watched warily as Dietrich came toward him.

Benji tried to get away, but Dietrich suddenly had him by the chest and lifted him. "I think you'll all be very proud of him," he said as he carried Benji to the door. "And I'll see you in a few days."

"Poor Benji," Cindy said as the door closed.

Paul smiled and shook his head as Mary picked up the phone again. "How about that? Benji's a spy."

"He is not a spy," Cindy protested.

"I'll bet that guy's a spy too," Paul said nodding at the man on the floor. Then he caught his breath. The man's hand was moving to his head and he was trying to pull himself up. "Mary?" cried Cindy and Paul in unison.

Mary looked and quickly clamped the phone between her shoulder and chin, holding the pistol out with both hands.

"Stay exactly where you are," she said striving to keep her voice under control. "Paul and Cindy, go around behind the bed."

The man was up on one knee, rubbing his

head. He blinked and looked around the room as if not certain where he was for a minute.

"Hello?" Mary said on the phone. "Yes. Will you please send the police to room seven-oh-one. Yes, that's right, the police. Thank you." She fumbled the receiver back to the cradle.

The man was on his feet now, frowning at Tiffany on the bed. "Where's the other dog? The brown one?"

"He's safely away from here," Mary said. She lifted the gun higher, pointing it directly at the man's chest.

The man's eyes narrowed. "Is he with Chandler Dietrich? Is that who hit me?"

"That doesn't happen to be any of your business," Mary answered. "Just stay there by the door and don't come any closer." The man had not moved, but she wasn't taking any chances.

The man snorted. "I suppose he told you he's an agent of the United States government."

"I told you, it's none of your business."

The man nodded and stepped forward. "Yes, it is my business, lady. You see, the body of the real Chandler Dietrich was found this morning at the bottom of a river in New Jersey. The man who was here is not Chandler Dietrich and he is not an agent for the United States government. Now please put that gun down so I can go after him."

Mary kept the gun up, not sure what to think. She had seen enough of Chandler Dietrich to know him fairly well, and he certainly seemed trustworthy. She didn't know anything about this man, and his appearance certainly did not inspire confidence. "And I suppose you're going to tell me you *are* an agent?"

The man sighed and shrugged. "What else?"

"I don't believe you," Mary answered promptly.

The man gave her a cold glance and turned away in frustration. "Well, we can wait for the police, and wait another hour for them to check it out. By then your Dietrich impostor can be halfway to Saudi Arabia."

It was clear that the man was getting impatient with her, and Mary wondered what she would do if he just walked out the door. If he did, she knew she couldn't pull the trigger. But she also wondered if he might be telling the truth. If he was, she could never forgive herself if Benji got hurt. She swallowed hard, keeping the gun up, at the same time trying to come to some kind of intelligent decision.

"Of course, it's not terribly important," the man said sarcastically. "I'm just trying to save the life of a top scientist, and preserve a project of worldwide significance. It's no big deal, lady."

Mary blinked, wondering if that was true. She knew about the scientist and how all the Athens police were looking for the man. But that didn't mean this man was on the side of the police.

"Well, say something!" the man suddenly shouted at her.

"I don't know what to say," replied Mary, on the verge of tears.

"Well, you can try saying goodbye to your dog, because that man who took him out of here will probably kill him when he's through."

Paul and Cindy moved closer to Mary, both of them blinking at the man. "I can't believe that," Mary said. "Chandler Dietrich is a very nice man."

"Don't you understand what I've been trying to tell you, lady? The man who has been traveling with you and escorting you around is *not* Chandler Dietrich! He's an international thief, and he's probably a murderer! And what your dog probably has tattooed somewhere on his body is worth nothing to him if anyone else gets their hands on it. Now, if he's killed a person, is he going to stop with a little . . . brown . . . dog?"

Mary crumbled into tears and Stelios grabbed the gun.

"I'm sorry I had to say those things," Stelios said. "But you won't be." Mary didn't know what to say. She felt a little ill.

The man looked at them for a minute and then disappeared out the door.

VIII

Dietrich kept looking in the rearview mirror as he drove through the city. Benji sat tensely on the seat, watching the streets and wondering where they were going. He'd never seen this part of the city before. Dietrich made a lot of quick turns into alleys and narrow streets and then accelerated sharply.

Benji sighed and settled down, not knowing what to think.

A few minutes later when he sat up and looked out the window again, Benji could see water and hundreds of boats moored in a harbor. It seemed to be where they were headed.

Dietrich parked the car, then, with Benji in arm, he hurried down a long pier where dozens of huge boats were moored. About halfway out he stopped and looked back, then moved up the gangplank of a big cabin cruiser.

"Well, Benji boy, we seem to have made it." He smiled and hurried to a cabin door.

Then a familiar voice stopped him cold. "Do you still plan to dispose of him?"

Dietrich spun around toward the back of the boat.

It was Ronald, the Englishman. He and Elizabeth appeared very comfortable in a pair of deck chairs sipping tall, cool drinks.

"The wife and I sort of like the little chap. We would be quite distressed to hear he was left at the bottom of the harbor."

"What are you doing here?" Dietrich asked angrily.

The Englishman rose and moved slowly across the deck. "Well, to be frightfully honest, old boy, we thought it might have crossed your mind to—as you say—run out on us."

"Run out on you? That's ridiculous. There's nothing to run out on."

Benji looked off at the woman, and then felt himself swung around as Dietrich opened the cabin door and shoved him inside. The door closed quickly behind him.

Benji didn't move for a minute. He glanced around at the fancy leather seats and the big table in the middle of the room. Outside, the two men were still talking.

"There's really no point in discussing it," Dietrich was saying. "You didn't complete your end of the bargain. You let him get away."

Benji moved away from the vent and circled around the table. There were cushioned seats along both sides of the room, with round windows just above them. Benji jumped up and pressed a paw against one of the windows. It was closed tight.

"Yes, of course," the Englishman was saying outside, "I do appreciate that full value was not received. Still in all, a partnership is like a marriage, you know. For better or for worse. And we *did* expose ourselves to enormous risks."

From the seat Benji looked around at the rest of the room. Then he jumped up on the table and studied the vent directly overhead.

"I suppose that's true," Dietrich agreed. "However, as I said, you did not deliver the goods."

The Englishman's voice was still casual. "I do hope this is not going to be a problem," he said. "Having become involved in a project like this, of course, could be very costly to us. I should hate to think we might have to recover the costs in other ways."

Benji couldn't reach the vent. He tried two or three times but he could get only his nose that high. He finally gave it up and stared back at the door for a minute.

"Well," Dietrich said after a silence, "I guess you deserve something for your efforts. Shall we say a compromise? Ten percent instead of twenty?"

"Under the circumstances I suppose that's a fair turn. What do you think, dear?"

"I think it's quite honorable of Mr. Thompson."

"Shall we go inside and have a drink on it?" Dietrich said.

"Excellent idea," the Englishman answered.

Benji looked over at the row of windows

again and his eyes suddenly locked on one of the curtains. It was moving, flapping gently against a breeze from outside. Benji bounded quickly from the table and jumped to the cushioned seats, pushing the curtain aside with his nose. It was wide open! He peered out, then looked quickly back at the door.

Through the glass he could see a hand reaching for the knob. He pulled himself to the top and struggled through the window just as the door flew open behind him.

"By the way," the Englishman said, "you never did say what you intend to do with the dog."

Benji crept softly along the deck by the side of the cabin. He stopped short of the corner and peered cautiously up through a window.

"After I get the code from his foot," Dietrich said coldly, "the dog goes overboard."

Through the window Benji saw Dietrich step aside to let the couple pass. Then, without warning, Dietrich suddenly lifted a heavy brass telescope into the air. As it flashed forward Benji saw the Englishman disappear and heard a loud thump on the floor, followed quickly by another. Then there was only silence.

"And to keep the dog company," Dietrich chuckled, "the two of you can go overboard with him." Then the door slammed shut.

"Benji?" Dietrich said inside the cabin.

Benji looked behind him and saw Dietrich's head suddenly pop through the open window. "Benji!" he screamed.

Benji was over the railing and onto the pier in one bound. Behind him he could hear the clatter of Dietrich running through the cabin and throwing the door open. But Benji was on his way by then.

"Benji!" Dietrich screamed again.

Benji didn't glance back. He heard the thump of Dietrich jumping from the boat to the pier, and then the running footsteps. By that time Benji was almost to the end of the pier.

As he reached the top of the ramp he slowed to a stop and glanced around for an instant. Then he jumped to the side and looked back as splinters of wood seemed to explode within inches of his paw.

Dietrich was holding a heavy pistol with both hands, the ugly black barrel pointing directly at Benji. Benji was running at full speed when the next explosion came. He heard the loud bang, and at the same instant there was a click on the pavement just behind him and the bullet went whining into the distance.

Benji quickly altered his course, keeping a row of parked cars between himself and Dietrich. When he reached the top of the hill he looked back again. He saw the door slam on Dietrich's car and then it was backing up, the wheels spinning.

As Benji raced up the street in the general direction of town, he glanced back and saw

Dietrich's car. Benji made a sharp turn onto a long street. He heard the screech of tires as Dietrich turned the corner behind him.

Benji had no idea which street he should take to get back to familiar territory but he took a sharp left at the next corner. Behind him he heard the screech of tires from several cars and he glanced back, hoping one of them had blocked Dietrich's path.

Two cars were stopped crookedly in the intersection, but Dietrich had gotten by them and was still coming. He was gaining fast now. Benji rounded the corner.

As quickly as he was on the next street he skidded to a stop, his legs spinning under him. Then he turned and quickly went back to the corner, watching.

Dietrich took a wide angle, crossing all the way to the other side of the street before he came into the turn. His tires were screaming as he sped around the corner past Benji, then screeched to a stop as he saw Benji dash off in the opposite direction.

Benji heard more squealing of tires as he ran on at top speed. He knew the car would be gaining fast. The streets were more crowded now and Benji angled across a corner, tearing by several pedestrians and then between two parked cars. He suddenly felt more hopeful as he raced down the street and saw a broad flight of concrete steps leading off the sidewalk and up to the right. Benji bounded up the steps, taking them three at a time as he heard the car round the corner behind him.

When he reached the top he stopped to catch his breath, and then watched as Dietrich skidded to a halt on the street below. Benji stared at him and Dietrich stared back for a minute. Then Benji took off again, galloping easily along the higher street.

Had he lost him? Benji felt a little more confident now. He went up another set of steps and turned back in the opposite direction at the top. He slowed to a trot to catch his breath.

Then his heart dropped and he skidded to a stop again, staring off at the intersection ahead. Dietrich's red sports car was passing along the cross street. It screeched to a stop and the chase was on again.

Benji darted out, heading in the opposite direction from the car. There were more screeches behind him as Benji rounded the corner.

Up ahead six or seven garbage cans were standing in a cluster near the curb. Benji covered the distance in three seconds, sliding to a quick stop as he ducked in behind them. He stuck his nose out just enough to see the car coming around the corner. Then his eyes widened and his muscles tensed. He couldn't believe it for a minute. But it seemed to be true. Dietrich was coming faster and faster, and he was angling closer and closer to the curb, heading directly at him.

Benji spun and bolted out from between the cans an instant before the car soared over the curb. Then the cans exploded in every direction, sending garbage and trash splattering over the street and sidewalk. One of the lids sailed over Benji's head and went clattering off in front of him as he raced on at full speed.

He wasn't going to last a whole lot longer.

Suddenly, Benji saw a cobblestoned alley sloping up the hill to his right. Behind him he could hear brakes squealing as Dietrich slowed to make the turn. Benji bolted toward the alley and up the steps, finally disappearing around a corner.

Dietrich screeched to a halt at the bottom of the hill, jumped out and started up the steps. But it was no use. Benji was long gone. He gazed angrily toward the top of the hill for a long moment; then a smile began to spread slowly across his face. He hurried back to the car, slid behind the wheel, and disappeared into the afternoon traffic.

Things were beginning to look familiar again. Off in the distance Benji could see the ruins and the hill where he and his big friend had their hideout. He moved faster, wanting desperately to get back to Mary, Paul, and Cindy.

He galloped on through the park, sending dozens of pigeons flapping into the air. Then he rounded a corner and sped past the open flower market.

Only when Benji was within a block of the

hotel did he finally slow down a little. He rounded the corner and then came to an abrupt stop.

Traffic was blocked and at least a dozen police cars with flashing lights were parked in front of the hotel. Policemen were all over the place, some of them standing on the grass, others milling around the street or standing across from the hotel. There was a babble of noise from the car radios and the policemen seemed to have an awful lot of guns.

Benji moved along a few feet, trying to get a better view of things. But he still couldn't figure out what was going on. With all that crowd around, it was pretty clear that he would have no chance of sneaking in the door.

He turned and trotted back toward the corner and then stopped again.

Two policemen were standing side by side near the corner, staring directly at him. Benji looked out at the street. More policemen seemed to be coming in his direction, all of them moving slowly and watching him.

What was going on? Benji turned and trotted a few steps the other way and stopped again. Then his ears pricked up as a voice crackled over a loudspeaker echoing something in Greek.

The policemen were slowly closing in on him from all directions except the direction toward the hotel entrance. He was confused.

He finally turned and moved slowly toward the hotel. Then he stopped again and glanced around. The policemen behind him followed, always stopping within a few feet of him. And the ones in front of him seemed to edge back, clearing a path toward the hotel. Then he tensed, staring off at the entrance.

The revolving door was no longer turning. Two policemen stood on either side, huge guns held tightly in their hands.

"Προσοχη!" the loudspeaker repeated, the voice suddenly very soft. Benji glanced over at a man holding a microphone next to a police car. The man seemed to be looking directly at him as he spoke.

Then Benji saw them—Mary and Paul. They were staring at him from the far side of the hotel door, and they seemed to be holding tightly to each other as if they were frightened. Benji gave his tail an uncertain wag. Then he trotted forward, angling across the walk leading to the hotel door.

"BENJI!"

The voice was Cindy's, and it was a frightened, anguished scream that stopped Benji dead in his tracks.

Then he saw it—Dietrich's red sports car was at the curb about fifty feet away, with all the policemen standing well away from it.

Dietrich was behind the wheel and Cindy was sitting next to him. Benji's heart sank. Dietrich had an arm around Cindy's neck and tears were streaming down Cindy's face.

Then he saw something that gripped his entire body with an icy fear. In Dietrich's other hand, just inches from Cindy's head, was an ugly black piece of metal.

Benji's thoughts raced back to a dark night in Silver Creek when he'd seen another man hold a gun like that. He remembered the loud explosion, the flash of light, and the smell of gun-powder. And his friend falling to the sidewalk.

"Benji?" Cindy called again weakly. "Here, Benji."

Benji stared for a full minute, scarcely breathing. Dietrich opened the car door and then tightened his grip on Cindy. Benji remembered Dietrich's attempts to shoot him and run him down with his car. Now he had Cindy. And a gun. Benji couldn't bear to see Cindy fall like his friend back in Silver Creek.

Suddenly Benji was in motion, gathering speed as he crossed the walk in front of the hotel. He could see Cindy's anguished look and the smile coming to Dietrich's face, and he was moving faster, digging in with each step, flying at full speed as he raced across the sidewalk. His eyes were fixed on only one thing—the ugly weapon resting in Dietrich's hand. The man was not going to make Cindy cry anymore and he was not going to harm her, and Benji didn't care what happened to him.

He was still ten feet from the car when he leaped, and for an instant he saw the look of doubt and fear cross Dietrich's face. Then Benji was through the opened door and his teeth clamped into the man's bared wrist.

There was a yell as the impact sent Dietrich's arm high into the air and the gun exploded right next to Benji's ear, the bullet tearing harmlessly skyward. Then Dietrich's arm crashed down against the car door and the gun sailed free, clattering down onto the marble steps as Benji's momentum somersaulted him out of the car.

Benji scrambled to his feet, ready to run. But suddenly it was too crowded to run. A dozen policemen were now surrounding the car and rifles were being thrust through the doors on both sides.

It was over. The loudspeaker was blaring out instructions, more policemen were coming at full speed, and Benji edged back, trapped for a minute by the mass of surrounding legs. Then he spotted Mary and Paul and Cindy standing at the curb in front of the hotel. Mary was hugging Cindy, and Paul was looking off at the crowd around the car. Then a big smile suddenly came to his face.

"Benji!" he shouted. "Come on, Benji!"

And Benji did.

IX

Benji had never seen a beach before. When they walked down from the hotel he stood looking at it for a long while, amazed at seeing so much empty sand in one place. He finally trotted to the shore and sniffed the clear, blue water, jumping back when the little waves broke and came chasing after him. Then he raced full speed along the edge, barking out at them, with Tiffany running along behind. The two of them finally jumped in and Benji leaped directly into the first wave that came along, showing off a little for Tiffany. She stayed in the shallow water and barked while he tumbled and thrashed around. Benji finally came back to shore and gave himself a good shake, looking things over again.

It was really a beautiful place. There were palm trees growing in the sand, and there wasn't another person or dog in sight for miles.

Paul and Cindy were in the water now and Benji watched them splash around and jump over the waves for a while. Up on the sand Stelios had strung a hammock between two

117

palm trees and was stretched out in it while Mary sat in a beach chair under one of the trees, slowly swinging the hammock with one hand while fanning herself in the warm sun with the other.

"Benji just happened to be going to the right place at the right time, and for security reasons someone decided to let him carry the coordinate code for a secret meeting with the scientist," explained Stelios.

"Oh!" gasped Mary. "And we never caught on!" Then she said, "But why is the scientist so important?"

"They think he's close to a formula that'll turn one barrel of oil into twelve," Stelios replied. "You can guess how many folks would like to get their hands on that."

"Well," Mary sighed, "the whole thing sounds to me like something out of a James Bond movie."

Stelios laughed. "If it were a James Bond movie, I'd be Robert Redford and you'd be Genevieve Bujold." Mary grinned at the thought and Stelios continued. "Anyway, the whole thing would have worked if Benji hadn't missed the plane change in Athens."

Stelios paused, pushed back his straw hat, and gave Mary a wry smile.

"Hey, you're not living up to your part of the bargain. If I'm gonna talk, you've gotta pull."

Mary laughed and gave the hammock a
118

gentle tug. Behind her, Benji and Tiffany were still enjoying a romp in the cool surf.

"How did the man we thought was Dietrich find out about all this?" Mary continued.

"I don't know," replied Stelios casually. "Security leak, I guess. It happens all the time. We've got spies . . . they've got spies . . . and we're all trying to earn our salaries."

A big wave chased Benji and Tiffany back toward the beach, and they both took off in the direction of Paul and Cindy, who now sat on a blanket enjoying the ocean breeze.

"By the way, how's Benji?" asked Stelios as Benji and Tiffany trotted under the hammock. "Any signs of wear and tear?"

Mary turned to watch as Benji neared a large picnic basket and nudged the top away with his nose.

"I don't think Benji has ever been better," Mary answered simply.

Paul and Cindy smiled as Benji stood proudly looking into the basket. Inside were four of the handsomest, liveliest puppies they had ever seen. Three were cuddly white, with soft fine fur like their mother's. But the fourth . . . well, he was the obvious heir.

His mixed brown coat was scraggly with a little white streak on his chest and he yapped and growled as he crawled feistily over the other puppies.

Benji reached down into the basket, nudged him away from the others, and gingerly picked him up by the nape of the neck. The tiny puppy gave his proud father a small lick on the nose as Benji placed him carefully onto the blanket.

If ever a son bore the marks of his father, it was this lively, brown puppy who sat looking admiringly up at a very special dog named Benji.

Woof.